"Not so loud!" She glanced around the restaurant, but no one seemed to have heard him. "And yes, that's the plan. It's complicated, but the short of it is my husband disappeared five years ago and was finally declared dead, and I'm looking to test the waters again, so to speak."

"All the men in L.A. must be either blind or stupid. Or both." He shook his head in amazement. "And if you want to test the waters, you sure as hell don't have to go all the way to the Bahamas. I'd be more than willing to help you take the plunge."

Their gazes met and held again, and this time the heat curled deeper and sharper. Almost as loud as words, their silence said, *Let's do it. Now.*

Hide in Plain Sight is also available as an eBook

From the bestselling author who "puts the snap-crackle-pop into the mystery-romance" (*Detroit Free Press*)—be sure to read Michele Albert's

ONE WAY OUT

"The outstanding Michele Albert's new adventure is roaring, and the romance sizzles. Settle in for a great ride."

—*Romantic Times*

"Exciting romantic suspense. . . . Action-packed. . . . Michele Albert provides a fine, exhilarating, way out tale."

—Thebestreviews.com

"A fast-paced, suspenseful book that's impossible to put down. This book has a kick-ass heroine and a hot, yummy hero. . . . If you like suspense, mystery, and action mixed in with your romance, this is THE book for you!"

—ARomanceReview.com

"Michele Albert has another winner on her hands. *One Way Out* is a brilliantly paced story. . . . The chemistry between Alex and Cassie fairly sizzles off the page. . . . The tension between the two is a palpable thing. . . . A wonderful, one sitting read that both touches the heart and the funny bone. . . . Snap this one up—you won't be disappointed!"

—Contemporaryromancewriters.com

OFF LIMITS

"Wow! Take one smart, by-the-book, beautiful cop and mix well with one hunky, devilish bad boy: the perfect recipe for a delicious romp of a romance. . . . Michele Albert gives us not only a wonderful love story with some hot sex, but also two people who stand up for what they believe in. . . . Fun, sexy contemporary romance."

—Curledup.com

"Intelligent characters and scorching love scenes. . . ."
—*The Romance Reader*

GETTING HER MAN

"Whoa, boy! Michele Albert outdoes herself with this sexy, sassy, and exciting book."
—*Romantic Times*

Also by Michele Albert

One Way Out

MICHELE ALBERT

HIDE IN PLAIN SIGHT

POCKET BOOKS

New York   London   Toronto   Sydney

An *Original* Publication of POCKET BOOKS

POCKET BOOKS, a division of Simon & Schuster, Inc.
1230 Avenue of the Americas, New York, NY 10020

ISBN-13: 978-0-7434-8503-6
ISBN-10:   0-7434-8503-3

This Pocket Books paperback edition May 2006

10 9 8 7 6 5 4 3 2

POCKET and colophon are registered trademarks of Simon & Schuster, Inc.

Cover design by Jae Song
Cover photograph by Nick Laham/Getty Images

Manufactured in the United States of America

For information regarding special discounts for bulk purchases, please contact Simon & Schuster Special Sales at 1-800-456-6798 or business@simonandschuster.com

Much love to my family for all their support over the past year, especially during the bumpy times—and thanks to my agent, Pam Ahearn, for going above and beyond. I appreciate that support more than words can express.

Prologue

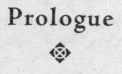

INTERNATIONAL SMUGGLING MADE FOR STRANGE BED-
fellows, and on this hot July night, in a tiny Hamburg
restaurant, the promise of large sums of money
changing hands had brought together a cultural melting pot of thieves, liars, and killers.

Gathered around a small table were two elegant
Iraqi men with a large briefcase that never left their
sight; a long-legged, big-busted, blond, blue-eyed
Finn acting as a liaison for the German who
should've shown up fifteen minutes ago; and himself.

Tonight, Griffith Laughton was playing the part of
the arrogant American with all the money; his dark
hair perfectly styled, his black suit immaculate, his
little round glasses making him appear every inch the
ambitious young businessman.

Griffith held back a small smile. He loved being in
the thick of it again and operating on his own script.

There'd be bitching about it at headquarters later, but as long as he got the job done and got his team out in one piece, Ben Sheridan would go easy on him.

Especially if he managed to reel in von Lahr.

Seated between the tense Finn and the equally tense Iraqi smugglers, Griffith didn't miss how their gazes kept straying to the leather briefcase tucked firmly between his ankles. Nor could he miss the fact that somebody was going to explode if von Lahr didn't make his appearance soon or his lover, Annamari Hakkinen, didn't get the show rolling.

The little restaurant was dark and mostly empty, except for a couple cooing at each other behind him; the cheerful, redheaded waitress folding napkins at the next table; and the bald-headed bartender polishing his bar. The bartender's massive shoulders eliminated his neck, which, along with his curling handlebar mustache, gave him the look of a turn-of-the-century circus strongman.

Catching Griffith's gaze, the bartender nodded politely—but didn't look away. And he was sweating.

That wasn't good.

Holding back a frown, Griffith turned to the blonde and said, in German, "Your associate is late. How much longer do you expect me to wait? I have other appointments this evening."

Although Annamari gave him a dazzling smile, it

didn't reach her cool blue eyes. "I fear Rainert must have been unavoidably delayed. Perhaps we should continue without him."

With no signal as yet from his lookouts, Griffith already anticipated von Lahr would be a no-show. He hadn't assumed it would be this simple to run to ground one of the most notorious art and antiquities thieves in all of Europe, but he wouldn't have minded catching a bit of blind luck for a change.

"But that was not part of our deal," he said, pretending not to notice the growing agitation of the two Iraqi men, al-Shadri Senior and al-Shadri Junior, as he thought of them. "Our deal was that von Lahr would be here to handle the final details."

Annamari's annoyance leaked through her encore smile, but Griffith had to admit von Lahr's excellent taste in arm candy. Then again, the man was an art thief; he had an eye for the exquisite.

"I believe we shall have to alter the plans, and I will act in Rainert's place." Annamari, her expression flat, looked directly at al-Shadri Senior. "I realize it is not your habit to do business with a woman, but unless you wish to leave this place tonight without what you came for, you have no choice."

The Iraqi men hadn't bothered hiding the fact that they disliked having to conduct their business in the presence of a woman—even worse, a European woman. Yet despite the palpable disdain, the younger

Iraqi had been eyeing Annamari with an insulting sexual interest.

Al-Shadri Senior, however, hadn't taken his attention off Griffith since he'd walked into the restaurant—which he could play to his advantage, if necessary.

"You must give me an answer now or this meeting is terminated," Annamari said after a short silence.

Her ultimatum didn't sit well with al-Shadri Junior, who turned, thin-lipped, to his companion and spoke in a low voice.

Ibrahim al-Shadri and his nephew Yousef were members of the notorious al-Shadri clan. The tribe was in the thick of looting and smuggling ancient artifacts, which the current upheaval in Iraq made frustratingly easy. Griffith knew they were extremely dangerous, even before Yousef spelled it out in a few concise, quiet words.

Unfortunately for Junior, Griffith understood and spoke a number of Middle Eastern dialects. "Shooting us and taking the money just isn't a good idea," he said pleasantly, enjoying their startled expressions. "Bad for business. Seriously."

Senior recovered quickly, smiled, and said in heavily accented German, "Forgive my nephew. He is young and rash—and justifiably angry. We have come here tonight at a great risk and were assured there would be no problems. Yet our contact is not here, and now you, Mr. Laughton, speak of leaving as well. I am not pleased with how the transaction is progressing. And I do not feel comfortable in this open place. We should return to my hotel room, where we will have more privacy."

Annamari frowned, and Griffith decided enough was enough.

"You don't trust me?" he asked al-Shadri Senior, his tone pitched low, friendly. "You think I'm armed? Wired?"

Senior shrugged elegantly. "It is a dangerous business we are in, this is true. Who can afford to trust blindly?"

"So how about you see for yourself that I'm clean?" Griffith stood, slipping off his suit coat and tossing it casually on his chair—and over the briefcase that held no money at all.

Annamari muttered, "Goddamn American cowboy!" then snapped, "What are you doing? Sit down! I am the one in charge here!"

"Everyone wants the money, right?" Griffith tugged his tie loose, then tossed it on his coat. "And since *I'm* the one with the money, that makes me the one in charge."

As al-Shadri Junior made a hiss of annoyance, Griffith started unbuttoning his shirt—and he saw the moment Annamari understood his intentions. Her beautiful, cold eyes widened.

"You cannot do this, not *here*," she said from between clenched teeth as the shirt joined the suit coat and tie.

He was unfastening his belt as she added more urgently, "Mr. Laughton, please stop this at once!"

"I don't think so." He gave her the act she expected, an arrogant wink and an equally arrogant smile. "We're just getting to the fun part. C'mon, honey, have a little fun. You people are way too serious."

Al-Shadri Senior gave a low and appreciative chuckle that echoed loudly in the silence of shock that had fallen over the small restaurant.

Got you, you miserable bastard.

His impromptu act garnered Griffith a rapt audience. The red-haired server was frozen in mid–napkin fold, staring. The couple at the next table, a boyish blond and a cute brunette, stopped their annoying giggles and love talk long enough to exchange startled glances, and the girl squeaked in stilted German, "What are you doing?"

"Isn't it obvious, sweetheart?" Griffith asked, his grin widening as the brunette's mouth dropped open.

Annamari had had enough. She stood, grabbing his arm, the talons of her nails sinking into the muscle of his bare biceps with a pain that was sharp and pleasant. "Idiot! You're going to ruin everything! You—"

"Be quiet and sit down," Griffith said, keeping his tone friendly but with enough edge that her mouth opened, then shut, and she sat back down.

He hopped onto the table, and every gaze in the place was focused on him.

"See? No wires."

Turning around slowly, Griffith kept his teasing grin trained on al-Shadri Senior, who looked torn between lust and embarrassment. His dark eyes kept straying to where Griffith played his fingers along the zipper of his pants.

"Take it all off!" called the tiny brunette from the next table. "Don't be shy now— Let it *all* hang out."

Annamari looked ready to have a meltdown, and there was a glint of fear in her eyes. Probably fear of him as much as fear of what von Lahr would do to her if she botched the transaction.

He almost felt sorry for her. Almost.

Griffith kept al-Shadri Senior's attention on him and slipped his hand down the front of his pants. The younger Iraqi stood, swearing in a rapid string of words, and beside him Annamari gasped and said weakly in English, "Oh, my God . . ."

Whether that was because of the gun she felt at the back of her head, held there by the redheaded waitress, or because of what he'd hauled out from inside his pants, Griffith didn't know or care.

"You look disappointed." He smiled as he aimed

his Smith & Wesson .357 Magnum at Ibrahim al-Shadri's astonished face. "Expecting something else, were you? And here I thought I was being so clever. I'm hurt you don't appreciate my humor."

"Goddammit," snarled the tiny brunette, who had her gun pressed against Yousef's back. "*That* was not the fuckin' plan, you asshole!"

"I improvised," Griffith said, smiling at Diva's show of temper before turning to her "boyfriend." "Hey, you—rookie. Tie up Senior here. And do it carefully. Both he and Junior are armed to the teeth."

"The name's Perry," the new kid grumbled, even as he efficiently disarmed al-Shadri, tied his wrists together, then pushed him onto the floor beside his bound nephew and Annamari Hakkinen.

Her eyes were still glazed with shock, but she was beginning to understand what had just happened.

"You don't look like cops," she said in English, and her full, pink mouth curled in disgust.

"Really?" Griffith reached for his belt.

"Cops have a look to them." Annamari leaned back, affecting an air of unconcern that Griffith didn't buy. "In the way they move, the way they watch people. You don't look like that."

Griffith smiled. "Nope, not a cop."

"You're Avalon, aren't you?" She was watching him carefully. "Rainert told me about you."

"Right. And speaking of von Lahr, where is he?" Griffith hopped off the table and crouched down beside her. Even in a situation like this, it did his masculine ego good to see that she was checking out his chest.

"He knows you are after him. He told me he has been playing games with you for a long time. So don't be so arrogant: you failed."

Griffith leaned close; so close that her attempt at bravado withered and her smile faltered. "I'm not the one going to prison, Annamari," he said softly. "Or taking the fall for somebody else."

"True." She was trying to tough it out, but not very convincingly. "But he made a fool out of you. If nothing else, that makes *me* feel a little better."

"So all along he was playing us. Again." Diva, tying back her dark hair, scowled as she stared down at the two Iraqi men sitting trussed up at her feet. "That won't go over well with HQ. I sure as hell hope what we came for is in that briefcase."

"Let's find out." Griffith had pulled on his shirt but left it open. He retrieved the briefcase the two Iraqi smugglers had brought and carefully opened it.

A rich gleam of old, beaten gold lay within, fragile and thin, amid beads of lapis lazuli and carnelian and amber. The princess's headdress was shaped like a flower and etched with lifelike details, and her necklaces, earrings, and bracelets were there as well.

"The Ur-Nammu treasure." Griffith turned to the two men stewing in impotent rage on the floor. "These little trinkets are over four thousand years old and rightfully belong to the people of Iraq. Shame on you for fuckin' over your country. But if I couldn't count on greed as surely as on the sun rising and setting, I wouldn't have a job now, would I?"

Leibowitz, the redhead, leaned over for a look and gave a low whistle. "Bingo. Good job, Grif. Even if you didn't follow the plan. And even if von Lahr got away again."

"That bastard," Annamari whispered. "He set me up from the start."

"And you're only now figuring this out?" Diva let out a derisive snort. "Let me tell you something about your boyfriend. His M.O. is to find a pretty girl with big tits and tiny brains to do his dirty work for him. Then when the law arrives, as it always does, he disappears and leaves her to take the fall. You're bimbo number nine—that we know of, anyway."

Leaning back, she added, "And not all of them survive. Of course, no one can prove he was responsible for killing any of them. You still feeling all smug and clever?"

Annamari said nothing.

Griffith shut the briefcase. "Okay. We got what we came for. Time to move out."

"Answer me a question first." The rookie, Perry,

stepped in front of him. "We have a few seconds before the police get here. Right?" He glanced at the "bartender," Kurt, who was actually one of the local cops and their inside edge with the Hamburg police.

"They are on the way," said Kurt.

"Okay, I'll make it quick. Tell me why you did . . . that." Perry motioned at Griffith's open shirt and unbuckled belt. "I mean, shit! You wouldn't have stripped bare-ass naked, right? And you wouldn't have . . . you know, gone and done anything with that little bastard over there. Right?"

God save him from naïve rookies. He'd never been that clueless, had he? "I do whatever it takes to get the job done," Griffith answered flatly.

The kid frowned. "That's not really an answer. I—"

"Sure it is."

"No, it's not. Look, I hear these stories about you, and I figure they can't be real. There—" Perry froze, his face paling and eyes widening as he looked down at the knife Griffith had against his belly. "Jesus! Where the hell did you pull *that* from? Your ass?"

Griffith laughed; he couldn't help it. "No, it's yours. Next time, pay more attention." He tossed Perry's knife back at him, and the kid nearly fumbled it. "Even if you're with someone you trust."

"So that's your answer?"

"It's all the answer you'll ever need," Griffith said, although he could tell the kid still didn't get it. "Think about it some more and it'll make sense. If it doesn't, you might consider another line of work."

Diva laughed, and Griffith exchanged grins with her before turning back to the red-faced Perry. "In the meantime, remember rule number one: Get the job done, no matter what. It's the only rule people like us live by."

"It is time, as you say, to ride into the mist," Kurt interrupted in his rumbling voice. "My people are on the way. You must go now."

Griffith had already picked up the sound of distant sirens.

"Yup," said Leibowitz cheerfully. "Time for our disappearing act, boys and girls, and we get to take—"

The sound of windows shattering cut across her voice, followed by rounds chambering, feet running, soft curses from his team, and the panicked shouts of the prisoners.

Diva had pushed the Iraqi men down, and Perry, closest to the woman, shielded her with his own body.

"Sniper fire!" yelled Kurt, ducking behind the bar.

Sonofabitch. It had to be von Lahr.

"Leibowitz, help Diva and Kurt get the Iraqis behind the bar," Griffith ordered. He grabbed the briefcase with the fragile, priceless treasure. "And stay away from the windows. I'll help Perry move the girl and—"

Perry slumped forward, silent and still, when Griffith grabbed his shoulder.

"Goddammit," Griffith whispered.

The kid was dead. A bullet had pierced his heart, killing him instantly. Beneath him, Annamari was dead as well, a neat hole through the center of her forehead.

"Oh, Jesus," Leibowitz whispered. "Is he . . . is Perry dead?"

Griffith nodded, and when she turned to run outside, he grabbed her arm. "Forget it. He's long gone."

"How did this happen?" Her voice shook with anger. "We should've known, we should've been prepared—"

"We were, and I had safeguards in place." Griffith caught Diva's grim expression, and suddenly, deep inside him, something snapped. Cold flooded him from head to toe. "It seems . . . they're no longer in place."

He stood, and before he even reached the door Diva was yelling, "Griffith, don't! You can't go out there, either and . . . Ah, shit!"

The restaurant door shut behind him. Moving fast, not caring that his open shirt didn't hide the gun shoved into his back waistband, Griffith dodged between cars, ignoring the irate honking, and slammed open the hotel door across from the restaurant.

People stared as he ran past them. Not bothering with the elevator, he took the stairs two at a time until he reached the floor where his lookouts had been stationed to keep watch on the front of the restaurant.

Banging on the door, he shouted their names, even though he knew they were beyond answering. Then he kicked the door in, gun drawn and ready.

It was dark, but he could smell the blood.

Carefully, he switched on the light.

Both his lookouts were lying on the floor, dead. Ramirez was sprawled on his back, staring lifelessly up at the ceiling, but Bouchet was positioned at the window as if still on watch, his rifle propped against the wall.

In his back, hilt-deep through a sheet of blood-stained paper, was a hunting knife.

Rage ripping through him like a white-hot fire, Griffith yanked the paper loose. Written in English in bold, aggressive black ink was:

Tag! You're it.

R. von Lahr.

For a split second, his mind blanked under the force of his fury, and when the haze had slowly cleared, he became aware of a burning pain in his left hand.

Looking down, he saw that he'd punched a hole through the dresser mirror. Blood and tiny shards of glass covered his knuckles.

At a sound from the doorway, he whipped around, gun drawn.

Diva raised her hands, her face pale. "It's just me! Just me."

Griffith lowered the gun, not really seeing her as she ran in, not really hearing her gasps of shock and grief, her questions, increasingly louder and sharper.

Tag! You're it.

One

GRIFFITH LAUGHTON DUCKED INTO A DOWNTOWN Seattle phone booth, glad to be out of the cold drizzle that made his back ache like a bitch. He went through the routine with the calling card, punching in a number he'd memorized a few days ago, and waited only seconds before a familiar voice answered softly, "Sheridan."

"It's Laughton. I'm heading to Sea-Tac. Any last-minute instructions or updates?"

"No new updates. The target is there, we're sure of it, and we know von Lahr was recently spotted in the States. There's a good chance he'll be close by as well. You're not going to have a lot of time on this one—and I want that woman kept safe."

"Understood." Griffith leaned back, frowned at a prickling of pain, then shifted to take the weight off the still-tender scars.

"Whatever you do, make sure she stays in your sight at all times. If von Lahr gets to her first, he'll use her as leverage. And if that happens—"

"Got it. You don't need to spell it out."

"You have everything you need? You know what the woman looks like? Where she—"

Griffith laughed. "Ben, stop acting like my mother, for Chrissake. I'm feeling good; no problems except an ache or two. I haven't forgotten how to do my job. I got shot in the back, remember? Nothing's wrong with my head."

His boss sighed. "Sorry. I'm still reacting to the fact we nearly lost you. It was a close call."

Hell, yeah. Tangling with the violent clans outside Al-Fajr was always dangerous, and this last chase had nearly ended in disaster. Nothing like being ambushed by a fourteen-year-old with an assault weapon to prove that the world was going to hell all around him.

Lately he'd started to think that if he died without ever having retrieved another cuneiform tablet or another cylinder seal, he'd die a happy man.

To put Ben's mind at ease, he said, "I've got this covered. Kennedy's a cute little redhead with lots of freckles. She's a genius when it comes to Marlowe, and the file you gave me lists more details about her life than she'd like any stranger to know. She sells antique books out of an old Victorian house near USC, address committed to memory."

"Take it easy on giving her information. The less she knows, the better."

"Right."

The manuscript in his briefcase was a brilliant fake that had cost a gullible and very wealthy man a lot of money. Its only real value was as a lure to draw their target out into the open. Once they had him, they'd have the information they needed to put a long-standing group of forgers out of business for good. Their anonymous tipster claimed that the fake manuscript contained a coded message only Fiona Kennedy could spot, which was why Griffith was headed to L.A.

Ben was skeptical about the coded message, but if it would bring von Lahr out of hiding, he didn't care if that tip was true or not.

Still, dangling an innocent woman as bait was risky, even if the chance of harm coming to her was minimal.

"For the record," he told his boss, "I don't like this plan."

"Nor do I, but we don't have much of a choice. I'm calling a few others to the Torrance office to back you up. I can't pull Kemal out of Iraq right now, but

Diva's in Milan working with the Carabinieri on the Pompeii looting incident, and Rico's in Amsterdam. I can bring those two back, though it'll be a couple of days before they can get to L.A."

"Then make sure the Bayview room is ready. I'll take her there if things go bad, and arrange for a pickup at the airfield. And if our contacts in the LAPD and the Torrance office are on alert for trouble or any cleanup work, that'll be a big help."

"I'm already on that. And I've arranged to have a car waiting for you at LAX, in the usual place."

A large delivery truck whooshed by, spraying the phone booth with water from the predawn rainstorm, and Griffith peered through the bleary wet at the traffic on the streets and sidewalks. He liked Seattle; always had. If he ever settled down like a normal human being, he'd choose Seattle.

"I fuckin' hate L.A., Ben."

"It's better than Baghdad."

"Not by much," Griffith muttered. "I'm still thinking we won't catch our target like this. After all this time, why would he be so sloppy as to make a personal appearance where everybody will be looking for him?"

"We said the same thing about von Lahr, and yet those two yahoos from Wyoming nearly managed to do something we haven't despite fifteen years of trying with the best professionals on the job."

Griffith stared balefully outside the phone booth, barely registering the traffic as it sped past in a blur of color and motion and streams of light: red in one direction, white in the other. "Dumb luck."

"If somebody nails the sonofabitch, it should be Avalon." Ben sounded impatient.

"It should be *me*. I've been hounding his ass for the past five years," Griffith replied.

"Just be careful. We don't want a repeat of what happened the last time we got this close to him."

"Not likely to forget." A brief image flashed to mind: the exploding glass, the blood, those three mocking little words: *Tag! You're it*.

The deaths still haunted him, constant reminders of the consequences of underestimating Rainert von Lahr.

"It's the first solid lead on him we've had in a long while. Since the Hamburg incident, there hasn't been a Western European sighting—"

"*Confirmed* sighting," Ben corrected, then sighed. "I still think he's operating out of South America, but he'll show up again sooner or later, and when he does, we'll nail him. So get your ass on that plane and check in with me once you're in L.A."

"Will do." Griffith hung up.

He stepped out and pulled up the collar of his grandpa's old bomber jacket against the drizzle, then walked briskly to where he'd parked his rental car. By the time he slid into the driver's seat, his jeans were damp, his hair was dripping, and his glasses were rain-spotted. With the bottom of his navy silk tie, he wiped the droplets off his glasses, then put the car in gear.

With half his attention on the rain-grayed highway, Griffith replayed everything he'd read in the file that Ben Sheridan had given him the day before. The first thing he'd noticed was that Kennedy was pretty. Maybe she was a brainy chick, but in his experience it was the quiet ones you had to watch out for. And then there was the red hair. If the folklore was true, she'd have a temper.

Temper or no, spending a few days with her would be like a vacation compared with his usual jobs.

As long as nobody started shooting at them, anyway.

A familiar buzz of adrenaline pumped through him, despite an encroaching sense of dread that threatened to blunt its edge.

"Goddammit," he muttered. Then, as if to remind him that he wasn't as invincible as he'd once thought, his back pinched in pain again. "I'm getting too damn old for this."

Two

10:00 A.M.

Rainy November days were best for daydreaming, Fiona Kennedy decided, and she arranged herself in an indolent slouch at the desk of her Los Angeles bookstore. Norah Jones crooned from the CD player, and the piquant smell of brewing espresso mingled with the pungent scent of old rooms and even older books.

The accounting software seriously needed upgrading, but she couldn't seem to muster the energy to boot up the program, much less do all that point-and-click stuff. The gentle pattering on the windows, the soft whistle of wind, and the cozy dimness lulled her into a state of self-indulgence. The only way she could be more comfortable right now was if she could trade in her casual rust-colored pants and the soft, ivory silk turtleneck for jeans and a sweatshirt.

The awful tension of the past few weeks was gone, now that the lawyers had finally gotten Richard declared dead—five years after he'd driven his car into a deep, fast-running river.

After years of searching for a body that had never turned up, and years of living in limbo, she was legally a widow, and the official stamp had lifted that last, shadowy weight off her shoulders. She could get on with her life without that thread of doubt holding her back, and her friends no longer had any reason to rag on her about "hiding" herself away from the world.

As if. Just because Diana was recently married and Cassie looked to be heading in the same direction, they suddenly felt an overwhelming urge to pair her up.

The idea of getting married again didn't make her want to run screaming in the opposite direction, but she needed some time for herself before she started thinking in those terms again.

Still, men were figuring in her thoughts more frequently lately—mostly as a physical itch of need. What she needed was a mindless fling, a few days or weeks of hot, guilt-free sex to clear the slate and get back into the groove. She was only thirty-six; there had to be lots and lots of grooves left for her to get back into.

Fiona settled farther back in her old leather desk chair, eyeing the dozens of brochures spread across her desk beside the new accounting software box she was trying to ignore.

Hmmm . . . work or play?

Work could wait. She shoved the software aside, leaving the colorful jumble of brochures to dominate the big oak desk.

Tahiti. Bahamas. Barbados. Caribbean. Jamaica. Oahu.

The names were like poetry: a cadence of the exotic, of blue seas and white beaches and warm winds, palm trees and lazy nights sipping fruity drinks in an outdoor bar with little white lights sparkling like stars.

Her daydreams had been of the tropical island flavor for months now, and today she'd pick a destination, book a plane ticket, and call Eddie to arrange for him to watch the store and feed her cat. Then she'd buy skimpy new clothes, maybe get her hair cut, and arrange for a facial, pedicure, and manicure before hopping on a plane and thoroughly indulging herself for two weeks straight.

"I want to go scuba diving," she murmured and was answered by a muffled meow from somewhere beneath her desk. "I wasn't asking your opinion, Faustus."

The cat emerged, a huge, pure black male that had

left his tomcatting ways behind long ago and packed on some extra pounds. Snobby, contrary, lazy, and solely hers, he was alternately her daily companion and a furry pain in the ass. He stretched, face to the floor, butt and tail arched, and gave another rumbling meow.

Smiling, Fiona scratched his ears on the side, where he liked it best. "Not that you have any idea about these things, but all the girls who've vacationed on the islands tell me the scuba instructors are gorgeous . . . and easy. I need an affair, Faustus. A hot, totally self-indulgent affair."

Faustus twitched his tail and lumbered down the musty, narrow stacks crammed full of old British books, which she fondly called the British Aisles—a pun too few people appreciated.

Outside, the wind picked up and the rain splattered against the windows with more force. They'd gotten more rain than usual this year, which was why the idea of sun-drenched tropical isles held such appeal. She had a feeling the lousy weather had also played a part in keeping business so slow this week.

She read through the brochures, weeding them out one by one until her choices had narrowed down to the Caribbean or the Bahamas. If the Caribbean *really* came with pirates like Captain Jack Sparrow, the choice would've been a no-brainer, but she kept coming back to the Bahamas brochures, which featured lots of diving tours and flashy shots of tanned, hard-bodied scuba instructors.

Fiona grinned. "The Bahamas it is then."

As she reached for the phone, it rang. She picked it up and said briskly, "Kennedy Antiquarian Books. How may I help you?"

Silence. She waited for a few seconds, certain she could hear someone breathing on the other end, then repeated, "Can I help you? Hello?"

The loud click of the line disconnecting was her answer. Fiona held the phone away from her, staring at it with exasperation for a moment before calling her travel agency. Fifteen minutes later, she had her trip booked for early January.

What better way to kick off this new phase in her life than starting the new year in an exotic locale she'd never visited before, and indulging in new experiences and adventures?

Several older women came in, browsed a short while, then left. After that, one of her regulars stopped by to pick up a first edition of Steinbeck's *The Grapes of Wrath* for quite a nice sum.

Fiona began dusting shelves—a never-ending chore in this old heap of a place—and was extravagantly flicking the feather duster along to the sweeping rhythm of Andrea Bocelli's magnificent voice when the door chimes tinkled, announcing another customer.

She turned and went still with amazement. Tall, blond, wearing an expensive leather duster, he had to be the most beautiful man she'd ever seen.

Next to him she felt plain as mud, and it took her a moment to find her voice. "Hello. May I help you?"

The man put his umbrella in the stand by the door and smiled.

"Is there something in particular you're looking for?" she added.

"I'm not sure, thank you. I thought I would browse for a few minutes." His voice was masculine but not too deep—a smooth, rich tone suited to his white-blond, blue-eyed good looks—and held a faint accent.

"Take as much time as you'd like. If you have any questions, please ask."

"I'm on my way to a meeting and time is short, but I'm certain I will find something of interest here." His gaze caught hers, and as she tried not to stare, he smiled again. "Then I will return later. What time do you close?"

"I close at five on weeknights, but I'm open until seven on Saturdays, if you can't make it back by then."

He walked closer, and she admired the way he carried himself. Men this well-groomed and handsome were, alas, all too often gay, but this one—this one radiated a sexuality that was most definitely for her benefit.

"Thank you. And might I say that I notice you have an accent. A lovely one. Irish, yes?"

"Yes, a transplanted Belfast girl. I can tell you're not from around here yourself. Are you in L.A. for business?"

"Ah, you notice! Then my English is not as good as I hope, despite all my practicing." He gave her a look of mock sorrow, and she couldn't help but smile back at him.

"Your English is very good, actually. I deal regularly with international customers, so I'm more attuned to it. I'm guessing Dutch. Or German."

"You have sharp ears." He made his way slowly toward the closest aisle, trailing a long, well-manicured finger along the worn and faded spines. "I'm a native Berliner, though business takes me all over the world. Even to great cities like Los Angeles."

"Are you a bookseller? Or are antique and collectible books a hobby?" Fiona asked, her gaze following him as he moved toward the case with several rare eighteenth-century French political treatises.

"Old things are my business, as it so happens. Finding, selling . . . you have a nice selection here."

"Nothing shockingly valuable or rare, but yes," she said, pleased that he'd noticed. "It's a nice collection. I'm quite proud of it."

Fiona returned to her desk. Her customer made his

way through a few more aisles, lingering now and
then over display cases, and she remained acutely
aware of his presence. Then, after ten or so minutes
of browsing with no intent that she could discern,
the man headed for the door.

"Nothing caught your eye?" she asked and then
went warm as she realized how her words might
sound to a man who looked like this. He probably
had to fight off women on a daily basis.

"There is much here to catch my eye, as I thought,
but not enough time to take advantage of it. I will be
back before you close today. You can count on that."

An interesting turn of phrase.

He flashed another wide smile, said good-bye, and
left.

Even if he was on the odd side, she hoped he
would come back. If nothing else, admiring him as he
wandered around would be an enjoyable way to pass
the time.

Now that she thought about it, perhaps he'd been
trying to flirt with her in his own way. She'd met
enough men from around the world to know that flir-
tation might be universal, but the cultural nuances
surrounding it were not.

Fiona smiled ruefully. Yes, indeed, she had men on
the brain. Still, how often did a guy who looked like
that walk through her door? It'd likely never happen
again.

By noon she'd made an appointment to attend an estate auction the following week because the executor had listed books, magazines, maps, and other antique paper items. Shortly after that, she'd sold a bundle of turn-of-the-century sheet music for a good sum to a visiting couple from Santa Barbara.

The customers had barely walked out the door when her phone rang. "Hello, Kennedy Antiquarian Books."

Silence answered.

Again, she could hear someone on the other end of the line, breathing softly. Irritated, she slammed the cordless back on its stand.

Seconds later, the phone rang again.

Knowing it was best to ignore such pranks, Fiona didn't pick up this time. If it was a genuine call—which she sincerely doubted, given the timing—the answering machine would pick it up.

She couldn't ignore that tickle of unease as she listened to each ring until the machine switched on—just in time to pick up the loud click of the disconnect.

Three

As Fiona was contemplating whether to order Greek or Thai for lunch, her door opened again on a whoosh of rain-scented wind and an airy tinkle of chimes.

Putting down the hideously dull software manual she'd been trying to read, she stood and smiled with what she hoped didn't look like desperate relief. "Hello! How may I help you today?"

"Hello," a cheerful, deep male voice responded, and then he turned from the umbrella stand.

Fiona straightened, resisting the urge to run a smoothing hand over her hair or glance at the dusty old mirror behind the desk and make sure she didn't have any lipstick smudges on her teeth.

Incredible. Two drop-dead gorgeous men in one

day! It had to be some kind of divine omen that her luck was on the upswing.

This man was tall and dark-haired. While not as untouchably perfect as her Berlin businessman, he had the sort of friendly, clean-cut, "brainy guy" good looks she'd always found irresistible. He wore round wire glasses, loose-fitting jeans, and a dress shirt with a conservative navy tie. Over that he had on what looked to be a genuine World War II–era flight jacket, which showcased a nice pair of broad shoulders.

His warm smile flashed beneath eyes made all the more blue by his dark hair. "I'm looking for Fiona Kennedy-McMahon."

"That would be me." Her smile faded, but only for a moment, and she walked around the desk toward him. "Can I help you find something? I handle a wide variety of antique books, as well as other collectibles. Are you here for something in particular?"

"I have a client who recently acquired a manuscript that's old and valuable, and would like to hire you to evaluate it."

Fiona nodded. After discovering old books, maps, hand-tinted prints, or letters and records in an attic while settling a family estate, people frequently came to her to learn if any of them were worth money. Most of the time the items weren't particularly valuable, but every now and then true treasures turned up.

"Of course. I'd be happy to hear more about your

client's manuscript, Mr. . . . I'm sorry, but I didn't catch your name?"

"Laughton." He smiled again, this time apologetically. "Griffith Laughton."

"Please have a seat, Mr. Laughton, and we'll talk. Can I get you some coffee? Soda? Bottled water?"

"That coffee smells great. I'll have a cup, thank you." He shifted his large, slightly worn briefcase and then sat in one of the two leather wingback chairs to the left of her desk. Most women, and more slightly built men, were swallowed up in the extravagant artifact of robber baron days, but Griffith Laughton looked right at home surrounded by all that worn oxblood leather and polished, carved mahogany.

Fiona turned to grab a clean mug. "Do you take cream or sugar?"

"Black is fine." As she was pouring, he asked, "Are you going on a vacation to the Bahamas?"

"I'm planning a trip, yes." Observant fellow. "May I ask your client's name, Mr. Laughton?"

"I'm afraid I'm not at liberty to divulge that information."

Startled, Fiona nearly spilled the last bit of coffee. This was rather unprecedented. She placed the cup on the edge of the desk near him, regarding him curiously. "Whoever it is must be familiar with me. I haven't gone by the name Kennedy-McMahon since my husband's death five years ago."

He looked surprised but quickly recovered. "I apologize for calling you by the wrong name. Is it Ms. Kennedy now?" When she nodded, he said, "My information comes from my client, who is familiar with your work regarding the Elizabethan playwright Christopher Marlowe."

"Ah. That would explain the name, then. I'm no longer in academics, Mr. Laughton. These days I'm in the business of selling books and manuscripts, not researching or writing journal papers on them."

"We're aware of that. However, my client feels you're the most qualified to evaluate this manuscript."

Anticipation, mixed with alarm, tingled through her. "Are you at liberty at least to divulge what kind of manuscript you'd like me to evaluate?"

"Under the condition that you don't speak of our conversation to anyone."

He certainly had her attention now—and as he leaned closer, she caught the tantalizing smell of wind and rain, old leather, and a darkly scented cologne.

"Any business discussion between us will remain confidential, Mr. Laughton."

"My client has acquired what appears to be a lost manuscript by Christopher Marlowe and would like you to verify its authenticity."

Fiona dropped onto her desk chair with such force

that its old springs squeaked in protest. "I don't believe I heard you correctly."

"Yes, you did. A lost Marlowe manuscript has turned up."

Before he even finished speaking, Fiona was shaking her head. "It's not possible. It must be a forgery. Or simply a mistake."

Either way she couldn't help him, and with an effort she squelched that flutter of academic curiosity and excitement—so long buried, she'd almost forgotten what it had felt like.

"I'm flattered your client considered me for such a project, but as I said, I've been out of the academic loop for some time now, and I don't feel qualified for this sort of work. I could give you the names and numbers of several of my former colleagues, if that would be helpful to you."

Again, surprise flashed across his face, and those strangely pale eyes widened behind his glasses. Obviously he hadn't expected her to decline. For that matter, *she* could hardly believe she had.

"My client doesn't want anyone else. I was given very specific instructions regarding this."

"I repeat, Mr. Laughton, that the chances of this manuscript turning out to be genuine are very slim." She picked up her coffee and took a quick gulp to ease the dryness in her mouth. "It would only be a waste of your client's time and mine. I'm sorry if my response will put you in an awkward position with your employer."

"Ms. Kennedy, no one expects you to be anything but skeptical, and while the circumstances under which my client acquired the manuscript are confidential, I was told to give this to you." Laughton pulled a file from his briefcase and slid it across her desk. "It's a photocopy, but it should give you an idea of what we're dealing with."

Fiona tried not to stare at the file, even as her fingers tingled with the need to pick it up.

A Marlowe . . . a *lost* Marlowe.

Poet, playwright, provocateur . . . Kit Marlowe had been her first crush. She'd lived and breathed the highs and lows of his short life, debated hotly with those who tried to pass off half-baked theories and fantasies as facts. When her school friends were squealing over the latest rock stars and movie idols, pinning magazine pictures on their walls, she'd been obsessed with a man dead for over four hundred years. In many ways, Marlowe had been a part of her life longer than her husband.

Now that the initial shock was fading, she couldn't help thinking it wouldn't hurt to take a quick look at this file. What if the manuscript *was* real? Could she ever forgive herself if she passed up the chance to see it? Or at least to be the first to see it?

"It has been such a long time." She couldn't keep the wistfulness out of her voice. "I'm afraid I'd be rather rusty at it."

"We're talking Elizabethan lit here, not rocket science." His tone was gently cajoling. "Not much about Marlowe could've changed in the few years since you left the university."

A valid point. And if she argued too much, he'd start asking questions about why she was so reluctant when she should've been leaping at the chance. The last thing she wanted was to dredge up that old scandal again. "All right. I'll look at these papers you've gone to such trouble to bring to me, but no promises beyond that."

"There's no need to explain yourself to me. I'm just the messenger boy." He smiled again with friendly, wholesome charm. "I'll leave you alone to read this over. You'd probably prefer no distractions."

Not immune to the charm, Fiona smiled back. "Oh, that's not necessary. There's not much to do here and—"

"It's a bookstore, Ms. Kennedy, so I'll look at books."

"Yes, but—"

"And I promise not to touch the expensive ones." His good humor almost twinkled, and how could that be? People didn't *really* twinkle or sparkle, yet he'd seemed to brighten up the place simply by walking through the door. "Don't worry about me. I can take care of myself."

As he turned away, his hold on her snapped. Almost as if she'd been under a spell.

She shook off the odd sensation. Then, steeling herself for the disappointment she was certain would soon follow, she reached for the folder—and noticed, to her dismay, how badly her hands were shaking.

The file contained only a few sheets of paper: Xerox copies, and not high-quality ones. Or else the source material was in very poor shape, which wouldn't be unexpected either.

It took a moment to adjust to the old writing, with its spidery flourishes and quirky spelling; she'd grown used to perfect computer-generated printouts. Yet it took only a moment before she slipped back into old habits, effortlessly reading the faded text:

Ay, pray for me, pray for me! And what noise soever ye hear, come not unto me, for nothing can rescue me and my soul is evermore lost to me.

"It's *Faustus*," she whispered.

And yet, it wasn't. There was an extra line: "And my soul is evermore lost to me" was in neither of the two surviving texts, the A version or the B version.

Leaning closer, frowning in concentration, she quickly skimmed to the ending, which she knew to be significantly different in the A and B versions. Again, this text was different. There were additional lines involving the devils taking Faustus away—more aggressively than in the A version but in not quite the gruesome dismemberment of the B version.

The changes, while small, were significant enough to add new shades of meaning. Nothing immediately screamed "forgery," but the teasingly few pages told her that this matter needed to be handled very carefully.

"Mr. Laughton," she called out, quite proud of how calm she sounded. Considering her pounding heart and sweating palms, she should've been squeaking as if she'd been sucking helium. "I believe I've seen enough."

"All right, then." Muffled by the stacks of heavy old books, his voice sounded distant. "We'll be there in a second."

Fiona raised a brow. "We?"

"I'm being stalked by a big, black cat."

She laughed. "That would be Faustus. Usually he ignores people."

"He's not ignoring me." Laughton emerged from behind the British Aisles, and at his heels, trotting with more speed than his girth would seem to have allowed, came Faustus. "I think he's herding me."

Laughton halted, bending down to pat the cat, and Fiona couldn't help but notice how nicely the denim tightened around the hard contours of what her blunt friend Cassie would call "a fine piece of man ass."

"Faustus believes he owns this place and everyone in it," she said. "It's best to humor him."

"Do you bring your cat to the store, or does he live here?"

"I've been bringing him with me to the shop since he was a kitten. I didn't like the thought of him being alone in my apartment." A little embarrassing, admitting she'd been such a hopeless softy. "Fifteen pounds and four years later, Faustus continues to tolerate the kitty cage so he can lord it over the shop."

"And why'd you name your cat Faustus?"

"Because he's black as the depths of hell, with the devil's own curiosity, which gets him into scrapes. Besides, it's the perfect name for the cat of a Marlowe fanatic."

Laughton sat again in the wingback chair by her desk, his smile fading to a more serious expression. "And so, what's the verdict? Will you examine the rest of the manuscript for my client?"

There was no good reason to say no, despite the little voice warning her she was foolishly getting her hopes up.

"Yes. Marlowe was the great passion of my life—I'd do anything for him." Knowing how that must've sounded, she added, "And on a practical note, the timing couldn't be better. I wouldn't mind extra money for my trip in January."

The consultant fee would undoubtedly be quite nice, since only a very wealthy man could've acquired such a valuable manuscript.

Or a very rich woman.

It suddenly dawned on her how careful Laughton had been not to reveal the gender of his client. He made the omission seem so natural that she'd only now noticed it, but avoiding the casual "he" or "she" in a conversation wasn't natural at all. It required considerable effort.

Catching her questioning look, he asked, "Is something wrong?"

"You can drop the act, Mr. Laughton. You're too well dressed and well spoken to be a mere messenger."

"It's not an act. I'm—" He broke off, looking faintly annoyed. "All right, the truth is that I'm a lawyer, but I'm so low on the food chain that I get stuck with the jobs nobody else wants. So in all the ways that matter, I am just the errand boy."

That he was a lawyer *would* explain the artful turn of speech and the ease with which he'd obscured telling details.

Laughton plucked the folder off her desk. "I'm afraid I can't let you hold on to this. My client wants to keep the manuscript a secret until you've had your chance to determine whether or not it's genuine, so I can't have copies lying around for anyone to see."

With a sharp disappointment, Fiona watched him return the file to his briefcase. "Not that I have legions of Marlowe experts wandering through my shop, but I understand."

Laughton sighed. "I really am sorry . . . And I'm noticing that I keep apologizing to you. It's kind of embarrassing."

And endearing. Fiona's smile widened. "It's quite all right."

"Good to hear . . . and I'm glad to see you smile. You know, you have a really beautiful smile."

A warmth of pleasure washed over her, in defiance of her common sense. Hmmm; maybe she could trade in the scuba instructor for a fling with a sexy messenger boy. Griffith Laughton didn't look like the type who'd protest a friendly, discreet overture.

"You're a flirt, Mr. Laughton."

"A natural consequence of growing up with sisters." He grinned, and again the room seemed to brighten around him. "And if our relationship has progressed to that level, you'd better call me Griffith. Or Grif."

"Griffith it is, and you can call me Fiona."

"Just Griffith, huh?"

Still smiling, she added, "I don't believe we've progressed to Grif *quite* yet, even if you have just bought me like a cheap whore."

He laughed, a rich, chest-deep laugh that warmed her all over. She'd always let the man make the first move before, but maybe it was time to let go of that habit as well.

Faustus meowed loudly and twined around Griffith's legs, which was surprising since he was very particular about the people on whom he bestowed his attention.

After Fiona shooed the cat away, Griffith asked, "What time do you close today?"

"At five. Why?"

"How about I meet you here after you close and take you out for dinner? Then you can ask me all the questions you'd like."

So much for her fledgling attempt at being more aggressive. "You seem quite devoted to your job."

He leaned forward with another of those irresistible smiles. "I wasn't thrilled about babysitting a file of papers, but the job's turning out to be much more interesting than I'd expected."

Her innate Irishness—and plain old female intuition—told her he was feeding her a line of blarney, yet he was so blatantly flirtatious that it was hard to be annoyed.

"I bet you say that to every antiquarian bookseller you meet."

He laughed again, and she noticed how his eyes crinkled at the corners and his cheeks grooved. "I don't meet many antiquarian booksellers. In fact, you're my first."

"Really? I feel so special."

How deliciously easy it was to flirt with him; something about him invited comfort, familiarity, and warmth.

"And you should. You are very, very special." He leaned his elbow on her desk and propped his chin on his palm, those very blue eyes of his amused. "You are the prettiest woman I've seen in a long, long time. I can't get over all those freckles." His smile widened. "Do you have them everywhere?"

A sudden heat suffused her face, and Fiona was certain she was glowing red. "That's a rather personal question."

He had the sense to look sheepish. "Guess it's a guy thing. I can't help wondering if it's possible to count them all."

If anybody else had spoken so outrageously, she would've been alarmed, even angry. But, again, because he was so straightforward, her discomfort faded. Or it could have been that she was just used to this kind of teasing. Richard had often joked about her freckles; once, he'd even tried to count all the ones on her breast. Predictably, he'd gotten distracted and never finished.

"I'm still waiting for an answer about dinner, Fiona."

Hearing him say her name with such familiarity

flustered her. But she managed to keep her tone professional. "I'd be happy to go out for dinner with you. It'll take me a few minutes to close the shop down for the night, so you should come back around a quarter after five, Mr. Laughton."

"I thought we were at Griffith."

"Until later, Griffith," she corrected herself, smiling. "And please let your client know that I am very grateful for this opportunity and that I hope the manuscript will turn out to be genuine."

He hesitated, as if he wanted to say something else. Instead, he gave her an odd little half smile. "Consider the message delivered. See you in a few hours."

Fiona watched him walk away, briefcase in hand. He'd been out the door for only seconds when she noticed he'd forgotten his umbrella. She quickly walked around the desk, intending to try to flag him down, but the phone rang.

She glanced from the phone to the door, then sighed and answered. "Hello, Kennedy Antiquarian Books."

There was no answer.

Oh, for . . . Not *again!* "This is the third time you've called me today, and my patience with you has reached its limit."

Nothing; only that same low, steady breathing.

"If you have something to say, say it. Otherwise, if you call again, I'm contacting the police."

The silence stretched on for a few seconds longer. Just as she was getting ready to slam the phone down, a muffled male voice said softly, "Don't get involved with the manuscript." Then the caller disconnected.

Fiona stared at the phone as alarm prickled across her skin, raising the fine hairs on her arms.

"Well," she murmured. "So much for them wanting to keep it a secret."

Four

AFTER LEAVING THE BOOKSTORE, GRIFFITH CIRCLED the block to the narrow, dark service alley behind the shop to sit in his car for the next few hours. He couldn't be two places at once, so he'd decided to guard the most vulnerable area of the shop: the back door, with its flimsy excuse for a lock.

How could Kennedy be so careless? Earlier, while she'd been engrossed in the file, he'd taken a quick look around and found everything else in her place reasonably secure. But that back door leading to the cellar was begging for trouble even from petty thieves.

The upper two stories were also a potential problem. He presumed those floors were storage and office space, but he hadn't been able to see beyond the velvet, tasseled rope that blocked the stairway.

And of course there was the fire escape.

It appeared they'd lucked out and he'd gotten to Fiona before either McMahon or von Lahr, but Griffith knew better than to relax his guard. Fifteen years of experience had taught him that trouble always hit the minute you started to relax.

Griffith didn't peg McMahon as the type who'd walk through the front door of his wife's shop five years after he'd supposedly died. No, he was the creeping-around-in-the-dark type. So any bad shit would come from the back door.

Still, things were going well. He'd clearly caught Kennedy's eye; he'd read those signals easily enough. She wasn't the sort to knock boots with whatever guy crossed her path, though, so he'd have to be careful not to push too hard later tonight.

As time passed, he tried to find a position to ease the chronic pinch of pain in his back. At a quarter past four, he pulled his cell phone from his jacket pocket and dialed Ben's number.

"Sheridan."

"Checking in. So far, so good."

"So we got there before our target?"

"It looks that way. If she'd heard anything about the manuscript or if McMahon had tried to contact her, she's not a good enough liar to hide it from me."

"Notice anything suspicious?"

"Not yet, but McMahon's made it this far without getting himself killed. For a spineless little bookworm, he's damn good at making himself invisible."

"Remember that we still don't know for sure it's McMahon. And we're fairly certain he was working with at least one other person, so don't count out that possibility."

Ahead, a moving shadow became two young men walking down the alley in his direction. "My job doesn't change whether he's alive or dead, Ben."

"So what's your next move?"

"I'm taking her out to dinner, then I'll get her into bed. That'll keep her with me 24/7. The manuscript's got her attention, and she'll be too busy looking it over to ask many questions until she gets to the part where she notices something's wrong."

Griffith shifted, aware of a slow burn of pleasure when he thought of Fiona. All that thick, dark red hair, the pale skin dusted with freckles . . . He couldn't wait to get her naked.

And because he wasn't a totally rotten bastard, he'd do everything possible to make sure she never learned the truth.

"She won't be a problem. And by the way, she's a hell of a lot better looking in the flesh than in the file pictures. This may turn out to be a sweet little assignment after all. Thanks for calling me in."

"You were the only one around, and *that* was only because you were half-dead until a month ago. Anything else I need to know?"

Griffith watched a scrawny mutt skitter down the alley, sniffing as it went. The two men were still walking his way.

"The security at this place is shit. If we can get an extra body in here to watch the back door, it'd make my job a hell of a lot easier. I did a quick check of her apartment, and the situation there isn't much better. She's on the second floor, but there's nothing to stop anybody from getting to her if they really want to. How are you coming with sending me some help?"

"Our LAPD contacts are alerted to your presence, and your backup has just called in sick, so he'll be on hand for the usual 'off-duty officer passing by' help if you end up in a mess. I'd appreciate it if you could avoid making any messes."

"I always try."

"Bullshit," Ben said, his tone exasperated. "The Torrance office is on standby. Diva and Rico are getting ready to fly back, and Noonie's leaving New York later tonight."

"Noonie's a rookie. I hate working with rookies. You know that."

"Tough. He's an *available* rookie."

"And that's better than nothing. Is Bayview ready?"

"Yes."

"All right. I'll check in again tonight when I get a chance. Or earlier, if something comes up."

Sheridan disconnected, and Griffith slipped the phone back into his pocket, readjusting the gun in his waistband as he did so. Damn thing kept digging into his spine, which didn't help matters. The Tylenols he'd gulped weren't working worth shit, either. Another couple weeks to heal probably would've been a good idea, but he was well enough to do whatever needed doing.

He hoped. And he'd find out soon enough.

The two men, one Latino and the other white, were trying too hard not to look at him even as they all but strutted toward him, hands in their pockets on their guns or knives, cocky bravado in every line of their bodies.

Nothing marked them as professionals.

Goddammit.

Tamping back the disappointment, Griffith got out of the car and kicked the door shut with the heel of his boot. The men stopped for a moment, then, glancing at each other, moved forward again.

"Looks like the welcoming party finally arrived." Griffith leaned against the car, hands loose at his sides. A buzz of anticipation sparked, lightening his mood for the first time in months. "Good."

Again they exchanged looks—then rushed him.

Griffith rolled over the hood, easily avoiding the Latino's punch, which instead slammed into the side of the car.

A flood of cursing in Spanish followed.

"Bet that hurt." Griffith balanced on his heels, ready to move again in a split second. "Better luck next time."

"Motherfucker!" With a snarl, the white guy surged forward, knife flashing in the dim light. "You're gettin' it!"

Griffith ducked and rammed his fist in the man's gut, then spun and kicked the backs of his knees. The man dropped to the dirty pavement with a thud and lay there, curled in on himself as he gagged and coughed.

The Latino at least knew how to fight. He was faster and smarter, not telegraphing his intent as easily as his partner. His knife snaked in and out with vicious speed, forcing Griffith to move faster to avoid each thrust and slash.

"Damn!" Griffith laughed. "You're actually making me break a sweat."

As the Latino circled, blade glinting in the pale yellow of a back-door light, Griffith moved with him, resisting the urge to go for his gun or his own knife. If he couldn't take out a punk like this with his bare hands, his ass should be fired on the spot.

"You like this?" the man asked in Spanish.

"A good fight, the promise of even better sex tonight . . . What's not to like?" The curved tip of the blade came a little too close for comfort. "Uh-uh.

Not Granddad's jacket. That's my good-luck piece."

Time to put a stop to this before he ended up with a cut he'd have to explain to Kennedy.

He deliberately left himself open, and the man took the bait, rushing forward so fast he nearly trampled over his fallen partner.

As Griffith spun and ducked, he grabbed the hand that held the knife and bent the wrist sharply backward until it made a dry popping sound. The man grunted in pain, and the knife clattered to the ground. Griffith kicked it out of reach beneath his car, then swung the man around to smash him face-first against the window glass.

Griffith pulled out his gun and pressed it into the stunned man's back, keeping a close eye on the partner, who was still moaning.

"I could've shot you both before you got anywhere near me." He spoke directly into the man's ear, his tone even and soft. "But because I'm in a generous mood, and because you're just street punks who did this for a quick buck, I'll let you walk if you tell me who sent you and where they are right now."

Von Lahr clearly hadn't hired them. They'd never stood a chance against him, and von Lahr wouldn't make a mistake like that.

"I don't know," the Latino said, between gritted teeth. He was holding up pretty well despite the shattered wrist and broken nose. "He didn't give us his name. He said to beat you up good. Make you hurt. Then he would pay us."

"What did he look like?"

"I don't—"

Griffith twisted the wrist, and the man cried out, quickly biting his lip. "I don't know . . . just some white guy. Brown hair. Not tall. He looks like every rich dude walking down the street. That's all I know. I'm tellin' the truth, man!"

Brown hair didn't help much. McMahon had brown hair, but so did a lot of other people.

Standing so close to the man, Griffith took in a lungful of stale liquor and sour sweat, the stink of unwashed hair and skin. He wouldn't get anything helpful out of either of them because they didn't know anything. They didn't even know, or care, why they'd been told to attack him.

Maybe they were more of a diversion than a genuine attack.

Griffith shoved the Latino aside, then retrieved the knife from his fallen partner. "Get the hell out of here before I change my mind about letting you go. Because the LAPD won't give a damn if I take out trash like you."

The Latino took off at a dead run, leaving his partner to stumble after him.

Griffith watched them for a few seconds longer to make sure they didn't come back at him, then turned and walked swiftly out of the alley, tucking in his shirt and shoving the gun back in its holster, out of sight.

If von Lahr hadn't sent them, then it had to have been the target—although what he'd hoped to accomplish with a couple of losers like that, Griffith couldn't guess. But McMahon was close by, all right, and watching over his ex-wife—just like everyone had anticipated.

Or maybe it was someone connected to McMahon; Griffith hadn't forgotten Ben's warning.

A glance at his watch showed that it was 4:30. He'd be a little early for his dinner date.

Griffith rounded the corner toward the shop: tall and hulking in all its faded Victorian glory, a relic of a bygone era stranded in a sea of modern motion and noise and brilliant lights. The russet awnings, printed with KENNEDY ANTIQUARIAN BOOKS in white, drooped beneath the weight of the pooled rain and dripped on him as he pulled out the glasses and slipped them on.

Then, smiling his friendliest smile, he walked inside on a gentle tinkling of chimes.

Five

IN A SMALL CAFÉ KITTY-CORNER FROM FIONA Kennedy's shop, Rainert von Lahr slouched elegantly in a booth and raised his chipped saucer and cup. He caught the eye of the counter girl and smiled slowly, holding her gaze until her expression softened and a faint color marked her cheeks.

"Hello there."

"Hi . . . um, did you want more coffee, sir?"

The last thing he wanted was more of the tepid, bitter brew.

Time to leave this too-visible place and retrieve his redhead. He judged it near enough to closing time to take her without raising any immediate suspicions—and the more time he had to work with the situation before the police interfered, the better his chances of getting what he wanted.

"The check, please," he said, still smiling.

The color in the girl's cheeks darkened. She was a pretty thing, with wide brown eyes and skin the color of caramel candy. If only he weren't pressed for time—but this girl wasn't likely to willingly satisfy his tastes anyway. She was pretty but boringly sweet.

"I'll get it right to you, sir."

A moment later she slipped the register tape toward him on a little plastic tray and watched as he peeled off bills, including a generous tip.

He stood and looked down at her, his gaze lingering on her lips just long enough for her breathing to quicken. It always amused him, catching their interest like this. It was like an athlete practicing. He had to keep his skills honed; he never knew when he'd need a warm, sympathetic woman to help him stay out of sight for a few days or weeks.

As von Lahr headed for the door, he smoothed back his hair and straightened his tie—and stopped short, frozen in surprise for a split second before he eased back from the window.

Fiona Kennedy was leaving her shop a good twenty minutes earlier than she should have been, and with a man he recognized all too well.

"Laughton," he murmured, eyes narrowing.

How long had he been in the city? When—and

how—had the Avalon operative learned about McMahon?

These people had been a major nuisance five years ago; lately, they were becoming a very real problem. Laughton's presence changed everything; his original plan was now useless.

He usually worked with several backup plans, though—when he didn't, he always regretted it. Like his recent carelessness in that backwater American town.

Von Lahr had a clear view of Laughton and Kennedy as they crossed the street. They were sharing an umbrella, and Laughton had one hand at the small of her back and a briefcase in the other—the manuscript, no doubt. The woman was laughing as she tried to hold the umbrella high enough to cover them both, but the wind kept catching it, threatening to pull it out of her hands.

How friendly they looked.

He'd always admired and respected Laughton's abilities. In another time and place, under different circumstances, they might have been partners.

As they walked toward him, von Lahr aimed his index finger at the center of Laughton's forehead, cocked his thumb, pulled an imaginary trigger, and whispered, "Bang, bang."

Headshot. Right between the eyes.

"You're dead. And I win."

Then, noticing how the waitress stared at him uneasily, he smiled until the tense lines of her shoulders began to relax.

"An old business rival. Sorry. I couldn't help myself."

The waitress smiled back shyly. "Yeah, I felt like that about my ex-boyfriend. Nothing wrong with a little revenge fantasy, I always say."

"Nothing at all," von Lahr agreed. "Keeps us honest, yes?"

It was time to turn that fantasy into reality. Killing Laughton would deprive him of a worthy adversary but also a galling thorn in his side. If he was clever, this trip would eliminate two threats rather than just the one.

He stepped out of the café, impervious to the rain as he held his umbrella low and followed his redhead and the Avalon man. They walked only a few blocks to a small Thai restaurant, and once they were inside, von Lahr turned and walked away in the opposite direction.

Reaching into his coat pocket, he pulled out his cell phone, dialed, and waited for the answer. "Laughton is here, and he's with the woman. Yes, *that* Laughton. This necessitates a change of plans. Get to the Thai place near her shop. You know the one, yes? Good. Follow them. I want to know their every move."

Whistling, aware of the deep inner thrum of excitement, von Lahr stepped up to the curb and hailed a taxi to return to his hotel.

It was a good game they played, he and Avalon. Someday it would end, of course, but for the time being, he would enjoy himself.

Ah, yes. Life was about to get very interesting.

Six

"I LOVE THIS PLACE. IT'S NOTHING FANCY, BUT THE SATAY is excellent." Fiona dipped her chicken on its bamboo skewer in the peanut sauce. "And the portions are so huge that I don't have to cook for a couple of days."

"Then I'll walk you home. You can't carry takeout and the cat *and* an umbrella," Griffith replied.

"Good point." Faustus was still at the shop, snoozing away in his usual spot. "I'll take you up on that offer."

The little restaurant was dark, filled to capacity with a low-level hum of conversation, and saturated in the scents of spices and curries and hot grills. Fiona was still thinking about that strange phone call. Since the moment Griffith had arrived and persuaded her to lock up early—she hadn't had a customer in over an hour, so it hadn't taken much persuading—she knew she'd have to tell him about it. Now was as good a time as any.

"Griffith, how many people know of this manuscript's existence?"

Across the candlelight flickering from its dark red glass holder, he regarded her with a neutral expression. If her question took him by surprise, he didn't let it show. "You, me, my client. The person who found it, and the one who arranged its sale. If there are more, which might be the case, I wouldn't know about it. Why?"

"I got a call right after you left. It was a man, though I couldn't clearly hear his voice, and he told me to stay away from the manuscript. Then he hung up."

"That's not good." Griffith sat back in his chair, with a look of concern on his face. "Are you okay?"

"Naturally I'm worried. Over the past couple days, I've had several hang-up calls. Until the last one, I'd assumed they were crank calls or wrong numbers." She paused. "I don't think that's the case anymore."

"To the best of my knowledge, only a select few know of this manuscript's discovery."

"I'd say somebody leaked your secret."

"It does look that way, doesn't it? If you want to back out of the agreement, at least until I have a chance to identify who's calling you, I'm sure my client would understand."

"I don't like getting creepy telephone calls. On the other hand, it's not every day a supposedly undiscovered Marlowe manuscript lands in my lap." She met his gaze squarely. "Do I have a reason to believe that I might be in danger because of this manuscript?"

"None that I'm aware of." His brows drew together in a frown, and his lips narrowed to a straight, grim line. "The decision to stay or walk is up to you, but if you'd like me to arrange a more secure location for you to work, I can do that."

"Do you have any idea who might be calling me?"

"There is . . . an individual who was my client's partner some years back, and they had a falling out. There's been bad blood between them ever since, and it's possible that, if he found out about the manuscript, he would try to intercept it for his own use."

Fiona detected nothing in Griffith's eyes or expression to indicate he was lying to her, yet she couldn't help noticing he was still careful not to reveal any information about his client. She realized then that one of the reasons she'd been so quickly attracted to him was the aura of adventure, excitement, and mystery—even a whiff of danger.

God knew, she was missing adventure and excitement in her life. "I suppose people in high places who make a lot of money also make a lot of enemies."

"It goes with the territory, yes." Griffith shrugged,

still looking grim. "I don't believe you're in any real danger, but it's possible that if you get caught in the middle, things might get a little uncomfortable for you."

It felt as if her belly had dropped to her knees. "So why would they warn me? That strikes me as self-defeating for any shady plots."

"Because his vendetta isn't against you. He fancies himself a gentleman and a ladies' man, and it would be like him to try to warn you off."

"Now that we're aware of a potential problem, we'll be that much more careful. And, really, you're the one who should be worried. You have to keep the copies with you at all times. This person is far more likely to try to knock *you* on the head than *me*."

He grinned. "Thank you. That's very comforting."

Her face warmed on a rush of embarrassment. "What I meant was—"

"It's all right. I was trying to lighten the mood."

"Though I don't *like* it, of course, I don't mind taking a small risk to continue examining this manuscript." She gave him a rueful look. "It seems my academic ego isn't as retired as I'd thought."

"That's your decision?"

"My decision right now is that I be allowed to revise my decision should the need arise," Fiona said with forced lightness. "For the time being, I will continue to look at this manuscript and take precautions, like calling the police if I get another hang-up call. If more risks than I'm willing to take arise, I'll walk away."

He smiled, and she could've sworn admiration crossed his face. "It sounds like a workable plan, although the sooner you finish up, the better. How long will it take you to decide whether or not it's genuine?"

"It's hard to say. I'll need to read it first to get a feel for it, and if anything obviously false jumps out at me, it won't be long at all. If that doesn't happen, then I'll need to do a complete analysis."

"And that involves . . . ?"

"Checking for references to other plays and popular literature of the time, as well as allusions to current political and religious events or philosophies. Marlowe was drawn to particular themes and symbolism, so I'll look for those. I'll also do an analysis of line length, word usage . . . and I have an acquaintance at the Getty who can work on dating the material itself."

"Wow. I had no idea it would be so complicated."

"It would be much more complicated if this were an undiscovered play or poem, rather than one scholars have long suspected had a lost, earlier version. Still, verifying it won't be easy. The preservation of Marlowe's work was left to the whims of friend and foe alike after he was murdered. We'll likely never have a complete or accurate account of his life or his works."

"Fair enough." He leaned forward, a smile playing at the corner of his mouth. "Now let's talk about something more pleasant."

"Fine by me. I'd rather not spook myself to death before the main course. Did you have any particular subject in mind?"

"You."

With that one word, the voices around her faded and the already small room narrowed to only the two of them.

Griffith Laughton had the most amazing eyes, so clear and light—and direct. Those little round glasses disguised that directness; without them, she had a feeling meeting his gaze would be more difficult. Maybe even uncomfortable.

And he smelled positively wonderful. The scents of leather and spiced cologne enveloped her, reaching deep inside and stirring a hot bloom of desire.

"Men like you should not be allowed to exist. You're very bad for the collective female peace of mind."

For all his wholesome good looks, he was a canny piece of work. But that didn't prevent her from wanting to get horizontal with him. And he was making it plain that all she had to do was crook a finger and he'd follow.

"If you want me to stop, I'll stop." His voice had a hoarser edge to it. "I'm usually not such a pushy bastard, but you're such an amazingly beautiful woman, and those freckles, and that sexy accent . . . Irish, right?"

She grinned. "With a name like Kennedy, what do you think? I'm sure my accent's much tamer these days, since I've lived half of my life in the States."

"Maybe, but I still want to keep you talking so I can keep hearing it."

"Really, now?"

"Really. Say something Irish."

Fiona rolled her eyes and then, in a thick, cliché accent, she said, "Now, then, boyo, you won't be gettin' away with me lucky charms."

Griffith laughed.

Still smiling, she added, "You know, you're the second good-looking man who's commented on my accent today."

Surprise crossed his face, then he merely looked intrigued. "A taller, darker, handsomer version of tall, dark, and handsome me? Please say it isn't so, or my fragile ego will be crushed."

"I'd say your ego isn't very fragile, or in any danger. And no, he was tall, blond, blue-eyed, and very Aryan handsome. Not my preference, to be honest," she added.

His focus sharpened, as if scenting a challenge

regardless, and his smile widened. "Aryan, huh?"

Fiona shrugged. Mentioning the other man had been a whim, but it had been silly. She was so rusty in this whole dating and mating thing.

"He was some businessman from Berlin who said he'd be back later." Which, she recalled with guilt, she'd forgotten about in her excitement over the Marlowe. "It's not a big deal."

"Then I'm glad I stole you away before he came back to tempt you with his Aryan goodness."

He *was* jealous—if only a tiny bit—which pleased her. Though she wasn't looking for a long-term lover, she liked knowing that she was pretty enough and sexy enough to catch the attention of a man who looked like Griffith Laughton.

This picking up a guy was harder than she'd expected, though. Old habits were difficult to overcome, and she wasn't the kind of woman who had sex with a total stranger.

"Can I ask you a few questions, Griffith?"

The dark, finely arched brow rising above the silver wire rims of his glasses was his only acknowledgment of her abrupt hijacking of the conversation. "Sure."

"Where are you from?"

"You mean like where was I born?" When she nodded, he said, "Gary, Indiana."

Fiona had a vague idea that Gary was near the

Great Lakes and was industrial. "I remember you said you had sisters, but any brothers? Other family? Wives or children?"

She was pretty sure he wasn't married, judging by his behavior and the lack of a ring, but it didn't hurt to make certain.

"Wives, as in plural?" He laughed. "No, no harem back in Gary. I have parents, grandparents, uncles, aunts, and cousins, two older sisters and one younger brother. The sisters are both married, and I have nieces and nephews. I don't see my family very often, though." At her questioning look he added, "I travel a lot. Like any job, mine has its drawbacks."

"Where is home for you now, if you don't mind me asking?"

"Wherever work takes me. At the moment, it's L.A. Next week it could be Dallas or New York City or Chicago. Or even somewhere out of the country."

"So what do you do when you're not babysitting valuable manuscripts and antiquarian booksellers?"

Griffith smiled. "I usually do acquisition work, which means I spend a lot of time reading books, taking notes, and hanging out in records offices, looking over dusty old papers."

"It doesn't sound all that different from what I do." She leaned forward and didn't miss how his gaze briefly lowered to where her breasts rested against the edge of the table. "Related to that, sort of, is how much I've been admiring your jacket. Is it vintage or a reproduction?"

"It belonged to my grandfather. He flew the Pacific in World War Two and left it to me when he died."

"It must be very special to you, then."

"Yes."

Fiona waited for more—some family anecdote at least—but when he didn't elaborate and she began to sense some discomfort in the silence, she left it at that. She held his gaze for a moment longer, enjoying that deliciously warm, liquid pull of desire before returning her attention to her dinner.

Mission accomplished. Technically, he was no longer a total stranger, so now she could banish that annoying little jab of Catholic schoolgirl guilt.

"Can I ask *you* a question?"

Fiona smiled. "Seems only fair."

"Why are you going to the Bahamas?"

"Why does anybody go on a tropical getaway? For rest and relaxation." Then, on a spurt of frankness, she added, "And to have a fling. All my girlfriends tell me the scuba instructors are easy."

Finally, she'd surprised him. He stared at her for a long moment, then said, "You're going all the way to the Bahamas to have sex?"

"Not so loud!" She glanced around, but no one seemed to have overheard him. "And yes, that's the plan. It's complicated, but the short of it is my husband disappeared five years ago and was finally declared dead, and I'm looking to test the waters again, so to speak."

"All the men in L.A. must be either blind or stupid. Or both." He shook his head in amazement. "And if you want to test the waters, you sure as hell don't have to go all the way to the Bahamas. I'd be more than willing to help you take the plunge."

That was what she'd been aiming for, but she still asked, "Why?"

"Does there have to be a reason beyond basic lust?"

To say otherwise would have been dishonest. "When you put it that way, I suppose not."

Their gazes met and held again, and this time the heat curled deeper and sharper, because now there were no subterfuge or pretending. The silence said, almost as loud as words, *Let's do it. Now.*

"Do you want to finish your dinner or—"

"Let's get the cat and go back to your place."

Fiona nodded, and once he'd paid the bill, they headed for the door.

Outside, the sky was still dark and moody, full of clouds that threatened to pummel them with rain again. The rain didn't keep L.A. inside, though; people filled the sidewalks and streets in a great, moving swarm, all hurrying to be somewhere else. Bright headlights streamed in one direction, taillights in the other, a constant reflection of red and white. Around them, faces were obscured behind bobbing circles of umbrellas in various colors, sizes, and patterns, little halos of misty rain hovering over them as they passed beneath the streetlights.

A chill breeze cut through her, bringing with it a familiar scent of leather, cologne, and damp denim— and a rush of desire so intense she couldn't look at him.

"We should hurry before it starts pouring again." As she walked by, Griffith caught her arm, pulled her against the solid warmth of his chest, and kissed her.

Not a gentle kiss, but hard and hungry. He tasted of ginger tea, his lips cool, his tongue hot, and Fiona sank against him, opening to his mouth. Her tongue played along his, and she was aware of every part of her body pressed against his, chests and bellies together, her hand on his shoulder, his on the small of her back.

Eyes closed, she lost herself to the intoxicating power, the inner need winding sweetly tight, the feel of his mouth on hers, his tongue, his scent filling her, while the rain misted on their bare heads and shoulders in tiny beads and people passed them by without a second look.

Fiona broke the kiss first, pulling back. Up close, she could see the shadow of his beard, the faint lines at the corners of his eyes. He still looked wholesome and collegiate, like the proverbial Ivy League frat boy, but with a harder edge of maturity.

Then his eyes slowly opened, and she couldn't look away. For a moment, she thought she saw something darker, more dangerous in them, but then he smiled and the moment was gone.

"I've been wanting to do that since I met you. And now I want to do it again. All over. I'd like to see if you have freckles everywhere." His voice lowered to a whisper. "And I really want to fuck you."

Fiona froze. "No one has ever said that to me before."

"That's a damn shame." Griffith brushed his fingers along the side of her cheek, his gentle touch a stark contrast to his language. "Somebody should've told you long ago just how beautiful and fuckable you are."

People always described her as brainy, respectable, practical, refined . . .

The shivery pulse of awareness throbbed, and she realized that his rough, honest words turned her on.

"Let's go. Your cat has food, a place to sleep, and a litter box." His hand on her back, Griffith was already guiding her down the sidewalk and toward her apartment. "We don't need to go back for him."

Fiona nodded in agreement—and didn't notice that Griffith knew what direction to go in without her telling him where she lived.

Seven

✦

WHEN HIS CELL PHONE BEGAN VIBRATING INSIDE HIS suit coat pocket, Rainert von Lahr had a black-haired, olive-skinned beauty in lime green silk on his lap, nibbling his ear. The dark hotel lobby bar helped obscure where his hands were and how much his "friend" had had to drink.

"A moment, please." He slid his hands out from under her skirt and retrieved the phone. "Yes?"

"I'm calling to let you know they didn't go back for the cat like you said they would. They went straight to her place."

Von Lahr arched a brow. Laughton was up to his usual tricks, then. He was almost disappointed in his redhead; he'd expected her to have more class than to hit the sheets so quickly with the likes of Laughton. "That man, he is such a tramp."

His companion—whose name was Rebeka, with "one k and no h," as she'd kept telling him—giggled and pressed her impressive breasts against his arm.

"So what do you want me to do next, Rainert?"

"They'll have to go back to the shop soon. Follow the earlier instructions I gave you."

"Will do."

Von Lahr returned his phone to his pocket and his attention to Rebeka. "My apologies."

"So who's a tramp?" she asked.

She was still pressed suggestively against him, but he didn't mind. She smelled nice, was pretty and attentive, and he'd paid for her for the night. She was his to do with as he wished.

"Someone you don't need to be concerned about."

"I've never heard anyone call a man a tramp before."

Over the top of her head, he watched the traffic lights change at the corner and pedestrians stream across the intersection. "It was an insult."

"I know. And of course *you're* no tramp. You just hang out with whores for the fun of it."

He indulged her, smiling. "I am virtuous, true."

She made a face of distaste. "Not too virtuous, or I'll be very disappointed later on."

"Then I am virtuous only when I need to be. Is that better?"

"*Ja!*" She smirked. "It's the only German word I know."

"Not a problem. 'Ja' is all I'll want to hear coming out of your lovely mouth tonight."

"Mmmm." She kissed him, tugging at his bottom lip with her teeth, and he tasted a light, fruity wine on her mouth. "Let's go to your room."

"No," he said. "Let's go to yours."

That broke through her haze of alcohol. "Mine? But that's . . . Well, okay. I guess we can do that, if you really want to."

"I do."

He wanted to be where no one, including his own people, knew to look for him, in case something went wrong and they turned out to be talkative under persuasive situations.

He was in a cab and on the way to his escort's place—which he hoped was at least clean—when his cell phone went off again. He flipped it open, murmuring, "I seem to be popular tonight."

The number on the small screen wasn't one he recognized, and he frowned.

Ordinarily, he wouldn't have answered, but given the current circumstances, it would have been more dangerous not to. "Yes? Who is this?"

A muffled male voice said, "Someone who has a deal you can't refuse, Mr. von Lahr."

Von Lahr sat up straight, all his focus on that

whispery voice on the other end of the line. "Keep talking."

"Patience." The voice was amused. "It involves the Marlowe forgery, Fiona Kennedy, Griffith Laughton, and Avalon. I'm telling you all this so you know I'm for real. If you're interested in hearing more, I'll call you later."

When the woman tried to snuggle closer, von Lahr shoved her away without a thought.

"Why not tell me more now?"

"Because I'm not in the mood."

The call ended, and von Lahr scowled and swore softly as his escort sulked in the corner of the taxi.

Eight

Surprises within surprises within surprises.

That was Fiona Kennedy, as Griffith was beginning to learn. She lived on a block of converted row houses in a subdued rainbow of yellows, browns, and grays. Considering the plain exterior, he didn't know what he'd find inside, but he'd expected a frilly cottage look or the darkly faded Victorian charm of her shop.

Instead, he faced a living room and kitchen with a big, blocky sofa and chairs, polished chrome and pale woods, and everything in hues of turquoise, gray, and an orange-pink the color of a plate of fresh shrimp. It had a Deco feel to it, helped along by walls filled with 1920s and '30s advertising prints and posters.

"Nice place, though not what I was expecting," he said as he helped her take off her damp coat.

"Everybody says that."

As she hung up her coat, he took in the trim body

and small breasts beneath her ivory turtleneck, the way her hips and backside filled out the rust twill pants. She wore her long hair in a French braid, and everything about her—her clothes, her hair, and even her subtle makeup—was in tones of red and brown. Close behind her, he could feel the heat of her body, and she smelled of rain and shampoo—and a wisp of a spiced, vanilla-like perfume.

Desire flared, heating him from head to toe so fast and strong and *real* that it surprised him.

"Would you like me to take your coat?"

"I'll hang it up. Did you want to go freshen up or something first?"

He had to stash his weapons, and the easiest way to do that was to get her into the bathroom for a few minutes.

"Thanks." Her relief was transparent. "I'll be right back."

The second he heard the door close and running water in the sink, Griffith moved to the bedroom.

He barely noticed the interior—beyond that same spiced vanilla scent—as he stripped off his jacket, the shoulder rig beneath it, and the holster at his back.

He needed to hide his things where she wouldn't easily find them yet keep the guns in reach in case he should need to use them.

There wasn't anything he could do about the scars. Even in dim light there'd be no hiding them, and he'd have to come up with more lies to explain them away.

Scowling, he dropped to his knees and peered under her bed, seeing a small clutter of boxes, magazines, and dust. He quickly hid his rig and gun behind a pile of travel magazines.

As he stood again, he stripped off his shirt, then folded his jacket and placed it on the nearby chaise lounge, which was surrounded by stacks of books in all sizes and genres.

He added his folded shirt to the pile, then turned off the lights except the one over the dresser. It was a small lamp with a beaded shade and a base shaped like an Oriental elephant. More vintage prints and ad art hung on the walls, and he noticed a shelf full of old mechanical banks. An oddly whimsical collection, and, again, something he wouldn't have expected.

What other surprises would she spring on him?

As the water continued to run, he sat on the bed and quickly punched in Sheridan's number.

When Ben answered, Griffith said quietly, "Heads up; we got big trouble. Both McMahon and von Lahr are here, and they've both made contact with Kennedy."

Ben swore softly. "Is she all right? Where are you?"

"She's okay. She has no idea who von Lahr is, and didn't recognize the guy who called her today and told her to stay away from the manuscript. I gave her some bullshit answer, and she's fine with it for now. I'm with her in her apartment. She's in the john and will be out soon, so I don't have a lot of time to give you details. Get Noonie to her shop. Tell him to go inside and keep an eye on things."

"I'll do that. What's your plan?"

"For now I think it's better if we keep her here and act like nothing's wrong. If she disappears, McMahon will disappear. Do you think von Lahr would have any interest in her, aside from using her to get to McMahon?"

"No, but you know he can be unpredictable. He could hurt her just because he can."

As if he could ever forget.

The water shut off. "I gotta go. I'll check in as soon as possible."

He barely had time to stash his cell phone under his shirt, and reach into his back pocket for his wallet and the few condoms he'd brought along for just this purpose.

Whatever it takes to get the job done.

It had always been his motto; the creed he'd sworn to live and die by. Now the words seemed trite and hollow. Sitting in the soft light of this bedroom, in front of her dresser mirror, he had a good look at himself and didn't like what he saw.

The door opened, and Fiona walked into the bedroom wearing a dark green terry robe. She stopped and smiled down at him.

"You've still got your jeans on."

"I had to leave something for you to take off." He leaned back on his elbows, grinning. One tug on the tie of that robe and she'd be naked.

Silence fell, and Fiona said, "I want to be honest with you, Griffith. I'm not looking for love or romance or a lifetime commitment. I'm just looking for a night of hot, sweaty, wonderful sex."

The blunt statement surprised him. "I'll do my best not to disappoint."

"I'm sure you won't."

She stepped between his open legs and bent down, and Griffith slipped his hands inside her robe, touching warm, smooth skin as he kissed her; a long, lingering, and surprisingly gentle kiss.

Her breasts filled his hands just right, and he teased her nipples as he kissed her, catching her little sighs in his mouth.

Then she broke the kiss and pushed him back on the bed. As he fell, he pulled her down with him. The robe gaped, giving him a perfect view of her breasts. He pushed the robe aside, brushing his thumb over her nipple, then pulled her toward him so that he could take it in his mouth.

She gave a little gasp, and then, when he circled the tip with his tongue, she moaned.

The sheets felt cool and soft against his bare skin, the nubbed fabric of her robe rougher. He was hot and hard for her already, even before he impatiently pulled her belt loose and tossed the robe to the floor.

She kissed him back with hungry need. She was fine-boned and slender, with a redhead's pale skin. Her breasts were small, but round and firm, with pointed nipples that made him want to kiss and bite and lick.

Freed from its braid, her curling, dark red hair fell halfway down her back, and when she bent forward to kiss him again, the ends of her hair brushed across his chest.

She was beautiful, and his for the night.

"Time to get rid of these jeans," she said, her tone huskier. "You've had your chance for a good look at me. Now it's my turn."

Fiona kissed him again on the mouth, then on the chin. Her lips made a slow, determined progress down his neck and chest and the faint line of hair on his belly. He arched, briefly closing his eyes, when her hair brushed the sensitized skin of his lower belly.

She quickly unbuttoned his jeans and worked the zipper down, making a low sound as she rubbed at his erection straining against the denim.

There was nothing better than a woman who knew what she wanted and went for it.

It mesmerized him, watching her hair and breasts

swing gently as she moved, the darker place between her thighs that he couldn't quite see and wanted to explore.

She tugged his jeans off and then held out her hand. "Condom?"

Whatever initial shyness or worries she'd had about this, she had apparently gotten over them.

Smiling, he tossed the packet toward her, and she put it on slowly, stroking him until he didn't think he could get any harder.

"Do I get to see all those freckles now?"

Fiona perched on his hips, bare and beautiful. "You really find them pretty?"

"Hell, yes."

"Some people don't."

"Some people are total morons." Griffith sat up, then ran a finger down her belly, touching freckles here and there as he went along. She made soft sounds that he liked; and he hoped she would keep making them. "Your skin is so fair, and your hair is such a dark red. It almost looks the same color as these freckles."

"I'm color-coordinated, thanks to Mother Nature."

"That's what's so amazing. This is your natural color."

Then Griffith kissed her again, and he could feel her lingering tension melting away. She liked to kiss, to nibble and tease, with just the right pressure, just the right touch of tongue against his lips to keep him hot and hard for her. Fiona closed her eyes, running her hands down the smooth skin of his back—and he knew the instant she found the hard ridge of scar tissue.

She hesitated, her eyes opening, and he quickly forestalled her questions, the lie slipping out easily and smoothly: "I was in an accident a few months ago. Stitches, surgery . . . the whole thing. The scar's still rough, but it's healed. You can touch it."

"It doesn't hurt?" Her fingers gently explored the long, puckered line of the incision.

"No." His hands cupped her rear, and without him having to ask, she lowered her hips until her moist heat brushed against him. "And especially not now."

She leaned down, kissing him again, her tongue boldly stroking along his, and all the while she circled over his erection, the teasing driving him to distraction. All he could think about was pushing her thighs apart, feeling to see if she was ready for him, and then thrusting his dick hard and deep inside her.

Finally, she pulled back and whispered, "I want you inside me. Right now."

Before he could even move, she straddled and mounted him, her warm hands closing over him and moving him against her opening.

For a moment, he almost forgot to breathe, she felt so damn good. Then she lowered her hips at the same time as he arched his, and he pushed inside her on a long, deep, strong thrust. Her heat surrounded him, and as she moved with him, Griffith let his body take over, surrendering to the sensations: her smooth, warm skin, the spicy vanilla scent of her body, the tickling strokes of her hair on his chest.

He massaged her breasts, rousing the tips to hard peaks as her breathing roughened and her eyes lost their focus. Her mouth was slightly open, and her fingers closed hard on his hips as he thrust harder and faster. He felt the tightening tension as he moved in and out of her, his own breathing sounding harsher with the effort to bring her to her orgasm. He was close; her every sliding squeeze of her inner muscles made it more difficult to hold on to his control.

The low light of the lamp showed the flush on her face and chest, and her breasts bounced with her urgent rhythm.

"Tell me what you like," he whispered roughly.

"I like everything you're doing," she whispered, then made a little whimpering noise when his fingers found her clitoris and stroked it rapidly. "Oh, God . . . harder. Move harder. I don't want gentle. I want . . . I want—"

"You want to be fucked," he whispered, his voice harsh with desire. "That's all you want. That's all you need."

"Yes." She gasped, her back arching.

"It's okay—come on, Fiona. You're there . . . feel it!"

She was panting, and he couldn't wait any longer. He rolled her over onto her back, pulled her legs up over his shoulders, then thrust inside her again. "Oh, Jesus," he muttered and began moving fast and hard.

Her entire body seemed to fold around him, and when she began to climax, he grabbed her hips and helped her along until she came with a high, sharp gasp.

His own orgasm shuddered through him again and again until he fell on top of her, hands on either side of her head.

Still breathing hard, he kissed her as she slid her feet down the length of his back and rubbed them against his thighs with a soft sigh of pleasure.

And he already wanted more. He started kissing her jaw and neck, and then lower. This time he paid more attention to her breasts, playing and stroking until she was arching against him and grabbing at the sheets. Griffith slid his hand lower and slipped his fingers inside her, making her suck in her breath as he coaxed another orgasm from her.

He enjoyed watching her; seeing her head drop back, her eyes close, and her mouth fall open as each spasm of pleasure shook through her.

When Fiona opened her eyes again, he moved back over her, smiling, gently brushed aside a strand of her hair, and gave her a long, lingering kiss. He wanted to taste her, to feel her breath against his mouth, to lose himself in those deep green eyes and her willing, welcoming body.

If sex had ever been this good this fast before, he couldn't remember it.

"How's it going?" he asked, his voice low. "Getting back into the swing of things yet?"

Fiona smiled, a slow, wide smile that was so warm and so full of life and passion, it made him want to do everything possible to keep her smiling.

"Mmmm, I think we're getting there," she said, stretching. "But not quite yet."

Griffith laughed. "Then we'll keep trying."

Sometime after midnight, the weather cleared enough for the moon to appear.

Griffith, lying wide awake with Fiona's warm body curled close against him, watched the pale glow as it filtered through the room, starting in the corner and slowly brightening, as it moved toward the bed.

Shifting to his side, careful not to wake her, he rested his chin on his palm and waited for the light to reach her face, revealing all the contrasts of her fair, smooth skin and freckles and dark red hair.

Sleeping, she looked peaceful, soft, beautiful. Safe. *Safe . . .*

Gently, he touched a strand of her hair, moving it

aside to reveal the curve of a cheekbone and the flare of her dark brows.

No matter what, he had to keep her safe. And it wasn't just about what had happened in Hamburg. There was something about her that had him wondering what it would be like to have a life like this. To have a place of his own, a place of peace and serenity, of warmth.

All of that, right here beside him: vanilla perfume and a woman all in tones of cinnamon red and warm toasty brown . . .

The thought brought a vivid flash of memory, of playing outside in the winter's brittle chill and running toward the glowing lights of his home, glad for the beckoning warmth that drew him inside.

Griffith smiled wryly. Fiona wouldn't be too pleased about reminding a guy of kitchens and comfort. But something about the way she'd brought back those old memories made him realize how much he missed that comfort and security. The sense of belonging, of knowing that no matter where he went or how long he was gone, there'd always be a place to come home to. A place where the lights were always on.

He grinned. And where the sex would always be incredible. The old saying "watch out for the quiet ones" was very true in her case; he hadn't expected her to be so open and passionate. Maybe it was because she considered him a one-night stand, and didn't care. But he could use a few more nice surprises like this.

Fiona shifted, burrowing into the covers against him. Her mouth, softer in sleep, caught his attention, and he leaned over and gently kissed her.

She made a sighing sound, and then her eyes slowly opened.

For a moment, he didn't say anything, didn't look away from her wide, somber gaze. "Didn't mean to wake you up."

She made another sleepy, sexy sound and cuddled closer. "Mmmm, I don't mind waking up to kisses."

Her voice was a little rougher with sleep, and sexy as hell.

And, *damn,* she was beautiful. The photos in the file hadn't gotten across that aura of warmth and softness, the full spectrum of the red hues of her hair, the green of her eyes.

Or all those freckles . . . those mesmerizing freckles.

He'd never before met a woman with so many freckles and hadn't expected they would look so goddamn cute. It hadn't been a lie when he'd told her he wanted to see if she had them all over and wanted to count them.

Fiona raised her head enough to look out the window. "Hey, look at that . . . we have moonlight.

Alleluia, maybe that means it won't rain tomorrow."
Yawning, she peered at the bedside alarm clock.
"How come you're awake? It's almost one o'clock."

"I don't know . . . just couldn't sleep."

He became aware of her fingers stroking his belly;
feather-soft and slow. "We could try to tire you out
more."

He grinned. If her fingers strayed a little lower,
she'd discover that he was very willing to do that. "We
could. I know now that you really do have freckles all
over, but I didn't get around to counting them."

"That would require more concentration than
anyone has at one in the morning."

Her gaze drifted lower, and a faint pink color
spread up her chest toward her cheeks. He watched
its progress, fascinated, then focused on her breasts,
with their scattering of freckles and the darker nipples, stiff and erect with the chill.

He bent, kissing one, and felt her squirm a little as
she gave a soft sigh. He instantly wanted to roll her
over, spread her legs wide, and take her from behind,
holding on to that pretty ass of hers as he drove in
and out until they were both blank-minded with the
pleasure.

He gave her other breast a teasing kiss, then
grabbed another condom, pulled the pillows together,
and said, "Lay down on your stomach. Here."

She did, her eyes lighting with anticipation, and

left him with an incredible view. In the moonlight, her long, slender back was almost blue-white, with the deep shadow of her spine rising up to meet the rounded curves of her rear.

Impatient now, he lifted her hips toward him, nudging her legs wide apart, and entered her in a single deep, hard thrust that made her gasp. His eyes squeezed shut, Griffith savored the feel of her surrounding him before moving again. Hearing her make another high, sharp sound of pleasure fueled his own needs, and despite his good intentions, he couldn't go slow. Already he could feel the pressure building fast, and he knew it wouldn't be long.

Fiona tipped her head back and whispered, "Like this, I can feel everything. It's so much"—she broke off, gasping, as he thrust harder, then sighed—"so much more intense. Don't stop."

As she arched up to meet him, it took all his self-control to go slowly, rather than ram into her the way he wanted.

Jesus, sex with nice girls was complicated.

But it hurt so good to go so slow for her, and he loved stroking her tight, hot depths, listening to her moans turn to urgent panting, and finally, hearing her cries, muffled in the pillows.

That did him in. He arched, eyes closed, and thrust one last time as the orgasm ripped through him with a shuddering force that brought a moan from between his clenched teeth. He trembled, lost in the power of her body as everything went momentarily hazy. Then he let out a long, shaking sigh and collapsed over her.

"Damn," he gasped. "That was incredible."

She was still breathing hard. "I thought I was going to . . . pass out for a second there. God, I've never . . . Yes, that was incredible."

He laughed, rolling off her, thankful for the touch of the cooler air on his hot skin.

She stretched, and wiped out as he was, a liquid-hot thread of desire wound through him again, head to toe. With a body like that, she should always be naked in the moonlight.

Fiona tipped her head toward him and smiled. "Feeling more tired now?"

"I can't move or think yet. Give me a second and I'll get back to you on that."

She sighed, snuggling close, and without even thinking he looped his arm around her as his eyes closed.

"Yeah," he murmured after several minutes. "I'm definitely sleepy."

When Fiona didn't respond, he looked down and saw that she'd already drifted off.

Griffith smiled, dropping his head back to the pillow. But while his body craved sleep—now he was really feeling the day's exertions in his back—his mind wouldn't shut down.

Maybe it was the sex. Maybe it was the stab of guilt for all the lies he'd told her and would keep on telling her. Maybe it was the awareness of danger closing in, or maybe it was just the anticipation of getting closer to von Lahr after all these years.

And maybe he just liked lying here, feeling his vanilla cinnamon woman warm against him under the sheets.

After an hour of staring at the ceiling, he eased away from Fiona and slipped out of bed.

If he couldn't sleep, he might as well work.

Nine

VON LAHR DIDN'T SLEEP MUCH, SO WHILE HIS COM-
panion lay sprawled in a satiated slumber in the bed
beside him, he opted for a smoke.

He sat on the edge of her bed, naked, then
reached for the pack of cigarettes and lighter on the
bedside table and lit up. As he leaned forward, resting his elbows on his knees, he took a drag and then
slowly exhaled, watching the smoke curl upward to
the ceiling before it dissipated.

Judging from the smallness of the apartment, its
worn furnishings, and lack of new appliances,
Rebeka-with-one-k-and-no-h didn't make a lot of
money at the sex business.

Still, she wasn't bad in bed and was willing to do
whatever he wanted—not that it had been particu-

larly strenuous, since he was somewhat distracted.

He kept thinking about that call, and its implications.

Who had called him?

It annoyed him to the extreme that someone had managed to get hold of his private cell number, although people attempting to run him to ground was hardly a novelty. Being in hiding was second nature to him by now, and even while hiding out he managed to squeeze in more living than most people did while going about their mundane routines.

Survival meant keeping the important matters to himself and delegating everything else to those who couldn't inconvenience him if they failed. He hired people smart enough to get the job done but not smart enough to start getting ideas about double-crossing him.

The few times he'd turned to smart opportunists had caused him no end of trouble, and McMahon and Hanson had been foremost on that short list. McMahon was supposedly dead, but no one truly believed it except for the pretty redheaded wife, and Hanson hadn't made an appearance in over a year.

So which one was it? Von Lahr was leaning toward McMahon, despite his convenient demise. There'd been rumors about Hanson, but there were always rumors. The trick was to learn to separate out those that might be true from those that were not, and von

Lahr prided himself on sniffing out fact from fallacy.

While cleaning up after others offended his sense of professionalism, he had no choice this time, since he'd been the one to bring in McMahon. Perhaps he should've kept a closer watch on the man, but at the time he'd had other pressing interests and McMahon had seemed desperate for the money and the opportunity to help his own career along.

Something had gone wrong, that much was certain. Perhaps McMahon had changed his mind or grown greedy. All von Lahr knew was that when the man had disappeared, the fake manuscript had disappeared with him, along with all the money he'd been paid.

Not good for business or von Lahr's credentials.

Even worse, as his last grand gesture before "dying," McMahon had threatened to expose von Lahr and the entire forgery ring operating out of Munich. The little bastard claimed to have inserted an encoded note to his wife in the manuscript so that she could not only quickly identify it as fake but also discover the name of his master forger and von Lahr's own base of operations. Naturally that made the manuscript worthless on the market *and* far too dangerous to exist.

What a complete waste of time and money.

And now, after all this time, the manuscript had finally resurfaced—and McMahon along with it.

What Avalon was doing made perfect sense, and von Lahr admired the simplicity of their plan. Nothing but a threat to the unsuspecting wife would draw out McMahon and, by necessity, von Lahr himself. Whether or not the encrypted passages truly existed, and despite his having moved his business to a new location, there were names that shouldn't be named, and von Lahr couldn't take the chance on having Fiona Kennedy finding them.

That would be even worse for business.

So much trouble for such a worthless pile of papers, and he'd had to delay a meeting in Milan because of it.

McMahon had to die, and the manuscript had to be destroyed. But the execution of that solution wasn't so simple, and this mysterious call was a further complication.

If McMahon were to contact anyone, it should've been Laughton or someone else with Avalon; they, at least, wouldn't kill him. So why hadn't he done that?

Von Lahr finished off his cigarette and crushed the stub into the ashtray, the presence of which struck him as a touch whimsical considering all the burn marks on the tabletop.

He stood, his mind busy. A nagging suspicion warned him that something about all this didn't feel right. He had a good sense about these things; if it smelled rotten, it probably *was* rotten.

For now, he'd wait for the next call; then he'd come up with a plan. A plan that would go so much more smoothly if the current one played out the way it was supposed to, and took out Laughton.

It would've been far more satisfying to kill the man himself, but he wouldn't let personal needs interfere with business. He'd be sorry to lose an opponent like Laughton; he liked the man's style. They weren't really all that different from each other, and both made a habit of using others to achieve their own ends.

He glanced over his shoulder at Rebeka. This time Laughton had gotten the better deal.

"Enjoy her, my friend," he murmured, smiling. "Your time is up."

Ten

✦

IN THE SMALL HOURS OF THE MORNING, WHEN THE ever-busy city had quieted down, Fiona woke with a chill—and realized Griffith's warmth was no longer against her.

Tipping her head sideways, she searched for him in the dimness of the room and found him by the window, a finger separating the blinds, looking outside.

He was nude, and she shamelessly enjoyed the view. The pale white illumination from the streetlights slanted through the window, keeping half of him in shadow, the other in a pale glow that deepened the contours of his muscles and softened his harder edges. He had a whipcord lean build, muscles sharply defined but not overdeveloped.

He was absolutely beautiful.

Before he caught her staring, she should probably say something. "What are you looking at?" she asked.

Griffith calmly let the blinds fall back into place and turned toward her. Now he was almost lost in the shadows, except for the faint pattern of lines marked across his skin by the light leaking between the narrow slats.

"Nothing much. I still couldn't sleep, so I decided to get up for a while. I was just watching the traffic."

"There's something strangely peaceful about it, isn't there?" Fiona sat up, keeping the sheet close against her. "It's mesmerizing, the constant passing of headlights, the same way a gentle rainfall is mesmerizing. Some people find it too noisy, but I don't even notice it anymore."

"The lullaby of the city."

She nodded. "I've always lived in cities, and I can't imagine living anywhere else, but there are times when it hits me just how alone you can be among millions of other people."

He smiled. "Like you, I prefer the sounds of people and city to the silence. I'm not really the country type." He leaned his head back against the wall—and then he stretched, a long, slow stretch that arched his back.

Wow.

Fiona glanced away to avoid gawking like a boy-crazy adolescent.

"Hey, can I ask you something?"

Fiona looked back. "Of course."

"Why me?"

She blinked. "Why you what?"

"For sex. Why'd you choose me over any other guy?"

"Well, for one, you're closer than the sexy guy in the tight rubber suit in the Bahamas."

"That almost makes sense."

"And you *do* have the required interactive bits," she said lightly, hoping he'd leave it at that because she wasn't sure how she'd try to explain.

Griffith smiled. "Yeah, and besides that? There had to be another reason."

So much for taking the easy way out.

Since he'd asked her seriously, she decided it would be best to answer in kind. "I don't think there's much more to it than you were in the right place at the right time. I was just . . . ready to do something more for myself, and you walked through my door when I was having a weak moment."

"Lucky me."

Fiona smiled. "And you always have a quick comeback, don't you? Something tells me you've had a lot of practice with these kinds of situations."

"Not as much as you're imagining," he said drily.

"Still, it's just for the moment. I'm assuming that once I give you my verdict on this manuscript, you'll be on your way and I'll never see you again."

"That would be the plan, yes."

"I'm okay with that." And she was, even if a soft, wistful voice whispered that it would be nice to keep him around for a *little* while longer. Not that many cat-loving, handsome, book-reading, clean-cut, and sinfully sexy men wandered into her life. In so many ways, he was just what she'd always wanted. "Why don't you come back to bed?"

He stretched again. "I'm not tired enough to go back to bed . . . but too tired for any more strenuous activity." He gave her a slow, languid smile that started the melting rush of lust all over again. "You should try to get more sleep. I'll come back to bed before long."

"I'm not feeling very tired right now myself." Fiona grabbed the twisted jumble of sheets and wrapped them around her. She wished she was as unself-conscious about her nudity as Griffith was about his, but if her spontaneous inner hoyden hadn't made an appearance by this point in her life, it was unlikely to ever do so.

"I'll keep you company until the sun rises or until we get tired, whichever comes first."

He watched her approach, but in the low light she couldn't see his expression. "You don't have to do that if you'd rather sleep. I don't expect you to keep me entertained."

Fiona peeked out the blinds to see what he'd been looking at. The City of Angels never slept, and the night creatures were still on the prowl, looking for one more party, sniffing out the places where excitement could still be found. The traffic was constant, if much lighter than during the day.

"I know that," she said, letting the blinds drop as she turned to him. "But maybe I don't like thinking of you sitting here alone."

"Being alone doesn't bother me."

"It doesn't bother me, either. But it's still nice to be with someone in the early hours of the morning. That's when the city feels its loneliest, I've always thought. People shouldn't be alone when it's that kind of lonely."

Griffith smiled again, and maybe it was a trick of the light and shadows, but the smile seemed wider, warmer. Almost boyish. "Nobody's ever said anything like that to me before."

"Oh, come now. I'm sure you have family, friends. Ex-girlfriends." Judging by those nimble fingers and teasing tongue, he'd had quite a few ex-girlfriends, who'd taught him all he needed to know about how to make a woman very happy. "Surely someone has kept you company over a lonely night or two."

"Not like this." He fell silent for a moment. "Hey, how long were you and your husband married?"

The question took her by surprise . . . and put a

damper on her burgeoning fantasies of him slinging her over his shoulder and taking her back to bed.

"We met my second year in college. He was a teacher's assistant at the time, and I was barely out of my teens. Totally smitten I was, from the first time I laid eyes on him." It felt nice to talk about it in past tense. The hurt had faded long ago, and now she could finally let go of all the ambivalence and lingering regrets. "We married a year after that, and had our tenth anniversary just a month before he disappeared."

The last few years of their marriage had been stressful, with Richard's problems in getting tenure and the bumpy research that didn't earn him the recognition he'd needed and wanted, the way it had happened for her. The pressure got to be too much, and finally he'd snapped and done the unthinkable.

Yet what she couldn't forgive him for was not that he'd stolen the work of others to pass it off as his own but that he hadn't come to her for help. That he'd believed she wouldn't have stood by his side, wouldn't have supported him. She'd made a vow to do so. In the end, she'd loved him more than he'd loved her. That was obvious now, though it hadn't been so clear at the time, and admitting it still hurt.

"He was in the same line of research as you were?"

"Yes. We were both scholars in Elizabethan literature. I focused strictly on Marlowe, while he studied

Shakespeare's contemporaries, which included Marlowe. He was very good at what he did."

"But you were better."

He'd claimed not to know anything about her, so how—"Why do you say that?"

"It's in your voice, the way you talk about it. You sounded apologetic, and you have nothing to apologize for."

She'd sounded apologetic? It troubled her that she might still be locked in that old, guilty mind-set; she had thought she'd moved well beyond it.

"It was a little more complicated than that, but when my research took off, his stalled, and that caused a few problems. While I realize I have nothing to feel sorry for, it doesn't mean dealing with the effects of that kind of stress was easy. Even when you love each other, problems can come out of nowhere to derail all those little dreams you'd dreamed as a couple."

"I shouldn't have said anything. It's none of my business."

Fiona sighed. "No, it's all right. I'm . . . still a little too sensitive about some matters. It's a habit I want to break. The sooner the better."

Not only had the shadows added contours of mystery to his face but they also made him look older. If it were possible, he was even better looking in the shadows than he was in the light of day.

How perfect for a one-night-stand man.

"So why'd you wait so long to look for someone to be with? A woman like you, smart and sexy . . . I'd have thought the guys would've been jumping at the chance to hook up with you."

Fiona couldn't help smiling. "You have no idea how often my friends have nagged me about that. The older I get, the harder it is to find attractive, single, straight, and normal men." She looked over at him, then away again. "Or at least that's my usual excuse. It's always been difficult for others to understand what it was like, not knowing if my husband was alive or dead. After the first few weeks, I knew he wasn't coming back, but hope . . . it's like the poem says, it's the thing with feathers that perches in the soul."

"I can understand that. Sometimes the dead can have a strong hold over the living."

What an odd thing to say. After a moment she added, "Looking back, I can see that I couldn't commit to anyone because there was that chance, no matter how small, that Richard would come back. Even when I knew he wouldn't, it was easy to use him as an excuse. The men I've dated these past few years, they all picked up on that. No matter how I tried to be friendly, to be interested, I think they sensed something missing in me. Like a connection that was broken. There were no fights, no bitter farewells, just a slow cooling and drifting apart that was . . . comfortable. Kind, in its way."

She paused slightly, embarrassed. "I can't believe I'm saying all this to you. I'm usually not the type to spill my life's story. I always hate it when it happens to me on the bus or at the airport."

"People tell me I have a trustworthy face."

Fiona smiled. "You do, but I don't think that's the reason. As for why now and not years ago, the answer is that I have to get on with my life. I have this kind of nagging worry that if I don't do it now, it'll never happen. I'm not the adventurous sort, so I think I was looking . . . for a bridge. A nice person to be with, to get closer to, but not too close."

It suddenly occurred to her what this must sound like, to be called a "bridge." She wouldn't like it; she doubted he did. "I'm sorry. I must sound cold and shallow, and you're really—"

"It's all right. I understand better than you think."

She waited, hoping he'd add to that, and when he didn't she said, "In the end, I suppose you seemed like a nice guy to spend a little time with. I really don't have any other reason. Maybe I should, but I don't."

Griffith smiled, and she noticed all over again that he had a wonderful smile. A little lopsided, but wide and friendly, with those deep lateral dimples. "You're a very honest woman, Fiona Kennedy."

"Never underestimate the power of Catholic

schoolgirl guilt. It is a force to be reckoned with."
She shifted, feeling a sudden draft on the small of her
back that told her the sheet was coming loose. "And
I'm old enough to know there's more to life than
that."

"More to life." He made a low, derisive sound. "If
you find what that is, be sure to let me know."

More puzzling comments, even taking into consid-
eration that it was threeish in the morning—a magical kind of hour when lots of things made perfect
sense that wouldn't after the sun rose.

"Then you'll need to leave me a business card and
a phone number, so when I fortuitously stumble
across the meaning of life a few months from now, I'll
know where to find you."

He laughed. "I didn't give you my card, did I? It's
because you keep distracting me from my job. I'm
usually not such a slacker."

"Maybe not, but you're definitely a flirt. Would
you like some tea? Or any other kind of drink? Beer,
wine, . . . and I think I still have a bottle of old
Scotch whiskey somewhere in the kitchen. The
really good, expensive stuff."

"You know, a shot of good whiskey would be
great."

Fiona still couldn't believe she was having such a
normal conversation with a man who was naked and
didn't seem in the least concerned about it. Richard

hadn't been a prude, but by now he'd have pulled on underwear or a robe or a pair of sweatpants.

Then again, she was wandering around in a sheet.

Come to think of it, what was the point of that? She'd gone all porn queen on him a few hours ago and hadn't died of mortification. Griffith would be out of her life in a few days. She'd never see him again, so why not push the limits of her comfort zone a little more?

Fiona let the sheet drop, and she heard him suck in his breath. Liking the sound of that, she sent him a wicked little grin as she walked toward the kitchen. She didn't turn on the light, though; she wasn't *that* brave. Besides, her eyes were adjusted to the dark by now, and she knew where everything was in her kitchen.

Still, it was a strange feeling, the air brushing her bare skin, the tingle of awareness that Griffith was watching her, and the cool, smooth feel of wood and Formica as she leaned against the counter and cupboards in search of glasses and Richard's old stash of whiskey.

An odd sensation in a good way, and a tiny bit decadent. She should've tried walking naked around her kitchen long before this, with or without a man. She'd lived her whole life with this body; she'd learned to maximize the good and minimize the not so good, and she mostly liked herself. Even all those freckles she'd hated as a kid and had cried buckets over in her early teens didn't seem so bad right now.

Griffith thought she was pretty, and more important, she felt pretty and sexy and desirable—something she'd gone too long without feeling.

Smiling to herself, she walked back to the living room with a shot glass of whiskey for Griffith and a glass of wine for herself.

As she handed him the drink, his gaze moved along her body, lingering below her belly button before rising to her breasts, sending a little tingle of pleasure and satisfaction over her.

"I like the sheetless look." He took a healthy gulp of the drink. "You should be naked more often. Daily, I'm thinking."

"I'm thinking maybe you're right."

In silence they sipped their drinks, and then, without warning, he leaned over and kissed her. It was surprisingly sweet, and she liked the taste of the whiskey on his mouth.

But for all the sweetness of that kiss, his gaze was uncomfortably direct in a way that made him almost look and feel like a different man—and Fiona didn't think it was just because he wasn't wearing his glasses.

It drove home a point she'd been trying to avoid: she knew absolutely nothing about Griffith Laughton, and her behavior was extremely risky. Yet she didn't care. Maybe she'd care tomorrow, or the day after, but right now she wanted only to get him back to bed.

As if he'd read her mind—or, more likely, the blatant lust in her eyes—he said roughly, "Okay. Let's go back to bed."

Once they fell back onto the bed together, Fiona rolled over onto Griffith. "My turn to explore."

"No problem. When a beautiful woman wants to have her way with me, I'm easy."

"So am I, as it turns out."

Fiona eased closer to him and for a moment simply enjoyed looking at him. She'd noticed older scars on his body; one on his left arm, another on his leg, and numerous other small marks of past hazards. She'd also noticed the faint, white scars across the knuckles of one hand.

But the scars didn't take anything away from his looks; if anything, they made him all the more intriguing and handsome.

She ran her hands across the lines of his muscles, enjoying just touching his lips, his shoulders and chest, the thin line of hair down his lower belly to his groin—and the erection that she could hardly overlook.

Stroking him, she watched his face, liking how his eyes closed, how his nostrils flared. How he arched and sucked in his breath when she rubbed the sensi-

tive head of his penis. Watching him got her all hot
and bothered, and she cut the exploration short.

Sliding up his chest, she gave him a long, hard
kiss, her fingers buried in his hair to hold him close.
Already she could feel his hands on her, moving
down her back to her bottom, then between her legs.

The feel of his fingers inside her almost brought
her to her peak, but before she could come, Griffith
had withdrawn his fingers and rolled her over to her
back. Then he was inside her again, and she couldn't
hold back a soft cry as she felt only the pleasure.

Nothing could ever match the exquisite sensation
of hot, hard flesh filling her, stretching her almost to
the point of pain. He made every thrust last, each
one slow, going deep, and Fiona could feel the gathering tension.

"Tell me what you want," he said, his voice low
and harsh in her ear. "You're the one with the power.
You tell me what you want."

It was hard to think through the haze of sensation,
but she didn't think she had any more power over
him than he had over her.

"I want this," she said simply. "Just this."

In his face she saw no pretending, no artifice, no
clever dodging. For this moment, at least, he
belonged solely to her.

The realization arrived at the same moment as the
gentle, tightening inner ache released its hold and

rolled over her in a hot, trembling wave that curled her toes.

Above her, Griffith dropped his head back, body rigid, his hips grinding into her—and there was a strange vulnerability in the intimacy of that moment that made her reach up and touch his face tenderly.

Eleven

As she and Griffith walked to the shop that morning, Fiona was surprised to discover she was a little sore. Aches twinged in places she didn't know could ache, and she was tired—but it was a good kind of tired and a very nice kind of ache.

Griffith was quieter, more subdued than usual. Or so she assumed, since she didn't know him very well. Maybe it took him some time to get energized in the morning and this was usual behavior for him.

"Tired?" she asked, glancing over at him as she opened the door to the shop and set the little chimes to tinkling.

He smiled and moved closer, brushing against her in a sort of reassurance that was casual and yet somehow intimate. "A little. How about you?"

"Mmm, yes." Surprisingly, she blushed and quickly changed the subject. "I'd better find Faustus and feed him."

Griffith grinned. "Not to mention feed us. I'm hungry."

Fiona lightly banged the heel of her hand on her forehead. "I don't know why I didn't think to stop at the café across the street. We could've picked up something to eat there."

"You must've been distracted."

True enough, which was a puzzle given the Marlowe manuscript. A discovery of the sort she could've only dreamed about had fallen in her lap, yet she was more preoccupied with a sexy, good-looking guy who'd be gone in a few days than with the Elizabethan hell-raiser who'd fascinated her for over half of her life.

"Quit fishing for compliments." Fiona couldn't quite hold back her smile at his lazy grin. "I already told you that you were magnificent."

"I don't remember that. I must've been distracted, too. How about we go to the café together, and on the way you can tell me again how magnificent I am?"

"We don't both need to go." She propped her umbrella in the stand and hung up her coat. "That way I'll have the coffee ready by the time you get back."

As he shoved the briefcase with the manuscript out of sight below her desk, she scanned the shop for Faustus. The second the door chimes sounded, he should've come trotting out to meow belligerently at her.

"That's odd. When it comes to food, Faustus isn't slow about making an appearance. I can't imagine where he might be." Suddenly uneasy, she started looking down the stacks, calling for the cat. "You don't think . . . No, he's just probably off sulking somewhere. Faustus, where are you, you lazy fluff ball? It's kibble time!"

A loud, plaintive—and slightly annoyed—yowl sounded from the second floor. With a sigh of relief, Fiona smiled. "Usually he sleeps by the back door, but he must've gone exploring and gotten himself locked in a bathroom or one of the storerooms. Stupid cat. I'll go rescue him."

"No."

The terseness of Griffith's voice brought her short, and she turned back toward him. "What?"

His brows pulled together in a frown. "Let me go look around up there."

"Why? The alarm's set, so nobody broke in. The cat's fine; you heard him. He's just pissy." Then she added, "Or is there something you need to tell me?"

A simple, reasonable question—yet she became aware of a sudden, growing tension. Only a few hours ago she'd had sex with this man—blissfully wonderful sex—and now, after such intense intimacy, distrust stirred.

Despite her new wariness, Fiona refused to give in to the urge to glance away from that uncomfortably direct blue gaze searching her face. It seemed as if he were able to read her every thought, and could see her unease and the reason for it.

"Is there something *you* need to tell me?" he asked mildly.

The question, wholly unexpected, caught her off balance. "Of course not."

"Then there's nothing to argue about. This isn't complicated, Fiona. If anything happens to you, my ass is on the line—and just so we're clear on this, *I* don't want anything to happen to you. What's up on the second floor?"

He hadn't actually answered her question, which did nothing to ease her mind. "A small office, lots of file cabinets, a bathroom, a break room with a kitchenette, and another small room with a sleeper sofa in it." The intensity of his gaze was making a hash of her nerves. "Sometimes I work late and spend the night, rather than walk to my apartment. Faustus has a bed up there, too, and that's where I keep his food dish. He probably locked himself in one of the file rooms. The house is off center, so some of the doors swing closed at the slightest touch."

Griffith drew her back to her desk. Hands on her shoulders, he sat her down forcefully in her chair. "You sit right here and keep out of sight. And that means staying away from the windows."

Too startled to do more than nod, Fiona watched him walk down the British Aisles, unhook the rope blocking the steps, and then disappear into the darkness of the narrow stairway.

What a strange thing to say, that she must stay away from the windows. Why was it a problem now but hadn't been last night? Or all day yesterday?

And now she was thoroughly spooked, even though she could hear Faustus yowling in agitation. He wasn't hurt or in pain; it was clearly the meow of a pissed-off cat.

Griffith was just overreacting—maybe because of what had happened between them he felt more proprietary now.

She listened to the soft, hollow sounds of his footsteps on the old floorboards above her.

A particularly loud creak made her jump, and she scowled, hand pressed to her chest. Lovely; now he'd stoked *her* paranoia. The old house creaked and groaned all the time, even more so when it was rainy and windy. Then the shutters rattled, rain pattered on the glass and siding, and all the noise outside made the silence inside the shop even more apparent.

Now she wished parts of the shop had better lighting. It was pretty dark in the rear stacks and at the back door that led to the alley and garbage bins. The low lighting and cool dry temperature were necessary for protecting the old books and papers, but now they made her shivery and jumpy.

For the first time since she'd opened the shop, she didn't feel safe in her own space.

And then the phone rang.

It was much too early to be a customer. Her heart still racing, Fiona picked up and said slowly, "Hello?"

There was a short silence, then that same muffled male voice said, "I told you to stay away from the manuscript."

It took her a few seconds to find her voice. She swallowed. "Who are you?"

"Someone who cares what happens to you."

"Is that so? Harassing me and being cryptic is a strange way of showing your concern," she retorted.

"Trust no one, not even your guard dog. Walk away and don't look at the manuscript again. It's for your own good. Please believe me. Please."

The pleading took her completely by surprise; it sounded so . . . genuine. "Give me one good reason why I should believe you and not my guard dog."

"I told you. I'm someone who cares about what happens to you. I always did, my little cat-eyed goddess."

Fiona sucked in her breath as the connection terminated. A cold sweat broke over her, and she started shaking so badly that she almost dropped the handset.

Little cat-eyed goddess . . .

It had been Richard's pet name for her, one he'd used only in private. No one else had ever known of the nickname.

Dear God . . . Richard was alive?

Griffith, a gun in each hand, carefully made his way through the nooks and crannies of the second floor. Goddamn Victorians; couldn't they have built houses that weren't so easy to hide someone?

He'd had to stop Fiona from coming up not only because it wasn't safe but because he didn't want her finding a dumb-ass rookie operative playing with her cat.

Still, he didn't like leaving her alone downstairs. For a brief moment, he'd considered telling her the truth and breaking every rule he'd sworn to uphold in his years of working for Avalon. But he'd resisted the need to do so and figured she was better off not knowing. If he did his job, she'd never learn how close to danger she'd come or the ugly truth about her dead or not-so-dead husband, and all she'd be left with would be a few memories of nice sex and a pile of papers that had almost been a dream come true.

Lies, lies . . . he'd been spinning them for so long that doing so was easier than telling the truth.

How the hell had his life gotten this fucked up? Where, along the line to doing something right and good, had it spun so far out of control?

At his back, beneath the jacket, he could feel the weight of his third gun. He also had a knife inside his right boot. He was armed to the teeth and trained to kill with his bare hands if the need arose, but none of that made him feel any less uneasy.

It was all about *her*.

He'd gone too far with her: sometime during the night, he'd made the mistake of forgetting what he was and what he was hired to do.

"Noonie?" he called, quietly. "Are you here?"

His only answer was a disgruntled meow that came from the office.

A fine perspiration dotted his upper lip as he made his way from the kitchenette and sleep area to the office.

No sign of Noonie.

Ben had said he'd send the rookie, and there was no reason to think something had gone wrong. Then again, Griffith hadn't had a chance to check in either. Maybe Noonie had never shown up.

And that would have been bad; it would've left the shop unprotected all night, even if their LAPD contacts had done frequent drive-bys.

A thump sounded behind a narrow, tall door, followed by another meow. Griffith cautiously opened the door, and the portly Faustus sashayed out as if he hadn't a care in the world.

Griffith immediately headed for the stairs, keeping his eye out for any movement.

Something was wrong here; he could feel it.

If he blew this assignment because of a stupid cat, Ben Sheridan would crucify his ass—and he'd damn well deserve it. Hell, he'd welcome it.

Too stunned to move, Fiona stared unseeing at the phone she still clutched in her hand.

But Richard was *dead*.

If he'd been alive, he never would have left her alone for all those years. He would've contacted her long before now, she was certain of it. There had to be another explanation.

And what of that warning?

Griffith had repeatedly expressed his concern about her safety and had been up-front about why. Admittedly, his mysterious "client" could be shady or even dangerous, but she didn't think Griffith himself was a threat to her. She felt safe with him. He'd been telling her the truth all along—or at least as much of it as he could—and who was to say this caller wasn't trying to stir up trouble by getting her to distrust those she should trust?

And even worse, doing so by pretending to be her dead husband.

She stood, weighing Griffith's warning to stay put with the need to call him back downstairs and get to the bottom of this.

Then, out of the corner of her eye, she saw a shadow move from the book aisle directly behind her.

Before she could scream, a hand covered her mouth. She tried to twist around, and suddenly a man's face loomed into view. He was a short, dark-haired man with a crooked nose, and he was grinning.

"Nuh-uh. No screaming. We want this to be a surprise," he whispered into her ear.

She went rigid at the feel of his breath against her skin, then she bit down hard on the finger against her mouth.

The man cursed quietly as he yanked her back and gave her a hard shake. "Don't do that again, or you won't like the consequences."

He forced her toward the dark back of the store. While he might be short, he was very strong. One look at the flat, dark eyes told her he wouldn't think twice about hurting her.

Or worse.

"Where's the manuscript?"

Since he had his hand over her mouth, she couldn't answer.

"Ah, right. I'd take my hand away, but I don't trust you not to scream. So nod if the manuscript is by your desk."

Fiona nodded, trying to breathe through her nose as slowly as possible; the last thing she could afford right now was to pass out.

"Let's hope it really is, and he's not pulling a fast one on you. We'll sit here and wait until your guard dog comes down to check on you, and then I'll take care of him. After that, you and me take the manuscript and go see a man who's very interested in that pile of papers. I think he may make you a very attractive offer."

Alarmed, Fiona stared up at the stranger. He'd used the phrase "guard dog," just as the caller had. Could he be the one who had made the call? And if so, how had he known of Richard's pet name for her?

She didn't have time to worry about it, though. Any second now, Griffith would come back down and walk right into a trap.

The man smiled and casually pressed a large, ugly gun against her cheek.

As he pulled her into the shadows, she stumbled on something. Looking down, she saw it was a body, tied up and lying facedown on the floor.

Twelve

❖

THE SECONDS SEEMED TO STRETCH OUT PAINFULLY; she was shaking as much from fear as from the agony of waiting. She wanted to do something, but the press of the gun against her face wasn't making her feel in the least heroic.

Nor did the inert body at her feet. Who was he? And what in holy hell was going on?

Just then floorboards creaked above her and the man said quietly, "It's about fucking time. I could've killed and raped you a dozen times over before he got his lazy ass down here. He's getting slow in his old age."

Fiona glanced in horror and confusion at the man, and he winked as he put the barrel of the gun to his lips in a "hush" gesture, as if the weapon were his finger.

The footsteps drew closer, then reached the landing.

Fiona tensed, wanting to call out a warning to Griffith. For whatever reason, she seemed important enough to keep alive, but she didn't think it worked that way for Griffith.

Her chest felt too tight, each breath an effort.

Then she decided to do it anyway. She sucked in as long a breath as she dared and opened her mouth—just as the gun pressed viciously against her cheekbone.

"Don't do it. I need him down here."

The little pig-eyed bastard would probably kill her anyway, just like he'd killed the man on the floor. Why make it easy?

"Police!" Fiona screamed. "Call the police! Don't come—"

The slap to her face sent her reeling backward, her eyes flooding with tears. Stunned, she hit a file cabinet behind her hard, then fell down across the legs of the body on the floor. Even through the haze of pain, she heard footsteps coming down the stairs, slow and even.

Why hadn't he run?

"Griffith, no! Go for help!"

She tried to get to her knees, but the man put his foot on her spine and pushed her back down. "He won't run. It ain't his style," the man said, sounding strangely pleased.

"Leave her alone."

Despite the heavy foot pressing her against the hard, musty floorboards, Fiona twisted around enough to see Griffith. He was walking toward them, his expression calm.

"No . . . get away," she whispered, even though it was too late.

"I can't do that." He never took his gaze off the man. "Let her up. Even for you, this is low."

"Oooh," the man said in mock surprise. "You insult me."

"You're not worth my time to insult, Bressler. But she's a woman, not a cockroach. Get your fuckin' foot off her back. Now."

The pressure on Fiona's back eased, and with it came a slow, cold realization. She pushed herself to her feet and whispered, "You know each other."

"We go way back," said her captor cheerfully. "What line did he feed you? That he's just the messenger? He sweet-talk you? It looks like he did more than talk, eh?"

Between the pain from slamming into the file cabinet and her numb mind, Fiona could only stare back.

The man laughed, but didn't take his attention from Griffith, who'd stopped a few feet away, hands in his jacket pockets, face expressionless. He glanced once at the body but showed no surprise or anger.

"It's okay, sweetheart," Bressler said. "It's his standard operating procedure, and I hear he's real good at it."

"How do you— How . . . ?"

"Fiona, be quiet and stay out of the way. I'll get you out of this."

"You will, huh?" Bressler taunted. "Seems to me I'm the one with the leverage, Laughton. So get your hands out of those pockets right now. Slowly."

"You need her alive. Even you're not stupid enough to forget that."

"Nah, we need him to *think* she's alive. I don't want to hurt her, but it don't matter one way or the other to me if she ends up dead. She'd just be . . . what do you call it again? Oh, yeah. Collateral damage. Allowable loss."

The undercurrent of violence in the deep, heavy silence was so strong it raised the fine hairs all along her skin.

Griffith's mouth had thinned, and there was a cold edge to his eyes that made him look like a stranger. She didn't know this man. She'd spent the night in his arms and he'd passed much of his night inside her, and she didn't know him at all.

Her heart seemed to miss its beat when Griffith removed his hands from his pockets—and raised not one gun but two. Sleek, dark, and as deadly looking as Bressler's.

"By the time you pull the trigger on her, I'll have

splattered your brains all over those books behind you. You'll never get a chance at me." Griffith's eyes narrowed. "And that's one of my men lying there. I'm not happy about that. If he's dead, I'll kill you no matter what."

Again silence, and this time Fiona could feel the tension radiating from the man who held her.

"Where's von Lahr?" Griffith snapped.

"Around. You know how it is."

Von Lahr . . . something about that name sounded familiar, but Fiona didn't have time to dwell on why. The gun against her head remained firm. Whoever this Bressler was, he wasn't about to surrender meekly.

Dear God, she didn't want to die like this.

The murky dimness and musty, old-book smell were smothering; the shelves seemed to close in . . . and Fiona had never realized the sound of silence could be so loud. Her heartbeat pounded in her ears, and tension hummed, low and edgy.

A split second before the man holding her moved, she felt his muscles harden in anticipation, and she was already ducking before Griffith shouted at her to get down.

The body on the floor suddenly jackknifed with such speed she barely had to time to register that he'd kicked Bressler in the back of the legs and knocked him down.

A short popping noise followed, then several more like it, and she realized they were gunshots. Bressler grunted in pain, and she looked up from her protective crouch to see him fall a few feet from her, clutching his kneecap, which had shattered into a bloody mess. Then she realized his hand was also a bloody mess and his gun had fallen aside.

Nausea rolled up inside her, but she held it back and scrambled away from the two bodies on her floor, one struggling to sit up and the other lying in a widening pool of dark blood.

She ran for the back door, just a few feet away, only to be yanked back by the hem of her sweater and spun around to face Griffith's dark, expressionless face.

"You're staying right here," he said, in that niceguy voice she'd so easily trusted. "Got that?"

Fiona nodded, but a spark of raw fury was burning under her cold, sick fear.

Bastard. The lying, rotten bastard.

As if reading the venom in her eyes, and the thought behind it, Griffith smiled, and she watched the grooves in his cheeks deepen. "Atta girl. No screaming or fainting or having hysterics. You're tougher than you look. And you," he said coldly to the bound man as he cut his ropes free. "You're not as dead as you looked."

"He got the jump on me, Grif." He was young and dark-haired, with a cut on his lip and a huge bruise on his cheek. "Sorry."

Griffith spared only a glare at him before he walked toward Bressler—curled up in pain but strangely silent, his gun no longer in sight—and hauled out a pair of plastic ties from his back pocket.

As he passed her, Fiona demanded, "Who are you?"

Her voice was shaking from shock and fear, and as she watched him quickly tie up Bressler and then stash his gun in a holster inside his leather jacket, she understood why he'd been undressed when she'd gotten out of the bathroom, why he never took off that jacket.

"Me?" Griffith moved to keep both her and Bressler in sight. "I'm exactly what I said I am— except for the lawyer part. I'm just an errand boy working for a very powerful client who needed you to look at a manuscript."

Not trusting her legs, Fiona leaned back against the shelves. What was going on here? These men, the call earlier . . . none of it made any sense.

"Lucky for you, you didn't kill my operative," Griffith told Bressler. "I guess this means you get to live."

"I didn't have time to kill him. He came in right

before you did. Things were hoppin'. It was a regular party for a second or two there." Bressler laughed, a tight, strained sound that made her shiver all over again. "I don't suppose this means you'll be nice to me now?"

To her shock, Griffith hauled Bressler up, then punched him hard in the stomach. As the man flailed back, making horrible noises in his efforts to suck in air, Griffith raised his gun and clubbed Bressler on the head with its butt. It was a neat, clean blow, and the man slumped sideways, bonelessly limp.

It sickened her how Griffith had struck him down so effortlessly, and without so much as a look of regret or care.

It was also the last straw.

If she ran, she might be hurt, but if she stayed, injury or death was certain.

Fiona backed away slowly, hoping this time she could get to the door before he noticed her movement. She took one careful step, followed by another—and then his head snapped around, his eyes narrowing.

She lunged forward, panic driving her as she fumbled with the lock.

A split second later the lightbulb above the door shattered, sending a burst of small, sharp splinters exploding outward. Fiona froze, her eyes squeezed shut.

"Don't do that again." Griffith's voice came from behind her, soft and calm. "Or the next one doesn't miss. I won't kill you, but I'll make sure you can't walk, much less run."

Thirteen

◈

HER MUSCLES WERE PARALYZED IN TERROR. SHE'D never heard him move, but she could feel his heat behind her, hear his soft breathing. Smell his cologne and a hint of perspiration.

Despite his nearness, he didn't touch her. "Don't make this more difficult than it needs to be. Stay quiet and do as I tell you, and you'll be okay."

She stepped away, trying to stay as far from him as possible. The young man was sitting up, shaking his head groggily and rotating his jaw as if to test it. He watched Fiona and Griffith, and whenever his gaze fell on Griffith, he looked wary.

"That was stupid," Griffith told him as he slowly pushed to his feet. "You're damn lucky you kicked the little bastard, or I'd be tempted to give you another black eye to match the one you've already got."

The younger man said nothing.

"If you know where your gun is, get it. And for being such a dumb-ass, you get to stay behind and clean up the mess."

The kid took a quick, deep breath. "Yes, sir."

"You got the number for the janitorial help, right?"

"Yes, Mr. Sh——" At Griffith's glare, the kid broke off, glanced at Fiona, and then swallowed. "Yes, I do."

Griffith turned and took her arm. "We need to leave, Fiona. You're in danger."

"Oh, that's rich." She shook free from his hand, and he was smart enough not to try to touch her again. "No one shot at me until *you* did."

Beyond him, she could see Bressler trussed on the floor, unconscious and still bleeding. The nameless kid was standing over him, pointedly not looking at either her or Griffith. More quietly she added, "And you *did* shoot *him*."

"Because it was him or you. Don't be stupid about this."

It didn't escape her notice that he offered no other excuses or explanations. "And now you think I'm going to be thankful and consider you my hero, simply because—"

"Look, I'm not a hero and never claimed to be.

But I'm your best chance of staying alive." Still holding Fiona's gaze, he added, "Hey, Noonie. Ms. Kennedy's cat is hiding somewhere. Make sure he's fed and taken care of."

"Yes, sir," the younger man said in a subdued voice. "Anything else?"

"Yeah, watch your ass. Both targets are here and probably close by. Try not to get yourself killed; I don't want any more rookies dying on my watch. Got that?"

Noonie nodded but wisely said nothing.

"Bring me the briefcase. It's by her desk chair."

Fiona watched Griffith through the entire exchange, understanding that something very strange was going on and she was central to it. The manuscript, that call from Richard, if it was indeed Richard. . . . While none of it made sense, it was all connected through *her*.

"I've been ordered to keep you under constant surveillance and to keep you safe," Griffith told her. "I realize you have no reason to trust me, but I'm your only option at the moment. Do exactly as I say and speak to no one. I'm taking you to a safe place. Once we're there, you can ask me all the questions you want and I'll do my best to answer them."

So calm. So polite. So *false*.

Fiona swung her fist and hit him square on the

side of his mouth. Pain radiated up her arm, and her knuckles burned.

Noonie, returning with the briefcase, stopped in his tracks and stared.

She'd hit Griffith with all her strength, and he'd reacted with only a faint grimace.

"You *bastard*. All along you lied to me. You used me!"

A drop of blood welled on his lip as he smiled. "That pretty much covers it."

"You're not a cop."

"Nope." He wiped the blood away. "But I am fighting for truth, justice, and the American way, so you can consider me one of the good guys."

He took the briefcase from Noonie, then pulled her after him out the back door and into the service alley.

He was stronger than she was, and armed, and as much as she hated what he was doing and distrusted him, she wanted to believe he was looking out for her, even if he was being a total bastard about it. And he'd ordered that kid to feed her cat.

Rain drizzled down on them as he led her toward a small, beat-up car that no one would consider out of place parked in an alley.

After a quick check around and under the car, Griffith unlocked the door and pushed her inside, buckling her up—and handcuffing her to the door handle in a quick move.

Staring down with disbelief at the circlet of metal around her wrist, she said, "You have all sorts of surprises in that jacket of yours."

"Tricks of the trade."

He shut the door and jogged around to the driver's side, and within seconds, he had the car moving. With a dull surprise, she noted that the engine sounded much more powerful than she would've expected from the car's dilapidated appearance.

Even his car was a liar.

Griffith didn't have to look at his reluctant passenger to gauge her mood; anger and contempt radiated off her in waves so strong he could feel it.

He didn't expect anything else, and because he'd known all along how this would turn out, a perverse part of him had been even colder to her than necessary. If she was going to hate him, he might as well give her a good reason to hate him with every cell in her body.

Putting up the wall up between them was better for her, better for him.

He was still running on an adrenaline high, his heart pounding. What a goddamn mess. He'd been so focused on Fiona, standing pressed against Bressler with a gun to her head, that he hadn't had time to really think about Noonie's close call with disaster.

Damn kid. Having to take care of Bressler, feed

the cat, and explain to Ben what had gone wrong would be punishment enough.

Jesus. His hands were shaking. When was the last time he'd felt like this?

Again the image of Fiona with the gun to her head flashed to mind. As angry as he was at Noonie, Griffith knew he'd messed up as well. Bressler would've killed her if he'd had the chance, and Griffith had all but given him that chance on a silver platter.

He'd gotten too involved, too distracted. And not only had he failed to protect Fiona when it mattered most, but he'd probably blown his chance to get to von Lahr.

Uneasiness nagged at the back of his mind, and his instincts warned him that he couldn't relax his guard at all, not even at the safe house.

Which might be a good thing. If nothing else, it would keep him too busy to focus on the regret that stung like a bitch whenever he glimpsed the hurt and anger in Fiona's eyes.

As he entered the freeway on-ramp heading out of downtown L.A., the silence grew so thick that he couldn't ignore it any longer. "Fiona—"

"Don't." She turned her face toward the window. "Whatever you're going to say, I don't want to hear it. Nothing will ever excuse what you've done to me."

She was right.

What was done was done; the best he could do for her now was to get her back to her quiet life as quickly possible, then disappear.

Inexplicably, that hurt. And he didn't dare consider why.

Fourteen

❖

THE DRIVE CONTINUED IN SILENCE, AND GRIFFITH soon left the freeway, keeping to side streets in a part of L.A. Fiona wasn't familiar with. Van Nuys? It wasn't one of the better parts of the city.

The streets were poorer, older, and the SUVs and expensive imports had given way to rusted vehicles held together by only luck. Stark buildings crowded closer, and the blocky apartments and run-down businesses had metal grates over their windows and doors. The faces of the people on the streets had changed, too; they all looked as if they were dealing with harder times than the people in the neighborhoods she was used to.

Before long, Griffith turned off one of the main thoroughfares and parked in a service alley behind a generic-looking block of brick apartment buildings. Their small windows were covered with dilapidated vinyl miniblinds, and the scrubby yards were full of crabgrass, empty cans, liquor bottles, and other . . . things.

This was the kind of place where nobody would look too closely or ask too many questions. A place where people were concerned more with minding their own business than with interfering in anybody else's.

Griffith guided her toward one of the buildings. "Don't make a scene or start hollering for help. We need to keep as low a profile as possible until the situation is secure."

She *had* considered running, trying to lose herself in the people and the traffic, but the chance of breaking free from his bruising grip was zero. He'd only get rougher with her—and then she'd never get answers to the hundreds of questions crowding her mind.

And what if he was right? What if he really was the only person keeping her safe? She'd realized by now his threat toward her had been only to intimidate her. He hadn't killed Bressler, though he'd threatened to, and she couldn't forget how he'd told his accomplice—partner?—to take care of Faustus.

Those weren't the actions of a stone-cold killer.

Maybe she couldn't trust him, but everything she'd seen so far told her that he was indeed trying to protect her, and doing so against rather daunting odds. Which meant *her* odds were better with him, than without him.

Griffith plainly knew where he was going and so she kept quiet as he led her up the stairs to an apartment on the top floor. He pulled out a key, unlocked the door, and pushed her inside.

Bare walls in a forgettable light blue. Generic low-pile carpeting. A navy blue sofa that hadn't been worth much even when it was new, years ago, and the same could be said of the discount-store end table and small dinette set. A daybed sat on the opposite side of the room, a patchwork quilt covering it, and she realized she was in a studio apartment. The door by the kitchenette—with its worn linoleum, counters, and plain cabinets—must have led to the bathroom.

It had the semblance of an occupied apartment, with a television and stereo equipment, outdated appliances, and vinyl miniblinds that had seen better days. The overall impression was that it wouldn't leave an impression. It was the sort of room and building in the sort of neighborhood you'd forget within minutes of leaving it.

But aside from the dust and the closed-room smell, it was clean. "Lovely."

"Hard to keep a low profile in a fancy hotel." He pulled her toward the daybed. "Sit."

Since he was pushing her down, she sat. She struggled a little when he handcuffed her to the scrolled wrought-iron side arm, but his only effort in subduing her was a frown of annoyance.

She tugged on the handcuff, but the daybed was solidly built. No doubt that was the whole point. Who knew when you might have to handcuff a kidnapped antiquarian bookseller to the furniture?

The more she looked around, the more she was sure there'd be nothing in this room she could use as a weapon. The windows were probably specially secured, despite being four stories up, and she wouldn't be surprised if extra insulation had been added to muffle noise—or calls for help. And a closer scrutiny of the lock showed that it was new and sturdy, despite efforts to make it look older and flimsy.

If she got out of this, she was going to look up who owned this building and then sic the police on them—provided, of course, she could remember how they'd gotten here, much less find the building among blocks of others that looked just like it. She couldn't even see out the window that overlooked the main thoroughfare because the blinds were closed.

"So now what?" she asked, since it didn't look as if Griffith was going to kick off a conversation anytime soon.

"Like I said earlier, we wait here until I can evaluate the situation and come up with a contingency plan."

"So there never was a client, and I was never going to get paid."

"There's a client. We do need you to look at the manuscript. You'll be compensated for your time and your trouble. Any damages to your store, and any insurance claims or other legal fees, will be paid for."

"By whom?"

Griffith dragged one of the chairs from the dinette set toward the main window. "Ultimately, by the same person or persons who pay me. I don't know more than that."

"You expect me to believe you?"

"I don't care if you believe me or not. It doesn't change a thing."

As Griffith shrugged out of his jacket, Fiona stared at him in amazement.

The man was a walking arsenal. He wore a double shoulder holster, with guns in both. Those big, black guns that definitely looked like they could take care of business as easily as they'd taken care of Bressler.

Hooked to the back of his belt was another holster and gun, although that one was smaller. He tossed another set of handcuffs on the floor by his feet, then dropped down on the chair with a sigh and rubbed his eyebrows.

He looked exhausted—and she could hardly believe that, even for a second, she'd felt a twinge of sympathy for him.

As the silence stretched on, Fiona observed how often he moved the blinds aside, although only enough to glance through. If people were standing outside and watching for movement at the window, they might not catch it, he was that careful.

Finally, unable to take the silence any longer, she blurted, "You don't even look like the same person anymore."

There was something harder and darker about him that not even his obvious weariness could blunt. Griffith glanced at her but didn't respond.

Not that she'd expected him to say anything. After all, he was no longer required to be nice to her.

Well, *she* didn't have to be polite, either. "But since that was all a lie, I shouldn't be surprised, should I?"

Again, no answer. His stubborn silence was stretching her already frayed nerves to the snapping point.

"I thought you said you'd answer my questions."

"And I will, once you actually ask one I can answer."

The dry, almost mocking tone of his voice sent a hot wave of anger washing over her. She waited until she was certain she could talk without her voice shaking, then asked, "So who are you, really? You said something about tricks of the trade. What, exactly, is that trade?"

Griffith didn't turn from the window. "I'm what most people would call a mercenary."

Fiona blinked, words failing her. She wasn't sure

what she'd expected, but it certainly hadn't been this. For one, he didn't look like a mercenary, unless mercenaries had started recruiting at frat houses.

"Most people, you say," she said after a moment, proud at how calm she sounded. "And what would those other people call you?"

"Nothing flattering."

"Uh-uh. I asked you a direct question. You're supposed to answer."

He glanced at her, but in the dim room it was hard to make out his expression. Assuming there *was* an expression. "Probably most of the names going through your mind right now."

"Lying bastard? Rotten sonofabitch? Asshole? Dick?"

It was childish, but satisfying to vent her anger.

Unfortunately, he didn't seem to care; he merely shrugged. "Those would be among the top contenders."

Time to try a different approach. "Are you planning on fending off a small invading army? There are international terrorists with fewer guns than you're wearing."

That earned her a longer look. "And what do you know of international terrorists?"

Nothing except what she, like most people, saw on the news or read in the paper. "What do *you* know of them?"

Griffith smiled, that same wide, beautiful smile that had so thoroughly charmed her when they met yesterday. It still warmed her, drew her in, as much as she hated to admit it. "A lot more than you, I can promise you."

He'd managed to avoid fully answering her original question, but it was unlikely he'd tell her the truth. "So just how many guns do you have? I see three."

He was looking out the blinds again. "The larger pair are Jericho firearms, Israeli-made. The smaller one is an old Smith & Wesson .357 Magnum. Like the jacket, it belonged to my grandfather."

"Anything else that could be considered a weapon? How much did you have to strip off and hide while I was in the bathroom last night?"

"Trade secret," he said again, and the slatted light filtering through the blinds illuminated a small smile. "If you're lucky, you won't ever find out."

"Lucky" wasn't a word she'd have used to describe the last few hours, and when she thought about the call at the shop, it only added to her confusion.

Little cat-eyed goddess . . .

On top of everything else, she might not be a widow after all, and she forced her mind to go blank before she gave in to hysteria.

"What is this all about, then? I understand it has to do with the Marlowe, but why?" She paused. "Is it a fake?"

"Yes, and we need it to help expose a forgery ring in Munich."

"Who's 'we'? Tell me about these people you work for."

"I work for a small, private outfit that operates in the black market art trade around the world. We recover stolen and looted art and antiquities. Sometimes that involves tracking down forgeries, since they're usually connected to sophisticated art theft rings."

Griffith's tone was calm and even, as if he were discussing the weather or what to eat for dinner. If he and the people he worked for knew all along that the manuscript was a fake, then . . .

Understanding dawned, and with it came a sickening twist in her belly. "You used me as bait."

"It was the most logical move to draw our target out of hiding."

"And who is this 'target'?"

But she knew the answer. Deep inside, she knew.

He turned to face her and spoke slowly, as if carefully choosing each word. "There was an individual who was paid to forge a Marlowe manuscript several years ago. When the deal soured, the forger disappeared and was presumed killed. However, we recently received a tip that led us to believe otherwise. Evidence from other sources suggests the involvement of another very dangerous individual, someone we've been trying to catch for years. If this individual had gotten to you first, he would've used you as bait as well, then killed you. We had to get to you before he did. You got me because I happened to be the closest."

The sick feeling in her belly worsened as she realized that he'd known all along who the "target" was, and knew everything about her as well. It hurt more than she could've thought possible to have such a painful part of her life used against her like this.

"Why won't you tell me the name of the target? If you're using me to catch this person, then I think I have a right to know."

"And I think you already do know, Fiona." He paused, then sighed. "I'm sorry it had to happen this way."

She looked down, tears and anger mixing with fear and disbelief, and with a little niggling of hope that only led to more anger. "Don't use my name. You have no right to call me that. We're not friends. Or anything else."

"I'm sorry."

The apology sounded neutral, automatic. As if he'd said this many times before to others like her. "I don't believe you. I don't believe any of it."

It *wasn't* Richard, this "individual" he spoke of. It simply couldn't be.

When Griffith went back to watching through the tiny cracks in the blinds, Fiona turned away, tears trickling down her cheeks.

As much as she didn't want to believe what Griffith had told her—and it sounded fantastical enough, with his talk of covert operations and black markets, looting and thieves and forgers—there was a shine of truth to it. Even if she hadn't received that last call.

Richard had been struggling to attain tenure as her career had taken off. His research had been lackluster, while hers had garnered international attention. He'd been caught falsifying data and stealing research from other scholars, herself included, out of desperation to keep up with her.

For years that had filled her with guilt, even though she'd technically done nothing wrong. She'd only been doing what she was good at, yet the very things that had brought her and her husband together had not only destroyed their marriage but must have compelled Richard, in a moment of weakness, to do something unforgivable.

As much as she wanted to deny it, it was totally believable that he would have involved himself in forging a manuscript, had it "discovered," and then reaped the benefits in research funding and accolades. If the forger had been careful enough and stayed within the known facts of Marlowe's works— as was the case with what little of the *Faustus* she'd read—it would have been that much harder to detect that it was a fake. It might never have been discovered.

It must've seemed like the perfect plan for the person who'd make a small fortune from selling the fraudulent manuscript, as well as for the one who'd attain instant recognition in his field for studying a lost draft. Simple yet effective. Nothing flashy; Richard had never been the flashy sort.

She asked quietly, "You said the deal soured. Why?"

"We don't know. The best guess is that the forger had a change of heart and tried to back out. Most likely, his family was being used as leverage to keep him quiet and cooperative."

"I see."

"At that point, he took off with the manuscript. We think he may have tried to use it as leverage as well. He knew who commissioned the forgery and who was involved in setting up the scheme to 'discover' it. There was likely a real attempt on his life, which he managed to survive. But instead of going to the police and seeking protection, he disappeared so that he would be presumed dead."

He paused. "It's doubtful the people who hired him believed he was dead, but there was no reason to do more than keep you under surveillance until the manuscript showed up. We still don't know how that happened. But once it surfaced, we knew that the target would try to contact you to warn you or that others would try to use you to draw out the target and kill him. If you'd died in the process, they would've considered it an allowable loss. Collateral damage."

The same words the man in her shop had used. Such cold, hard words for talking about the death of another human being.

She'd often listened to her friend Diana talk shop and had heard firsthand what sorts of people operated in the lucrative black market art trade and what they were capable of. If that hadn't been enough, Cassie had recently had a scare when someone tried to steal her precious infant *T. rex*. It had turned out to be connected to a notorious international art thief who had a penchant for using gullible women to do his dirty work; in the end, they were always left holding the bag.

More than anything, though, it was that voice on the phone that convinced her. Richard's voice.

He'd never died. Perhaps a part of her had somehow sensed it, and that was why she hadn't been able to move on. She should have been more shocked at learning the truth. But once the initial jolt had passed, it all felt . . . right.

"While you were upstairs looking for Faustus, I got a call." She hesitated, still reluctant to put what had happened into words because then it would be all that more real. "I think it was Richard. My husband."

"I heard the phone and figured it was him." Griffith's tone remained neutral, calm. "I was waiting for him to contact you, hoping to grab him then, but he managed to get past me. For someone not trained in undercover work, he's very good at remaining elusive."

"He told me not to trust you."

"And you shouldn't."

She frowned. "But—"

"Fiona, listen to me. You have a kind, warm heart, and you're an all-around nice person. And I'm telling you this because you shouldn't believe a single word I say to you, beyond the explanation I just provided. And don't trust me to do anything more than keep you alive and return you safely home when this is over."

Fiona didn't know *what* to think any longer. He was honest with her—and yet not. Still, his words made her feel a little better. "And telling me this helps you keep up the illusion that you're one of the good guys."

An expression of annoyance flashed across his face.

Good. She was getting under his skin.

"I'm a mercenary, for Chrissake. I'm in it for the money. I like to think I'm doing something worthwhile at the same time, sure. But at the end of the day, I do the dirty work no one else can get away with, and I do it because it pays well."

"And if you find my husband, what will you do with him?"

"Turn him over to the police."

For a fleeting moment, Fiona was almost sorry, for the sake of his long-suffering family, that Richard wasn't really dead—then immediately she felt guilty for even thinking it.

"It would be the right thing to do," she said after a moment. "It's what he should've done to begin with. I suppose that'll put Richard and me back where we left off five years ago, with him doing something stupid. Only this time, I'll actually get the choice of whether or not I should stay by his side."

"Will you?"

The conversation had plunged into the surreal. She was talking about her recently declared legally dead husband with the man she'd had hot, sweaty, and wonderful sex with last night?

"He's no longer my husband. After all he's done to me and to others, I owe him nothing. But . . . for my own sanity, I want to talk to him and see him again. To find closure, maybe."

She was grateful, in a way, that he'd miraculously returned from the dead to try to "save" her, but it had been his own greed that had put her into this position. Beyond her gratitude for that phone call to warn her, he was still dead to her in all the ways that truly mattered.

As was the man sitting across the room; the man who'd used her, manipulated her, and worst of all, used her vulnerabilities against her with the skill of a master. Never in her life had she known such absolute humiliation. Or such anger at herself, for trusting him simply because . . . he was cute and looked good in a leather jacket and jeans.

How stupid and shallow she'd been.

Tears welled again, hot and stinging. She didn't want to cry in front of Griffith, but she couldn't hold back the tears. She had enough dignity to keep her crying quiet, though she could feel their wet heat rolling down her face, one after another.

Great. She was crying.

Griffith continued to watch the street activity outside, but it was hard to concentrate knowing that she was crying—and it was worse somehow, that she was trying to be brave about it instead of bawling out loud.

He hated everything about this; hated himself for what he was doing to her, for having failed yet again to be quick enough, and he even hated her, a little, for making him question himself.

Now was *not* the time for an identity crisis.

He wished he could reach out and comfort her; it sounded like she needed a hug. But he didn't have the right to offer her even something so simple now.

What could he give her that could help? Protecting her was a given, and it wasn't enough. All he really had to offer was a reason for her to hate him. Making her angry, stoking her hate, might keep her strong, keep her clear and focused.

Well, being an asshole was easy—and he'd had plenty of practice at it.

Griffith shifted, discreetly watching her. If not for the white of her sweater, it would've been hard to see her at all in the darkness. She sat stiffly, her shoulders square and proud, facing away from him, but he could see those shoulders shaking with telltale regularity, and every now and then he heard a little catch of breath.

It filled him with an overwhelming sense of despair and helplessness, which scared the shit out of him. He closed his eyes, willing himself to tune out her crying, and then returned his attention to the window.

Someone was out there watching them, even in this supposedly secure place. He could feel it with a bone-deep instinct born of years of sitting in dark rooms and waiting for all hell to break loose.

Fifteen

"CRYING WON'T DO YOU ANY GOOD."

"Like I give a damn what you think." Fiona glared at him. God, how had she let him inside her body, allowed him to be so close, when all along—

"How does it feel to use people? Or do you just not care? It must be so amusing, watching people make such fools of themselves. What I might be thinking or feeling never mattered to you. None of what happened meant anything to you, did it?"

He didn't bother defending himself; he simply stared out the window, and she wondered how he could sit so still. Already she had to shift, squirming in the confines of the cuffs, her bottom feeling numb.

She didn't know how much time had passed, but the room had begun to darken. Maybe the rain clouds had gathered again, but as the shadows grew longer, she rested her head against the wall and let her eyes drift shut. She had to sleep; if only for a short while.

"I keep wondering if there should be more."

His unexpected words caused her to jump with a soft gasp. Confused, she opened her mouth to ask Griffith to repeat himself when he said, "I think there should be more."

He was answering her question. Hours after she'd asked, but something she'd said must've bothered him.

Good. She hoped guilt was making him soul-suckingly miserable.

"I've been at this for a long time, but lately I've been thinking there should be more to life. Even for someone like me . . . there should be more."

Her interest piqued, Fiona tried to get a clearer look at his face. Something about how he sat in the darkness, coupled with what he'd said and his tone of voice, roused another little prickling of sympathy.

She immediately quashed it. After everything that had happened and his warning not to believe a word that came out of his lying mouth, how could she *still* be pulled in by him?

Fiona looked away, disgusted. She might be able to excuse having trusted this man because he'd been handsome, flirtatious, and she'd been desperate for sex, but there'd be no excusing any softness toward him now.

Instead, she said flatly, "I'm hungry."

"I hope you can tolerate bottled water and protein bars. You'll have to hold out until tonight for real food."

"You're going to keep me locked to this bed all *day?*" she demanded, her voice rising.

"Distrust is a two-way street, Fiona," he said as he walked to the kitchenette, "and I don't trust you any more than you trust me."

As he passed her on his way back to the window, he dropped an icy-cold bottle of water and three wrapped bars on the bed beside her. Fiona took a long, deep breath to keep her temper in check. Screaming at him wouldn't do any good.

And suddenly she wasn't that hungry anymore. On top of all the stress and fear and abject humiliation, being chained to a railing like a dog was just too much.

What if something happened to him? She couldn't do jackshit, handcuffed to the heavy iron bed. Perhaps she had to stay with him out of necessity's sake, but not like *this*.

"If you unlock the cuffs, I promise I won't try to get away."

That got his attention. He turned from his post, brows drawn together. "Nice try, but no."

"Why not? I feel like a dog. A *helpless* dog at that." She tore open one of the packages with her teeth and took a bite of the bar. Hungry or not, she needed to keep up her strength. "I accept that you'll keep me safe, so I'm not going to run, but what if something goes wrong and you get killed? I wouldn't even be able to try to run or hide, like this."

"Good point, but no."

"Why not?"

"As I already said, I don't trust you. Second, I need to be in control of the situation, and if you're a free agent, I no longer control you. It's basic strategy."

"Complete control of any situation isn't possible." She arched a brow to match his own. "That's basic common sense."

"Not in my experience."

"What is this?" She made her tone as mocking as possible. "Are you telling me you make mistakes? Miscalculations? Like trying to protect me by shooting at me? Hauling me away against my will and then still acting like you're some kind of hero?"

Griffith turned back to the window. "Trying to make me angry won't work. I've had a lot more experience in situations like this than you have. There isn't a trick I'm not familiar with."

An unpleasant reminder that she was so out of his league she should simply stop trying. Giving up, however, wasn't an option. Whatever she had to do to get out of this alive, she'd do it.

"Why not just let me go? The secret's out, so nobody is likely to come near me now. I'm probably in more danger with you than I would be back at the store."

"Your connection with the manuscript keeps you a potential problem."

"In what way? I've seen only a few pages of it!"

"They don't know that." He let out a sigh. "Look, we have reason to believe that your ex left you a personal coded message somewhere in the manuscript. The rumor is that only you would be able to find it, and that he also provided the names of the people responsible. It's those names that make the manuscript worth killing for, and that's why we really do want you to look at it. I suppose you might not be inclined to be helpful now, though."

"You can go rot."

"No matter how much you hate me, think it over. People like this need to be in prison. You can help put them there."

Unsure if she should believe him, Fiona settled for glaring. "Maybe I don't care about that. If you hadn't shown me that fake, I'd be buying new shoes and a swimsuit for the Bahamas. I'm not too impressed with you or the people you work for."

And deep down inside, she'd wanted to believe the manuscript was real. One more disappointment she could lay at his feet.

"So who's this other mysterious individual you're after?"

"Somebody we've been hunting for a long time."

"Is giving me a name breaking some mercenary rules of conduct? Do you *have* rules of conduct? Like a Miss Manners for mercenaries?"

"It'd be safer if you didn't know."

Fiona laughed; she couldn't help it. "Safer? I don't feel safe at all. You've done a fine job of putting me smack in the middle of danger, thank you very much."

"You were in big trouble before I even showed up. You just didn't know it."

The thought made her feel a little sick all over again.

"The man I'm referring to is a master criminal. He's been operating for nearly twenty years, and he's ruthless and smart and very, very dangerous. He specializes in antiquities and art thefts, and lately he's making a fortune by selling looted Sumerian and Babylonian artifacts from Iraq. With two wars over there, it's a free-for-all, and he's been one busy guy. We'd lost track of him for months when he showed up out of the blue in August and—" He sighed. "It doesn't matter. Just know that I want to nail this sonofabitch really bad."

Fiona shifted, trying again to find a comfortable position. Since she had to go to the bathroom, no amount of wiggling would help for long. Yet uncomfortable as she was, she hadn't missed his hesitation.

Griffith had mentioned a man's name back at the shop to Bressler, and she couldn't quite remember it. It had sounded foreign, though.

Something else he said bothered her, but she couldn't put her finger on it. Was it something Diana might've mentioned about art thefts? Maybe at her wedding back in August?

August . . .

Fiona straightened, suddenly remembering. Not Diana, *Cassie*.

God, what had been that man's name, the one who'd recruited one of Cassie's lab workers and nearly whisked away an invaluable prehistoric fossil? It *had* been a foreign-sounding name. German, if she remembered correctly.

Chewing her lip in concentration, she tried to remember those conversations when she and Cassie were in New Orleans for Jack and Diana's wedding. She was certain Diana had said the man was extremely dangerous and was wanted by a number of countries.

She suddenly remembered the handsome Berlin businessman who'd come to her store hours before Griffith had arrived, and then the name came back to her.

"Rainert von Lahr!"

Sixteen

GRIFFITH WHIPPED AROUND, THEN HE WALKED SLOWLY toward the bed. "What did you say?"

Judging by his reaction, she'd guessed right.

"Rainert von Lahr. He's the man you're after." In the face of his silence, she added, "You mentioned him back at the shop, and now I remember where else I've heard his name."

He smiled, cheeks grooving—and looking so painfully handsome and *trustable*. "Ah, yes. Your friends."

Even though she'd expected his answer, it still angered her to hear it. "You studied up on me. How thorough of you."

Griffith leaned back against the wall by the daybed, arms folded over his chest, his expression flat. "Your P.I. friend in New Orleans is someone we're aware of, since we're sort of in the same line of business. As for your incredibly lucky pal in Wyoming, she only recently caught our attention. We'd been handling more dinosaur thefts over the past few years and picked up rumors about a group of fossil looters operating out west. With her high profile and knack for finding valuable specimens, she was someone we identified as a high-risk target."

Whoever he worked for, they sounded quite organized. Fiona didn't want to be impressed, but it was hard not to be.

"Von Lahr also came to my shop and paid me a little courtesy call, right before you showed up. But you knew that already, didn't you?"

"I figured it out from your description, yes." He stretched, and she tried not to be impressed by that either. "The world of black market art theft is small. The players are well known, as are the global hot spots, and the people I work for have been at this for longer than I've been alive."

That took her by surprise. "And how long have you been with them?"

"Over fifteen years. Since I was nineteen."

That made him thirty-four. "So you graduated from high school and decided to become a mercenary. Such a natural leap, from geometry and pep band to mercenary."

He smiled again. "Funny you'd put it that way. I

wanted to be in a rock band, but I joined the army instead."

She found herself smiling back. "Another natural leap, from rock star to army grunt." Fiona did the math and said, "You were in the first Gulf War in Iraq."

"Yup."

"And this most recent one?"

"Not in a combat capacity."

Griffith pushed away from the wall and headed back to the kitchenette, and she couldn't help but admire the way he moved, the confidence and strength hidden so effectively beneath the understated clothing. Desire bloomed, warm and deep, as she took in his broad shoulders and narrow hips beneath the jeans and striped cotton shirt—and she couldn't deny there was something sexy, on a very primal level, about a man wearing guns in a double shoulder holster.

She wasn't proud that she could still lust after him, but she wouldn't lie to herself. There was already enough of that going around.

He opened the refrigerator, snagged a bottle of water, then started to eat a protein bar. She nibbled on her own, the fudgy chocolate taste almost too rich after not having eaten in so long.

"When are we leaving?"

"Not until after dark. Then you'll go to a place a lot safer than this."

"For how long? How can I . . . You can't just take me wherever you want whenever you want! That's kidnapping, regardless of good intentions. Which, in your case, are doubtful anyway."

"They're going to have to make their move soon, and we hope we can grab McMahon before they do. Once we have him, the heat will be off you. Until then, you stay with me whether you like it or not. When we decide you're safe, I disappear and you never see me or hear from me again. That's the way it works."

The mention of Richard's name brought her short. How incredibly awkward. "You slept with me knowing he was not only alive, but somewhere in this city and watching me. That's revolting." Embarrassment melted into anger. "And was having sex with me part of the plan all along?"

"I do whatever it takes to get the job done. I'm very good at what I do."

And how. Goddamn him.

Taking a deep breath, she met his gaze. "I need to go to the bathroom. And does the plumbing here work?"

"Of course."

"Then I want to take a shower. I feel dirty."

If he was bothered by her words, and their implication, it didn't show on his face. "I'll unlock you, but don't think you can outmaneuver me. You wouldn't stand a chance against me if you tried to fight or run."

"You manhandle and seduce women for a living? My, your mother must be proud of you."

His eyes narrowed a fraction. "I haven't seen my family in ten years. They don't really care what I do one way or another. I live my life for myself, no one else."

"As long as there's a paycheck at the end."

Griffith unlocked the cuffs but didn't answer. She sensed a simmering anger in him, which gave her a renewed flush of satisfaction. There were different ways to fight, and not all of them depended on guns or brawn. Fiona decided she'd use whatever means she had at hand to her own advantage. She'd found a little crack, a sliver of weakness, and she'd use that against him. Just as he'd used her vulnerabilities and weaknesses against her.

Without another word, Griffith led her to the bathroom. Once inside, she waited for him to leave. When he didn't she said coldly, "You're not seriously going to stand there while I pee, are you?"

"I don't let you out of my sight."

Fiona stared at him for a moment longer. Then, mouth tightening, she slammed the toilet lid up. It gave a solid, gratifying smack against the tank as she began to unzip her pants.

"A decent man would at least look the other way."

"And in what little fantasy world are mercenaries decent?" His close-lipped smile was cold. "We're selfish pricks who'll do anything for money—not the heroes you see in the movies."

Fiona couldn't look at him as she sat down. It was utterly humiliating, but she had no choice. Whatever she had to do to get through this, she'd do it.

After flushing the toilet, she turned the water on in the shower—it wasn't the cleanest shower stall, but it didn't look like she'd catch anything fatal from it. There was an unopened bar of soap, like the kind you'd find in a hotel, and little bottles of shampoo and conditioner.

Hotel amenities. It would've been amusing had it been someone's idea of a joke.

She quickly stripped down, well aware of his gaze on her. Those long hours together were fresh in her memory—the feel of him inside her, hard and urgent, the sound of his breathing, the smell of his skin . . .

There was nothing sexier than a tall, lean, dark-haired man wearing jeans that hung low on his hips, and she had an overwhelming urge to tug them down.

She yanked the curtain closed.

What was *wrong* with her? She was lusting after a rotten bastard who'd used her and seduced her, landed her square in the middle of danger, and even shot at her!

There had to be some clever psychological explanation for her response to him. She'd been practical and sensible her whole life long; now was *not* the time to change that.

Squeezing her eyes shut, she stepped under the showerhead. The hot water helped to soothe the tension tightening every sinew and muscle in her body. Eyes closed, she let the steam surround her, washing away, if only for a short while, the worries and fears that pressed in on her from every direction.

Seventeen

❖

"I'M NOT USED TO HAVING CLIENTS STICK AROUND." Rebeka, wearing only a black thong, paced up and down the bedroom. Since it was small, she looked like a twitchy cat in a cage.

The harsher light of day was not kind to her, but she was still pretty, in a worn and desperate kind of way.

Von Lahr, lounging in a papasan chair by the window with his pants unbuckled, shirt unbuttoned, and tie looped around his neck, watched her in amusement. "Do I make you nervous?"

"Kinda, yeah."

"Would you like me to leave?"

She stopped and eyed him warily, clearly unsure

how to handle a man who didn't just fuck, pay, and run. "Do you want to?"

He shrugged. "I'm in no hurry, as it happens. I have business to attend to, but not yet."

Mainly because the business hadn't checked in with him.

Bressler should've called hours ago. Apparently all had not gone well since his cell phone had been quiet all day. He could only assume Laughton had somehow gotten the upper hand—again—and the redhead was with him.

"No, you don't have to leave. It's just that—"

"I'm paying you, in cash, for every hour I spend with you," von Lahr interrupted. "Whether you choose to report that to your handler is up to you. I don't care one way or another."

She stared at him, and he could almost see the effort it took for her to add up the sum. Then her eyes widened as she understood what he was saying. "You wouldn't tell?"

"Why should I? You earned it; you keep it."

He had nothing to do but wait, and it might as well be here. He couldn't go back to his hotel. When he'd called the bookstore that morning, he'd gotten the answering machine. Not a good sign, since he knew the store was open on Saturdays.

Rebeka was still staring at him. "It's not the way the rules work, that's all. I just—"

"Forget the rules." She was beginning to get on his nerves; he definitely preferred her in bed, where he could give her mouth something else to do. "You don't need them. They will only keep you from having what you want. Even if you were to do something very bad, something everybody talked about, in a few days something else would happen and they would talk about that instead, forgetting all about you. In the end, nobody cares. People obey the rules only because they're afraid of what will happen if they don't. Once you get over that fear, you will be much stronger."

"You're not just an out-of-town businessman, are you?"

She was pacing again, a glint of fear in her dark eyes, which was good. That would make her easier to control, should the need arise.

"I *am* just an out-of-town businessman." And one whose business deal was souring.

Something had certainly transpired at the bookstore, but the other people he had in place had heard nothing. No gunshots, no sirens, nothing on the police radio, not even a whisper of a rumor. That told him someone had come in afterward and cleaned up. Someone with help in the police department, which could mean only Laughton.

Now all he could do was wait to see if his mysterious caller checked in. If he did, the game wasn't over yet.

Preoccupied as he was, von Lahr still found Rebeka's bare breasts, bouncing with her every step, distracting. "Perhaps you should get dressed."

That made her smile, gave her enough sense of power over him that her fear faded. "So should you."

"Am I distracting you?"

"You'd distract anybody," she retorted. "And in a city like L.A., that attracts beautiful people by the busloads, that says a lot."

As she turned away to pull on a T-shirt, he said, "Is that why you came here? To be in the movies?"

She snorted. "Yeah, another starry-eyed, stupid kid who thought she'd be a star and ended up a whore instead. Not that anybody cares."

"At least you're still alive."

When she turned, the fear had come back to her eyes. "Yeah. I guess so."

His cell phone chirped, and he pulled it out. The number wasn't one he recognized. Still, it might be Bressler. Thievery, kidnapping, and killing weren't exact sciences; sometimes things went right in all the wrong ways.

"Yes?"

A familiar, whispery voice responded: "Have you thought over what I said yesterday, Mr. von Lahr?"

Excitement gripped him. The game was still on. "Hold on a moment, I'm not alone." He glanced at the woman. "Leave."

"But I live here! Where—"

"Go take a shower. A long shower, and keep the door closed and the water running until I tell you to come out. Do you understand?"

She went to the bathroom without a word of protest. He waited until he heard the lock click— which made him smile—and the shower come on before saying, "What do you want from me?"

"I want to make a deal. In exchange for something I need from you, I will tell you where Laughton is hiding the Kennedy woman. And I'll tell you where Avalon is and who's giving the orders."

Von Lahr stood and began buttoning his shirt. "I know about Ben Sheridan."

"You know the puppet. Wouldn't you like to know the puppet master?"

For a moment, he froze. Then he said casually, "You know I would. Do you have this information?"

"I have lots of information. I hacked into their private computer system."

"Did you now?" von Lahr said mildly.

Probably a lie, but what if it wasn't?

"Yes. That means you could take them down. You, alone. You'd be a hero in your little world, Mr. von Lahr. Maybe even a god."

"Are you trying to appeal to my vanity?" he asked, injecting a quiet menace into his tone as a warning.

"Yeah. Is it working?"

"Let us just say that I try not to mix vanity with business. You do, however, have my interest. What is it you want from me?"

"I give you Avalon and the manuscript and you let me live and don't ever come near me again."

Finally the pieces were beginning to come together, if not as neatly as he would have liked.

"No money?"

"I don't want money. I just want my old life back."

Von Lahr smiled. "Richard, is that you?"

"Richard McMahon is dead, and I am whoever I need to be, if it means you'll agree to my deal."

Von Lahr deliberately let the silence stretch out, and he checked his gun, then slipped it into his jacket pocket. "If you try to betray me, I will kill you."

"Not if I kill you first. That's the way this game is played, right?"

Von Lahr laughed softly. "If you deliver me Laughton, the manuscript, and the real power and money behind my dear friends in Avalon, then you are free to live as you please, wherever you please, and to me, you will have never existed."

"I have your promise?"

"As there is honor among thieves, you have my word."

Silence again. McMahon, or whoever it was, didn't like that.

"I was hoping for an unambiguous yes or no answer, Mr. von Lahr."

"Ah, but that's not how the game is played."

"Very well." Even the whispery tone sounded tight with frustration. "As a gesture of my goodwill, I'll give you Laughton as a freebie. Do you have a pen and paper?"

"Tell me. I'll remember." When von Lahr had memorized the address, he said, "And then what? He holes up there with the woman until . . . ?"

"Until tonight. There's an abandoned airfield on the outskirts of the city. They'll fly her out of there to a more secure location, which I haven't discovered yet."

"Give me the address for the airfield."

Again, a hesitation. "Why should I?"

"Why not?" He glanced at the closed door of the bathroom, where the shower was still running. "Why should I bother with only one, when I can take out three or more? It's a more efficient use of my time and effort."

His mystery man gave over the address. A little too easily, in von Lahr's opinion.

"Do I have your word that you won't shoot me on sight when you see me?"

"I don't trust you," von Lahr said flatly. "But don't take it personally; I trust no one but myself. If I see you, I will listen. If you give me any reason to believe that you are trying to set me up or that you're actually working for Avalon, I will kill you."

"Fair enough." A rough laugh sounded. "So are you going after Laughton?"

"Wouldn't you like to know?" von Lahr asked, and then disconnected.

Let *him* stew for a few hours in uncertainty.

After he'd tucked the phone back in his pocket, von Lahr pulled on his suit coat and, as he knotted his tie, walked to the bathroom door and pounded on it.

The water shut off abruptly, then the door opened a fraction, letting out a hot swirl of steam and revealing half a face with a wide, dark eye.

He knew what she feared, but wasn't in the mood to dissuade her of the notion. He wasn't a killer, he was a thief. And not just any thief, but a master thief; a professional. Sometimes he had to kill people, yes, but only out of necessity; something Griffith Laughton would understand, since he followed the same code.

"You can come out now. I am off to play a few rounds with the guys. I'll be late, though, so don't wait up for me."

"You're not really coming back, are you?" she

asked, looking ready to slam the door shut at any second.

"No." He smiled. "And for that, you should be grateful."

He turned and walked away, but not before seeing her face turn pale.

Eighteen

◈

AFTER SCRUBBING HER SKIN VIGOROUSLY AND WASHING her hair twice, Fiona shut off the water and pushed the curtain aside.

Griffith was sitting on the toilet, his clasped hands between his knees, watching her.

Belatedly, she realized there were no towels. "I don't suppose there are any towels somewhere around here."

"Nope. Nobody actually lives here; it's just for show. There are a few basics, like the soap and shampoo, but that's about it."

She stepped out of the tub, and a perverse part of her wanted him to look at her. Naked, wet, right in front of him. Maybe that would be enough to put him off balance, enough for guilt to wiggle into some crack in his self-control . . . anything that would tip the balance of power back in her direction.

Fiona moved in close enough that she could feel his heat. While it was likely the heat and humidity in the bathroom bringing out those little beads of perspiration across his upper lip, she wanted to believe he wasn't as calm or cool as he acted.

"Then I'll have to drip dry. You've already seen all there is to see of me anyway."

He arched a brow. "It was dark most of the time."

"You told me I was pretty. Or was that a lie as well?"

"Fiona, stop." He sighed, lashes dropping to obscure those blue, blue eyes. "I know what you're trying to do, and it won't work. I'm enjoying the show, but you're going to be mad at yourself in a few minutes if you don't knock it off."

He was probably right, but she didn't care. "You didn't answer my question. Though I can't believe anything you say, I'm curious to hear it anyway. Did you mean it when you told me I was pretty? Sexy?"

Surprising herself as much as him, Fiona took his hand and placed it on her lower belly. His hand was large and dark against her pale skin, his fingers long and strong-looking.

And dangerous.

She'd witnessed the violence he was capable of, the scars on his body proving the violence he lived with—a violence he'd so easily kept leashed and hidden from her.

The desire pulling at her, so sweet and thick, was wrong. She knew it; and again, she didn't care. This wasn't normal life. All bets were off, all behavior allowable if it got her what she wanted. And what she wanted was Griffith under her power. Already she could feel the pull of heat and need between them. His body didn't lie; she could see his reaction.

"Other women have thought they could use sex to persuade me to let them escape, or entice me to their side. It never worked, and I always knew what they were doing."

Maybe she wouldn't succeed, but she didn't have anything to lose.

"And I bet you had sex with them anyway." She spread her palm over the top of his hand, sliding it lower until his fingers brushed against her curls. "Am I right?"

She couldn't do anything about the faint trembling in her knees, but maybe he wouldn't notice. Or he might simply assume she was afraid.

"Sometimes, yes," he answered her question, though it took him a few seconds.

"And you want to touch me now, don't you? Right . . . there." She pushed his fingers lower, widening her legs just enough so that he touched her, and her breath caught.

"It feels like you want me to touch you, too." A

half smile played at the corner of his mouth, and his frank gaze both unnerved her and made her hot.

Yes, she did want him to touch her—and more. "Seems that way," she said softly.

"But I'm not playing your game, Fiona." The half smile widened to a full one, grooving his cheeks. "Sorry."

"Then I'll play my game myself." Hardly believing she could behave so outrageously, Fiona pressed his hand against her and moved it, stroking and teasing herself with his fingers. He didn't stop her; he didn't participate . . . but there was a tension in his face that told her he wasn't immune to the sensation of lust and heat heavy in the humid air of the small room.

Spreading her legs wider, she straddled his knees, still holding his hand against her, and then she gently slid one of his fingers partway inside. The sensation seemed all the more intense because of how it occurred. She'd never done anything like this before, even though she'd often joked with her friends that a man was passé when a woman had a massaging showerhead.

But there was no substitute for a man, not one who knew a woman's hot spots as well as this man did.

She pushed his finger in a little farther, and this time she felt him push with her. She gave a sigh, briefly closing her eyes—and then her eyes flew open at the sensation of a hot mouth covering her nipple as he slid a second finger deep inside her.

"Oh, God." Fiona braced one hand on his shoulder for support even as she kept her other hand over his, guiding him to where she wanted to feel him.

He was using his teeth on her nipple; light nips but sharp, and the pleasure ripped through her so intensely she almost cried out.

She was going to come, right here in the bathroom, as he slid his fingers in and out of her with a steady, slick rhythm and his teeth tugged and raked her nipple. The orgasm gathered her tight in its power, squeezing harder and harder until it suddenly spun her loose and she came with a high, sharp gasp of pleasure.

She met Griffith's eyes and didn't look away. Even if she couldn't trust him, the raw desire in his face and his harsh breathing didn't lie.

It wasn't much, but it was something to bind him closer, to make him see her as a woman and not a mission objective, make him feel guilt and remorse and responsibility.

If there was any decent place left inside him, she would find a way to crack through his cold control and find it.

"Do that again," she whispered.

Griffith pulled her down so that she was nearly on

his lap, her legs straddled over his thighs, completely open to his exploring hands.

"You are so goddamn responsive," he muttered harshly, but in a way that told her he liked it.

His fingers teased her, fanning a warm glow, and she arched, pressing her breasts toward him. Again, he lowered his mouth over her breast, his tongue sliding across it as his fingers moved more quickly, and his teeth rolled her nipple between them, making her moan.

"Harder," she said, losing herself in the new sensation. "Please."

He was rougher this time, but it was a good, sweet kind of pain, and she came again, so fast and sharp and hard that she shook from the force of it.

Before she could do anything else, she found herself sitting on the toilet seat as Griffith roughly spread her legs and then bent down. His tongue was hot and wet against her, and she shuddered at each stroke, her hands in his hair. God, he was going to make her come *again*. She'd die; it would feel so good her heart would just stop beating right here, right now. Panting, she arched, feeling his tongue inside her, a strange and wonderful kind of invasion.

With a sudden clarity, she realized that his guns were within her reach. All she had to do was move her hand a little and grab one; he might not even realize until it was too late.

Instead she took his head in her hands, feeling the silky slide of his hair as she held him tight while another orgasm took her, so gentle and sweet that she dropped her head back with a little sigh.

Griffith moved back, and she sat straight. "Oh, no." She eyed his jeans, and the telling swell of his erection. "Not so fast."

She quickly unzipped his pants, then hooked her finger over his loosened belt buckle and pulled him close. Within seconds, she had the belt unbuckled and had slipped her hand down the front of his boxers.

The smooth, hard heat of him filled her palm, and she wanted it filling her elsewhere.

"Dammit, stop this. It won't make any difference."

He always lied. He'd told her as much, so Fiona ignored him, cupping his warm, thick weight. She licked him once, and he went still, his head dropping back, his nostrils flaring as he sucked in a long, deep breath.

"What do you want to do with me?" she whispered.

"Something I'm not doing in the goddamn bathroom." Griffith grabbed her hand out of his pants and then pulled her back to the bedroom area. She was aching for him, needing to get that hot, hard length inside her, and she sank back on the daybed. He leaned over her, grabbing both her wrists and pulling her arms up over head as he kissed her breasts, lightly flicking his tongue over her nipples until she was squirming and arching—

And then she felt the cold touch of metal on her wrist and an ominous click.

Fiona's eyes flew open to see Griffith looming above her, his gaze grim. She twisted her head around enough to see that yes, indeed, she was again handcuffed to the daybed.

Only this time, she was naked.

Griffith stood, putting his clothing back into place, his expression impossible to read. "You're more dangerous than you look."

"I thought you'd seen it all," Fiona said, faintly breathless. "And nothing I could do would matter."

The grim expression turned to a genuine frown. "I can't afford distractions, so knock it off."

That didn't sound "uninvolved" in the least.

Fiona raised a leg and watched a muscle in his jaw tense.

"The least you could do is finish what you started. Frustration is no fun," she said.

Griffith turned on her with a look of amazement. "Finish what *I* started? That's not how I remember what you were up to a few minutes ago."

"It's still a rotten thing to do."

"We've been down this road already. I'm a shitty

person. Deal with it." Despite his flat tone, his gaze kept straying toward her bottom.

"And I'm in a really bad mood, and don't feel like it. *Deal* with it."

"Jesus." The expression of surprise on his face might've been comical if she wasn't in such a lousy mood. "I don't believe this."

Then, he gave her a narrow-eyed grimace that looked a lot like anger.

"You want sex?" He slipped his shoulder holsters off and dropped them to the floor with a loud clunk. "Then you get sex."

As he unbuckled his belt again, Fiona's eyes widened. She wasn't sure why he'd changed his mind, but the look on his face alarmed her—and excited her.

"And then maybe you'll stop taking jabs and pokes at me every goddamn chance you get."

He dropped his pants, then moved over her, forcing her back. She tried not to let him intimidate her, but it was hard to stay calm with his lean, powerful body looming above her.

And she had nowhere else to move, shackled to the daybed like this. When he slipped on a condom, she couldn't mistake his intentions.

Moving too quickly for her to anticipate, Griffith trapped her free hand against the wall, then nudged her legs apart with his knee and entered her.

No teasing, no preliminaries, just that single thrust straight to the core of her. She gasped at the suddenness of it, and the immediate soothing of her restless need.

Without a word, he moved his hips slowly at first, then increased the rhythm and pressure. His breathing harshened, and the rawness of the sex aroused her with a quickness that took her by surprise. Maybe it was because she could see everything he was doing to her, or that he wasn't bothering to hide his own frustration or anger or need.

And then, without warning, everything changed.

Lost in a daze of pleasure, Fiona felt him gentle his actions, touching her in a way he'd not touched her before. His kisses weren't as hard, and there was comfort in how he held her, an intimacy that shouldn't have been there.

She couldn't think clearly; already aroused by the earlier play, her body found release quickly. As she clutched the bedrail with one hand and Griffith with the other, shuddering from the feelings sweeping over her, she suddenly realized what had felt so wrong.

Or so right.

The difference she'd sensed was emotion, too close to the surface for him to hide.

It had felt more like making love than having sex.

Griffith reached his climax a moment later, and

when he looked down at her, Fiona found herself staring into furious, icy-blue eyes.

Maybe she'd imagined that gentleness after all.

"Happy now?" he demanded, the sound of his voice rough against her ear.

Subdued, she whispered, "Yes."

Nineteen

❖

WHEN SHE COULD BREATHE NORMALLY AGAIN, FIONA
said, "I can't help wondering if my life is really in
danger, or if you're trying to scare me into doing
whatever you want. We're talking about a fake manuscript here. Is it really worth killing over?"

She'd hardly forgotten the morning's events, but
still . . .

"People are already dead because of it." Griffith's
frowned deepened as he stood and pulled his jeans
back on. "And while it's possible your ex was the one
who contacted you, we can't rule out the possibility
that he was working with someone else. That person
may have been the one who actually called you."

"No. It was Richard."

"How can you be so sure?"

"He called me by . . . an old pet name."

"So? He could've told someone about it."

"It was a rather unusual pet name, and one he used only when we were intimate or alone. I don't think he would've shared that with anyone else."

Griffith didn't looked convinced. "Did you recognize his voice?"

"The voice was muffled, as if he didn't want to be heard clearly, but there was something familiar to it. At least, I think so now." She heard the uncertainty creeping into her voice. A few minutes ago she'd been positive her husband was alive. Now, with only a few words in that flat, logical tone, Griffith had stirred all kinds of doubts.

He'd also neatly redirected the conversation.

Eyes narrowing, she asked, "Why is it so important to you that I'm safe?"

He arched a brow. "You mean besides the obvious, which is that I prefer innocent bystanders alive rather than dead?"

"I notice that you're going out of your way to avoid answering me directly."

For a long moment he stared at her, and then his mouth curved in a slow smile. "It's that obvious, huh? I must be losing my touch. Either that or you're more of a distraction than I'd thought."

"That almost sounds like a compliment."

Instead of responding, he turned and headed back to the window.

Fiona wasn't sure, but she suspected she'd won that round. Maybe she should keep the questions coming—one more might break through to him.

Best to start slow, though, or she'd piss him off and he'd clam up. "What are you looking for outside?"

"Any sign that we've been followed."

"If someone had followed us, wouldn't we know by now?"

"The people after the manuscript are professionals. They won't make another mistake like they did back at your shop."

Mistake? As she remembered it, the man—Bressler—had very nearly succeeded in getting his hands on both her and Griffith.

"How did that man get in?"

"It wouldn't have been difficult. Your locks and alarms are adequate against the average burglar, but a professional thief—or one of my guys—wouldn't find it any challenge to break in."

He was answering her questions, but only superficially. He was very good at avoiding revealing any real information, especially about these shadowy people he claimed to work for.

A secret organization that prowled the ugly underbelly of the world, looking for stolen art and looted antiquities. Who would ever believe such a thing? She could imagine the reaction of the police if she tried explaining she'd been held captive, and sort of rescued, by a mercenary who worked for something that should exist only in a movie script. Even to her it sounded ludicrous.

And then she imagined trying to explain to a police detective why she'd had sex—repeatedly—with a man she'd known for only a few hours, and she shuddered.

"Tell me the name of this top-secret organization of yours. It must be something catchy or clever. Isn't that the way it works?"

"It has a name, and, no, you don't get to hear it."

"All right." Fiona hadn't expected him to tell her; she just wanted to keep rubbing that burr against his sore spot. "So tell me again why we're just sitting here." She looked down at herself. "Vulnerable *and* embarrassingly naked."

He ran a hand through his hair, brows lowering. "Because I have a bad feeling about what's happened. They moved too quickly, too easily. And this man I'm after—"

"Von Lahr."

Silence. Then, "This man has a personal vendetta against us as well. It wouldn't be above him to kill you just for the fun of it and to make us look bad."

A cold chill settled over Fiona as she remembered the rest of the story she'd heard from Cassie—how von Lahr's plane would've run down his own accomplice had Alex not acted selflessly to save the stupid twit.

"If he's such a hotshot master criminal, how come my friends nearly caught him while he was hanging around some dot on the map in Vermont? Doesn't sound so clever to me."

Griffith smiled. "A situation that had us all in amazement, believe me. What I wouldn't have given to have traded places with that paleontologist. I would've taken von Lahr out."

"Alex decided to save a life instead."

"Good for him. But I'd have taken out von Lahr before anybody had been put in danger to begin with. Your friends did well, but they just got lucky. It could've ended up a lot worse for them."

For all she knew, he was telling her one long lie. He seemed honest right now, but he'd seemed so honest and trustworthy when they'd met yesterday, too.

"You didn't kill that man at the bookstore. Why not?"

"I'm a mercenary, not an assassin. I don't kill unless I have no other choice, and part of my job includes not ending up in the position of having to make that choice." He hesitated—hardly enough to notice, had she not been in such forced proximity for so long. "Or at least I try not to. Usually I get it right, but sometimes I miscalculate."

Maybe it was only her imagination—or wishful thinking that her frat-boy mercenary had a decent part to appeal to—but she sensed something regretful or pained in the tone of his voice, something that told her he'd made a very bad mistake once.

Fiona itched to press him on it but resisted the urge, and she wasn't even sure why.

She must've eventually dozed off, because it was completely dark when she felt the bed dip, and she rolled against something warm and sturdy as her eyes flew open.

"Don't get excited," Griffith said. "I need a little sleep. We'll be moving out soon and I have to be alert. I'm going to sleep for about twenty minutes. Don't disturb me—and don't think you can try to grab any weapons. They're within my reach but not yours, and I'm a really light sleeper."

"You do realize that threatening me again undercuts all your efforts to persuade me you're really one of the good guys," she said mockingly.

"I *am* one of the good guys." He leaned back against the wall. "I'm just not one of the *nice* ones. Where exactly is this rule that the good guys always have to be nice?"

Stung by *his* mocking tone, she retorted, "I believe it's a general expectation."

"Which is why people shouldn't have expectations. That way they'll never be disappointed."

Fiona frowned as his eyes slowly closed. She didn't know why she should care, but his words bothered her. His fatalism filled her with a sense of dread that had to do more with him than with her. She couldn't shake the feeling. "Do you get disappointed very often?"

He didn't open his eyes. "All things considered, I don't exactly catch humanity at its finest."

"So why do you do it?"

"Because it needs doing and somebody is willing to pay me. It's no more complicated than that." He shifted closer to the wall. "Don't look for any deep meanings or self-sacrificing nobility. You won't find it in me."

She watched him a little longer. "So I suppose it would be pointless to ask for my clothes? I shouldn't look for any profound meaning or nobility in your keeping me naked?"

Although he still didn't open his eyes, his lips curled in a smile. And it struck her, again, that he had a beautiful mouth: firm, and with just enough roundness in the lower lip to invite a nibble or a kiss. "Hell, no."

"I would really like my clothes."

"You're less likely to cause me trouble while you're naked."

Fiona scowled. "I believe I feel insulted."

"Don't. It's the highest compliment you'll ever get out of me. I usually control myself better than this."

What? But . . . she was *naked*.

"That doesn't make sense. Wouldn't it be easier to control yourself if I were wearing clothes?"

"I guess."

"Now I'm even more confused. Why *am* I naked? Really?"

Griffith opened his eyes. "Jesus Christ, Fiona. Why do you think?"

Understanding dawned—and suddenly she was even more grateful for the shielding blanket. "You miserable, low-life, manipulative *bastard!*"

"I told you I wasn't nice, and now you're shocked?"

"The free peep show is over. I want my clothes. *Now.*"

He regarded her for a long moment, so long that she feared he would refuse. Then he reached down and tossed her bundle of clothing onto her lap.

"I can't get dressed while I'm cuffed to the bed."

"Give me one good reason why I should trust you enough to cut you loose, Fiona."

"Because it's the right thing to do!"

"Your Irish comes out when you're angry. Did you know that?"

She narrowed her eyes, not in the least amused. He'd taken advantage of her in so many ways, and enough was enough. "Take. Off. The handcuff."

"You promise not to do anything stupid? Like try to claw out my eyes, run for the door, or grab a gun?"

"I'm not an idiot. You'd knock me halfway across

the room before I could get near you or the door."

His lids dropped, mouth thinning again. He was still watching her, but she couldn't read his expression. Not that it mattered; the eyes might be the mirrors of the soul, but not for this man. "All right, then. Make sure you do as you say. I don't want to have to hurt you."

Leashed power and danger emanated from him, and her instincts for self-preservation, cutting through the confusion of her brain, kept her still and silent. She'd seen him in action, observed how he'd morphed into a totally different man.

Yet despite that, a strong, pulsing need to run seized her, and it was all she could do to ignore it. He was a rotten sonofabitch, but she was still better off with him than by herself. She had no illusions about her own ability to keep safe. She'd already been stupid enough to trust this man just because he was nice to look at and charming. What else would she bungle if she tried to escape alone?

Fiona dressed in silence, angry at her helplessness, furious with Griffith just for being what he was, and furious with her husband—who might not be dead after all—for being so weak and foolish as to have gotten himself into such a mess to begin with.

When she was dressed, she sat back down. "So now what? Are you going to lock me up again?"

"I'm still deciding," he said tersely. "I really wanted

to catch a few minutes of sleep, and it'd be easier to do that with you safely cuffed to the bed."

Fiona could see the weary lines around his mouth, the shadows beneath his eyes, and she pushed back that stubborn pang of guilt. He'd just chained her naked to a bed for no reason other than to look at her, so why was she feeling sorry for him at all?

Because, a little voice whispered, *he can't protect you if he's half dead with exhaustion, you idiot.*

"You can sleep if you want," she said stiffly. "I won't try anything. I was telling the truth when I said I believe that I'm safer with you than without you. Which isn't a vote of confidence, in case you're wondering, and it doesn't mean I trust you."

"Forget it. I'll be all right."

She frowned. "You won't do either of us any good if you're too tired to think straight or your reflexes are slowed down by exhaustion."

"I've gotten by on less sleep than this. We won't be here for much longer, anyway. I have to get you out of L.A. My gut's telling me this place isn't as secure as it should be."

"Then that's all the more reason not to lock me up again. It would be quite embarrassing if you went and got yourself killed, leaving me trussed here like a virgin sacrifice to the evil villain."

Griffith arched a brow. "I wasn't planning on getting killed."

"Most people don't—but most people don't play against the kinds of odds you're dealing with right now. If you lock me up again and I need to run, I can't. So much for all your big talk of protecting me."

A smile curved his mouth. "You've got me there. That *would* be embarrassing."

"Even more so for me. I really don't want my obituary to read 'Killed in a spectacularly messy and painful way while chained to a daybed.' I was hoping for something more along the lines of 'died peacefully in her own bed of old age.' "

"You shouldn't talk like that." He sounded angry.

"It bothers you? Why?" When he didn't answer, she added, "I'd think someone like you would hold life rather cheaply, for all your claims otherwise. Why should you care if I live or die?"

"Because."

"Isn't that a mature and helpful response?" Her instincts prickled, and she narrowed her eyes. "Although easier than telling me the truth."

Griffith stood up and walked away, pocketing the cuffs. "You win this time. But if you try anything stupid, I'll lock you up again."

Certain she had his number now, Fiona asked quietly, "Who was she? How did she die?"

He stopped in his tracks, then wheeled around. Several seconds passed as he stared at her, blank-faced. "What?"

"Was it your fault?"

"I have no idea what you're talking about."

"Oh, that's not true." She was right; she could tell by the way his gaze shifted away from hers. It was only for a moment, but it was all she needed to know that her little shot in the dark had found its mark. "There was someone in your past, maybe more than one. People who trusted you to protect them, and you failed."

"Even if it were true, it wouldn't matter. It has nothing to do with you."

"Not only are you lying to me but you're lying to yourself. It does matter. And it has everything to do with me."

"And why do you think I'd explain myself to you?"

"You don't have to; I can figure it out for myself." She leaned against the wall behind the daybed. "When I was in college, I met my two best friends. Everybody always remarked on how different we were, and I think that meant they didn't expect our friendship to last beyond college. It has; we've stuck with each other through boyfriends from hell, weddings, divorce, death, birth . . . all those big moments in life."

He stood still, plainly unsure where she was headed. "I was never as cool and clever and elegant as the one. I was never as outgoing or brassy or stubborn as the other. I was the detail girl, the one who watched and put things together. I'm rather good at reading people, and while it's a skill that's failed me from time to time, it's mostly helped me along in life. Whether you realize it or not, you're leaving lots of bits for me to read, between the lines or otherwise."

It was quite the bluff. She wasn't lying exactly, but she hoped he couldn't tell.

"You're not totally right, but not all that wrong, either," Griffith said after a moment. As she watched, he turned himself back into a walking arsenal, then sat in the chair by the window, looking away from her. "I made a promise, and it's a promise I intend to keep."

Finally, after what must have been at least five minutes' worth of heavy silence, broken only by the sound of traffic and muted shouting from outside, he added, "Not that they heard the promise, since they were dead. You were right about that part."

"I wouldn't have minded being wrong."

"I wouldn't have minded, either." He shifted the blinds and frowned.

"Is something wrong?"

"Not that I can tell . . . But something doesn't feel right to me. It's that gut feeling again, and I can't shake it."

She probably should've asked him to explain the gut feeling, but what came out was "Who were they?"

Griffith sighed. "Three members of my team, one of them a rookie. Like Noonie. The fourth was von Lahr's lover. Her name was Annamari, and she was no wide-eyed innocent who happened to get caught in the cross fire, like you. Annamari was a player; she fenced very expensive antiquities looted from Iraq during the first Gulf War."

"But you still wanted to protect her."

"She was involved with someone who sold her out without a moment's hesitation, then killed her just to mock me and the people I work for."

"This would be von Lahr, I take it."

"Yes . . . and part of me wishes your friends had caught the oily bastard, because it would serve his arrogant ass right to get nailed by a couple of upstanding citizen types. But the other part of me, wants to be the one who finally catches him. That's the promise I made: that I'd make him pay for what he did."

"I'm sorry."

The little smugness she'd felt on sniffing out his weakness had faded at the genuine pain in his voice.

Or what she could only hope was genuine; she didn't want to believe he was lying to her about something like this.

"For the past five years, I've chased every wisp and rumor about von Lahr, and I've never managed to get as close to him as I am right now."

"That's . . . good, right?"

He didn't meet her eyes, and his silence brought her upright on a fresh rush of cold fear and understanding.

"Except . . . that you've used me for bait just as you used *her*. That's how it happened, isn't it? She was bait, and she died for it—and now you're hoping that keeping me safe will make up for her death."

Twenty

❖

GRIFFITH WANTED TO BE ANYWHERE BUT IN THIS little room, facing this woman who could see through him better than people he'd known for years.

Fiona Kennedy said things that made him look at himself in a way he didn't like and couldn't ignore. "Technically, I was bait as well."

She stood very still, silhouetted against the pale wall, half in the shadows and half out, like a little moral lesson come to life.

Black and white. Dark and light.

What might have been and what couldn't be.

"Why don't you tell me what happened?"

Hell, why not? He hadn't really spoken about it over the past five years, and everybody he knew always tried to avoid it. Maybe the ghosts would fade if he faced it once and for all.

"There's not much to tell. We were tracking a couple Iraqi opportunists who'd looted a mother lode of artifacts from tombs and unprotected sites during the war. We hadn't yet cleaned up from the first invasion when this latest one happened, and now the situation's really bad. It's even worse than what the Nazis did to the museums in Europe during World War Two and what the Russians did when they got into Berlin . . ."

God, he was talking way more than he should. He glanced at her but saw only genuine interest. Everything about her was honest and real. He looked back toward the window. "We had an undercover guy in Hamburg who used von Lahr's lover to set up a deal between the Iraqis and von Lahr and an American buyer, which was me. We were going to sweep in, grab von Lahr, the Iraqis, and the artifacts, and wrap up a long chase. It would've been a hell of a score for the good guys."

"But?"

"But . . . there's always a but." Try as he might, he couldn't forget those moments when the high of the victory had sunk into a nightmare. "Von Lahr didn't show and sent his lover to take the fall for him, although she didn't know that. At least not at first. I was in charge of the mission and had everything set up according to plan. It should've gone off without any major problems. Since von Lahr was dangerous, I took extra precautions. I even had guys on guard in several nearby buildings. We took the Iraqis and von Lahr's girlfriend into custody and retrieved the Sumerian artifacts, just as planned. But von Lahr's girlfriend—"

"She has a name, remember? I'm certain she wouldn't have wanted to be remembered only as 'von Lahr's girlfriend.' "

Even saying her name was difficult. "As it turned out, Annamari knew more about him than we'd expected. That was one of the reasons he killed her. To keep her silent."

"One of the reasons?"

"The other reason was to get to my outfit. To get to me." Which, he feared, might be the case now as well.

She was quiet for such a long time that he wondered if she'd made the connection, too.

Yet he'd been tracking von Lahr for years, and he knew how the man's mind worked. His suspicions didn't *feel* right for von Lahr; this kind of setup just wasn't the bastard's style.

Unless he'd changed his style.

"Grif, has it ever occurred to you that you might be the real person in danger here, and not me?"

Bing! Bing! Bing! And the prize goes to the little lady . . .

"Yeah . . . about three minutes ago."

Her eyes widened.

Pushing himself to his feet, Griffith paced the small distance between them. "But something about it is off."

"I don't understand."

"For starters, there's no audience. Von Lahr is vain, megalomaniac, calculating . . . but above it all, he has a flair for the theatrical. Sometimes it's only small touches, and other times . . ."

He trailed off, on a flash of memory so vivid that it hurt even to consider speaking of it. "And other times, he goes for the grand gesture. To me, this feels . . . too small for von Lahr."

"Maybe he got smart and changed tactics."

"Already occurred to me. It's possible. The mistake he made last August—" He cut himself off and forced himself to stop pacing. "I can't recall him ever being that careless. Yes, he has been known to take risks, to push things to the limit in order to make his presence known, but that was a huge mistake. It wasn't like him."

"Maybe he's overextending himself. Become over-confident."

"Mmm." He was only half-listening, thoughts and possibilities coming to him almost more quickly than he could process. "If it's me he's after and not you, then it's likely I'm just the bait to land a larger fish."

Fiona's puzzled voice broke across his thoughts: "Who's the larger fish?"

"The guy I directly answer to, who's probably the only one who knows the identity of the person, or persons, who really run this show."

"Then you can let me go."

"No." Griffith let out his breath in a long sigh, shaking his head. "Because I can't be one hundred percent certain it's *not* you, and those aren't odds I'm willing to bet against. Or that he'd kill you anyway just for the hell of it."

"Then what are you going to do? Look, it's not as if I don't appreciate your help, and I'm well aware that I'd likely be ineffectual if I had to protect myself in a gunfight. But I have a business to run, other responsibilities, and you can't just take me away like this and—"

"You want to go to the police?"

"Yes!"

"And tell them what?"

He couldn't help but smile at the consternation that washed over her face at his reminder. She had the most expressive face; and that simple honesty kept a hold over him.

Fiona sighed. "They'd never believe me. Even for Los Angeles, it would be too strange."

Griffith leaned back, briefly closing his eyes. "If von Lahr or anybody else wanted you, there were a dozen times they could've grabbed you. The real trouble didn't come until I showed up, did it?"

Fiona nodded. "The phone calls started before you arrived, but not by much."

"If I'd known that . . . Ah, hell, it probably wouldn't have made a difference. Goddammit. I've been such a dumb-ass about this. I kept trying to keep it impersonal, but—"

Again, he cut himself short. He'd already opened up to her far more than was sensible.

Of course she picked up on it. "But what?"

"You are a very dangerous woman, Fiona. I'm not sure what it is about you, but you make it really easy for me to talk. That's not good for me. Nor is it good for you."

She sat down again, a little limply. "So you really *did* want to protect me. That's why you were there all along."

"Yeah. That was the plan. And to grab whoever came sniffing around while you read the manuscript. If we got lucky, your ex-husband's secret message really did exist, you'd find it, and then we'd have a few people for the cops to arrest." He hesitated, then added quietly, "There was also that promise I'd made, but it's beginning to look like I can't even do that."

He ran a hand over his face, trying to chase away the weariness pressing down on him. "But it doesn't matter to any of them now, and I'm not the kind of guy people believe in anyway."

"Why do you say that?"

"After everything that's happened, you have to ask?" He couldn't help smiling. "I have spent years lying and using people. Sure, it's for something worthwhile, but I'm not deluding myself about what I am. I chase around the world after priceless treasures that aren't mine and never will be, and at the end of the day all I have to show for it is a lot of money in a bank, but no time to spend it and nothing in my life that's . . . real enough to spend it on."

Fiona walked toward him, and he shifted uneasily, not wanting her near the window, even in this darkened room. "Don't come any closer. I don't want you to be seen."

She stopped. "A little while ago, you said there should be more to life."

And she seemed to have an uncanny knack for remembering every stupid word that came out of his mouth. "It wasn't important."

"But there *is* more to life, Grif. You're right about that. I think you're wrong about people not believing in you. That's really not your problem."

For some reason, her words caused his temper to flare. With an effort, he kept it in check. "Is that so? I don't need you to—"

"I believe in you."

Taken completely by surprise, he turned to stare at her. "Are you fucking crazy? After everything I said, all the warnings—"

"I know. I heard you, and I understand. I'm not blind or stupid, Griffith—though I've been pathologically naïve these last two days. I don't exactly trust you, but I do believe in you. Enough to believe that you'll keep me safe."

"That could be a mistake."

"True, but as bizarre as all this is, enough pieces fit and make sense for me to believe a lot of what you've said. So I believe in you, Grif. Now all you have to do is believe in yourself. If you want something more out of life, make it happen."

Twenty-one

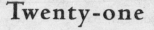

FIONA WASN'T SURE WHO WAS MORE SURPRISED, HERSELF or Griffith. A few hours ago she'd hated this man, and now she was going all Mary Poppins and telling him to believe in himself.

Yet she'd meant every word she'd said.

"You shouldn't put any faith in me at all," he said after a moment. "It's not smart."

In every word, in his body language and tone of voice, she heard a man who didn't want anybody to believe in him because he was afraid to let them down. She wasn't sure what standards his way of life had set for Griffith Laughton, but they must've been brutally steep.

"Everybody makes mistakes."

"My mistake cost a woman her life, along with three of my men—and they trusted me not to make stupid mistakes with their lives. We're not talking about losing a pair of socks here! If I had been more careful, if I hadn't been so goddamn overconfident—"

"They might still have died even if you'd done everything right. Is it so hard to believe that you were simply outmaneuvered, despite your best intentions?"

"But it's my job *not* to be outmaneuvered! Don't you see that?"

She did, sort of. "So now you're in a similar situation. What are you going to do about it? I don't know how much help I can be, but if you need help, ask. I'm quite motivated to save your hide if it means saving my own. And I truly believe you will keep me safe, Griffith."

But I really need you to believe it, too.

For a long moment he didn't answer, then he turned away. "After all those years hunting von Lahr, this is the first time I've ever had a real chance to keep that promise I made." He paused. "And yet, I've been wondering lately if there comes a point when something like that, something that started out for all the right intentions, could drag me down so far that I could never find my way back again. The truth is, if I fail, they won't care. Nobody will care. Except *me.*"

Silence fell over the room, tense and sharp.

"For the past five years, I've just been living my

life for people who are dead. How fucked up is that?"

And for people who could never give him the forgiveness he needed. He didn't have to spell it out for her.

"Everything I do, everything I've ever done, has been for somebody else. Never for me . . . And I'm tired of it. So goddamn tired."

He leaned against the wall, and it was all Fiona could do to keep from going to him and holding him.

"So what do we do now?" she asked softly.

"This is not a 'we' situation. This is me keeping you safe." He pushed away from the wall, and she watched as he stood taller, straightened the line of his shoulders. Put the barriers back up.

He took out his cell phone and dialed. "It's Laughton. I'm taking her to the field. Meet us there—and be damn careful, because I have reason to believe our security has been compromised."

He fell silent as the person on the other end spoke, then shook his head. "No, no. I don't have time to go into details, but there's a good chance I'm the one being targeted here. You can guess why." He paused again, listening, then said tersely, "That's good enough. We're leaving now."

Then he hung up and said, "Let's go."

Fiona took a long, steadying breath. Her emotions these past few hours had been all over the map. After everything that had happened, she should have been exhausted, but to her surprise she was anything but tired. "All right."

"Do exactly what I tell you and you'll be okay."

From beneath the daybed, he pulled a dark bundle that turned out to be trench coats and Kevlar vests. Separating out one for her, he said, "Here, put this on. I'll help you."

The fear came back with a vengeance, and Fiona stood very still as Griffith secured her vest. It felt strange, too tight, too blocky. But considering the alternative, she wasn't going to complain. As she pulled on the large dark coat, he quickly put on his own vest under his jacket, plainly having done so many times before. Then, his arm around her, he led her to the door, grabbing the briefcase along the way.

They didn't exit until he'd determined it was safe.

Because of the weather and the late hour they didn't encounter as many people on the streets, and those they did meet were all in too much of a hurry to get out of the rain to pay any attention to them.

As they approached the junky car she picked up her pace, only to be pulled back by Griffith. "Slow down. I have to check it out first."

Fiona stared at him as he hunkered down. "For what?"

"Do you really want to know?"

She considered it. "I think I can guess."

"I figured as much; you're a smart woman." He ran

his hand beneath the carriage and used a small flashlight to look for anything that shouldn't be there.

"We're drawing attention."

"Can't be helped. This won't take long."

The next thing she knew, sharp pops sounded as gunshots hit the pavement, showering them with stinging shards of asphalt. Griffith shoved her down roughly, and she hit the ground with a painful thud as he covered her body with his.

"Then again," he muttered, "it may take a few minutes longer than I'd anticipated."

He eased away, drawing both guns, and met her gaze. A grim smile curved his mouth. "I think this confirms the security problem."

"No kidding," she retorted. "Where did that come from?"

"I'm about to find out."

She didn't understand what he meant until he lunged up from behind the car's cover, just long enough to draw fire.

"Grif, no!"

He'd already fired in the direction the other shots had come from. "Dammit! The shooter's inside one of the apartments."

Then, twisting fast, he raised his hand and fired. Fiona looked up in time to see a man, dressed in black, drop on him from a fire escape. She'd never seen him, hadn't a clue there'd even been someone above them until that blurring shadow swooped down like a giant bird.

Griffith didn't have time to fire again, and the two men crashed back onto the pavement.

In the distance Fiona could hear people shouting in panic, in anger, but her entire focus, as she crouched back against the car with the briefcase, was on Griffith struggling with the assailant who'd dropped on him.

She didn't dare move, or do anything that might distract Griffith. The two men struggled in silence, except for noises of effort, harsh breathing, the scrapes of bodies against the pavement.

The soft, muffled sound of flesh and bone meeting.

She'd never seen a real fight, with people doing everything in their power to hurt each other. Lips drawn back in a grimace of effort, veins standing out on his forehead, corded sinews straining at his neck, Griffith made a low grunt and managed to get the upper hand long enough to jab his elbow into his assailant's face, stunning him.

Then, with brutal efficiency, he raised the man's head by the hair and slammed it back onto the pavement. It made a sound that she never wanted to hear again, and she squeezed her eyes shut, swallowing down a rise of nausea.

The shouting hadn't let up, and it would be only minutes, or even seconds, before police sirens started wailing.

His voice sounded in her ear, low and urgent: "You okay?"

Fiona opened her eyes, nodding. "I—"

"Get inside the car." Reaching above him, he pulled the back door open. "Stay low, don't make yourself a target. Don't move until I tell you to."

She scrambled into the back of the car and tossed the briefcase on the seat. She huddled in a tight ball, feeling the car rock as Griffith jumped into the driver's seat.

He had the car moving down the street before he'd even shut the door.

"Hang on!" he yelled, and a scant second later he turned sharply. Horns blared irately, cars squealed to sudden stops. The briefcase flew across the seat to hit the side of the car with a loud thump, and Fiona banged her head into the back of the seat.

It hurt, but she managed to hold back a yelp of pain.

As the car gained speed, the vibrations of its powerful engine reverberated in her body, and every bump and dip on the road jolted her.

After what seemed like forever, the car slowed. "You can move now," Griffith told her. "No one is following us."

Fiona pushed up to the seat, rubbing the back of her head, and then maneuvered into the front passenger seat and quickly buckled up. To keep her shaking hands under control, she clasped them in her lap as he turned down another street.

"You're sure no one is following us?" She wanted to turn and look but resisted the urge.

"Yes." Then he added, "At least not yet."

"That's good, right?"

"Ordinarily, yes. Now, I'm not so sure. If someone knew where to find us before, they're going to know our destination point."

"And where is our destination point?"

"An old airfield outside the city limits."

That would explain the "field" he'd referred to on the phone. "What else are you expecting to go wrong?"

"Anything and everything." He let out a long breath, his expression frustrated.

He hadn't escaped that tussle unharmed. He had a nasty scrape on the left side of his face, a cut on his jaw was still oozing blood, and the knuckles of his right hand were scraped raw.

"While we're in the car, we're protected," he added. "It looks like a piece of shit but the windows are bullet-resistant, the body is armored, and the engine is capable of more speed than you'd expect."

"I'd already figured as much."

He glanced at her and smiled faintly. "It's also equipped with a security system to discourage your average carjackers—not that they'd generally bother with this pile of junk—and anybody who might want to plant a bomb or two."

Fiona had already figured that was what he'd been looking for right before they'd been attacked, but hearing him actually say it made her heart pound. She tried her best to be brave about it and asked lightly, "It doesn't come equipped with rear cannons, lasers, jet engines, or any other James Bond gadgetry?"

"Nope." He glanced at her, brow raised, then patted his jacket and the guns stashed inside. "From now on, it's my driving and my shooting, though I hope I won't have to put either skill to the test. But if I tell you to duck and hold on, you do it with no questions. I'll be busy enough without having to try to keep an extra eye on you, understand?"

"I'm not an idiot, Grif. Deferring to your judgment won't be an issue."

"Sensible, as always."

"My only true talent."

He smiled lazily, his gaze intimate and warm. "I wouldn't say that."

She looked away. "Don't. I believe you'll keep me safe, but that doesn't mean I've forgiven you for what you did. Or for lying to me."

"As you shouldn't," he said after a moment.

Silence settled between them, and for miles neither of them broke it.

Once they were on the freeway and heading out of the city, Fiona couldn't keep quiet any longer. "So why were you so honest with me earlier? You didn't have to tell me anything."

She wasn't referring only to the danger level, and by the sharp glance he sent her way, she could tell he knew it.

"I don't know. Tired, maybe."

She could still hear the weariness in his voice. Beneath his smooth, controlled surface, he was a man, after all, not an emotionless machine. He couldn't hide everything every second of the day as she watched his every move. And though he claimed to be on the side of good, that side came with a heavy gloss of moral ambiguity.

"How is it possible for someone to have broken your security if it's a secret organization that doesn't exist?"

"The big wheelers and dealers in the black market know about us. Some know more than others. We work under the cover of a legitimate business that allows us to move around the world quickly and at a moment's notice. The smarter elements of the underworld have a pretty good idea what that cover company is and who heads it up."

"And the smarter elements include von Lahr?"

"Yup."

"Don't you ever worry that they'll come after you?

Like . . . you know, when you're off duty?" Did that sound as ridiculous to him as it sounded to her? "Or whatever you people call it."

"It's not much of a worry. I don't have a regular address."

She thought that over, then asked, "Is your name really Griffith Laughton?"

He glanced at her, and she couldn't read his expression.

"Never mind," Fiona said after a moment, looking away. "It's not as if it matters."

"It's my real name."

"Should you even be telling me that?"

"It seems the least I can do."

Fiona wasn't sure what to make of that, either. "How long until we get there?"

"Hard to say. Depends on the traffic, and traffic in L.A. is never good. I fuckin' hate this city."

"So why did you come here, if you hate it so much?"

"We don't have any people in L.A. And as I explained before, since I was on hand, reasonably recovered, and willing, I said yes when I was asked to take the assignment."

"But why don't you have people in L.A.? It's one of the world's major art hot spots."

"Because the LAPD has a very competent art squad. We need to be here only in cases like this, where it's all about shadows."

No matter what she asked, he had an answer. She hadn't been given any facts that would compromise his cover or the people he worked for, but that he'd offered as much as he had showed a huge measure of trust.

Or so she wanted to believe. But why did she keep caring about what happened to him, about what he thought of her, what she thought of him? Once she was safely away from Griffith Laughton, she'd never see him again.

"What will you do after I leave?" Fiona asked. "The truth, Griffith. I'd really like to know."

"I go back to what I'm paid to do."

"Oh." She looked out the window, at the gray rain, the gray sky, the dark, wet road. The rain smeared the lights in front of them, and all the world seemed out of focus, indistinct. Surreal. "And is that what you want?"

He was silent for a moment, then said, "There are times I don't like the work much. Every now and then, I wonder what it would be like to have the kind of life where I know that . . . no matter when I get home, the lights will always be on, waiting for me."

He quickly added, "But there's no other way of life for me; it's too late. I had my chances and my choices, and this is where they brought me. I don't regret what I've done. Even when I find myself wanting more, I know that what I have will be enough."

"That sounds like you're just settling."

He frowned but didn't look at her; his attention was focused on the traffic. "The job prospects for guys like me are on the thin side. It's not like I can put down 'undercover work, lying, and shooting bad guys' on a résumé at the local accounting firm. My outfit pays well, even if—"

He cut himself off and glanced at her. "Anybody ever tell you that you ask too many questions?"

"You said you'd answer them," she reminded him.

"So I did." He leaned back. "So how about you? I hear Ireland is pretty, though I've never been there. Do you ever think of going back?"

She couldn't miss his hint, since it was delivered with all the subtlety of a brick upside the head.

"Parts of it are beautiful. Nearly paradise, some would say. I don't remember much about it, since we moved away when I was young. Before that we lived in the city, and Belfast, as I remember it, was worse than L.A. So no, I have no desire to go back." Then, with belated concern, she said, "I shouldn't be talking. I'm distracting you."

To her surprise, Griffith laughed. "Fiona, I've slept while RPGs were exploding around me, and played poker while hiding out from Iraqi tribesmen who wanted nothing more than to shoot me and my buddies into unrecognizable pieces. Talking with you

while driving in L.A. traffic doesn't really compare."
He paused. "Though L.A. traffic sucks. I stand a better chance of dying in a car wreck on an L.A. freeway than of getting gunned down by Rainert von Lahr."

"That's not very comforting."

He grimaced. "Sorry. I probably shouldn't make jokes about car crashes with you of all people."

"Nice attempt to distract me . . . getting me all tied up in knots about the husband who may or may not be dead. Can I ask you something? How long have you been watching me?"

"My people, or me in particular?"

"Both."

"We've kept tabs on your whereabouts since your husband's disappearance. I've only been watching you since yesterday."

Strange, hearing that for the past five years she'd been watched by a shadowy organization and never once suspected it. "I can't help wondering why Richard waited until only a few days ago to contact me."

"I don't know. I'm sure he has his reasons."

"It just feels so . . . orchestrated. Staged. Why would they target you? Do you know something important?"

"I'm a senior member of the group. I know a lot of things, and a lot of people."

"Including the name of the person who's in charge of everything?"

"One of them, yes. I'm not sure if anybody knows the real show-runner."

"So what would be the point?" Frustrated, she shifted to face him. "None of this is making much sense."

"Tell me about it," he said with feeling. "But it could be a lot of reasons. Could be as simple as revenge. I've made my share of enemies over the years."

He shifted, and the stiffer lines of his body made her wonder if he was in pain and trying to hide it.

"Maybe somebody thinks they can use me to get to my boss. Or it could be something completely different . . . or nothing at all. You're not exactly in the clear yet as the prize cow in all this."

She gave him a dirty look at the "prize cow" comment. "The man in my shop only wanted the manuscript. He said it didn't matter if I was dead."

"That's because Bressler was working for von Lahr, who's only trying to cover his own ass. Eliminating the manuscript and your ex is all that's required. The only reason he needed you was leverage with your ex. As Bressler said, even then McMahon only needed to think you were alive."

Fiona fell quiet for a moment. It was still so strange, hearing him refer to Richard as McMahon, and with such familiarity. There was a nightmarish feel to it, so that she found herself hoping she'd wake up and this would all have been a bad dream.

"But if von Lahr has managed somehow to break your security, why not skip you and me and go straight to the source? If he knows so much, he shouldn't keep missing his chance at us."

"Running in the dark with the lights off, that's me." He sighed. "I never said I had all the answers."

"What a mess," she muttered. "If I do see Richard again, it'll be hard to resist the temptation to sock him."

Griffith laughed. "Take a number."

"What will happen to me once we're at this airfield?"

"We should be met by my backup. If they haven't arrived by the time we get there, we'll lie low and wait until they do."

"And then?"

"Then they'll transfer you into the care of the police after a few days. By the time they let you go back home, everything will be public, including the existence of the forged manuscript. With any luck we'll have McMahon in custody as well, and that'll remove the need for anyone else to threaten you. Once my people are no longer associated with you, you won't have any value to von Lahr and his like."

"And what if you don't catch Richard?"

"Once he knows that the police are involved, that you're safe, and the manuscript has gone public, your not-quite-ex will disappear again to save his own hide, and you can go back to living your life just as it was. He won't challenge the ruling on his death. He knows you're better off with him dead than alive. That's why he faked his death in the first place." After a moment, Griffith glanced at her and added quietly, "But I'm sorry you had to find out the truth this way. I would've spared you that, if it had been possible."

"There's nothing to apologize for. Well, except for you telling me that once all you superhero types vanish out of my life, I return to being just a boring antiquarian bookseller who's not worth the trouble to anybody."

Griffith smiled. "I'd never call you boring."

"But you know nothing about me, really. For all you know, I'm the most boring person on the planet." She slumped back in her seat. "You only met me yesterday, remember, and nothing about these past couple days has been ordinary."

"Regrets?" he asked, after a moment.

She knew what he was really asking. "I'd be lying if I said it's been all fun."

"None of it was your fault. I want you to understand that."

"I know."

"And nice people almost never get dragged into the middle of shit like this."

Fiona, unsure what point he was trying to make, said nothing.

"The thing is, I've spent so many years in the company of thieves, looters, and bastards who'd sell their own flesh and blood if they thought they could make a profit, I'd almost forgotten what it was like to be with a nice, normal woman." After a moment, he added, "You didn't ask for any of this and deserved better. And that is why I'll do whatever it takes to get you out of this mess safe and sound."

She glanced at him as he pulled off on an exit ramp. "Promise?"

"Promise." His mouth tightened. "And I really *am* sorry. For all of it."

After that, there wasn't much to say, so she let the conversation die as the windshield wipers swished back and forth, blearing the gray emptiness of the road stretching out before her.

Twenty-two

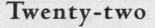

9:10 P.M.

GRIFFITH SIGHED WITH RELIEF WHEN HE FINALLY turned onto the rough road that led to the old airfield. Before the monster that was LAX took control of the airspace over L.A., this had been a small, private airport that catered to Hollywood studio moguls, stars, and starlets.

It had a main runway, a few service paths to the side, a cinder-block building with boarded-up windows and a padlocked door, and four rusted corrugated aluminum hangars. All were secured with old chains that had bled red rust down the metal doors.

Overrun with weeds and grasses, it was drab and dilapidated—but if people looked closely enough, they'd notice the main runway was in remarkably good shape for an abandoned chunk of real estate that should've long since been converted into a housing subdivision or a Wal-Mart.

Griffith checked his mirrors again for any sign of a tail he might've missed over the last twenty minutes or so, but there was no way a car could've followed him out this far without him noticing. Tall grass waved gently in the night breeze, and there were the sheds, but there were no trees or other outbuildings that could conveniently hide a vehicle. It was one of the reasons Avalon owned the old place: it was close enough to L.A. to use in an emergency but both secluded enough and open enough to discourage unwanted visitors.

"I was expecting them to be here by now." He turned off the car and looked up at the thick darkness of the sky.

Following his cue, Fiona tipped her head back against her seat, her expression puzzled as she looked out the window. "Why are you looking up?"

"Helicopter."

She turned to him, eyes wide. "You have a *helicopter?*"

After the armored car, the body armor, everything he'd told her—hell, everything that had happened to her since that morning—it amazed her that she could still be surprised.

"They're faster than a car and less trouble than an airplane." Griffith gestured around them. "We use this to land helicopters or small planes when we need to get out of L.A. fast or when we want to keep a low profile, but we don't actually keep any aircraft here."

"Planes *and* helicopters." Fiona shook her head. "You can't possibly expect me to believe that a helicopter can buzz around a city the size of L.A. and be at all inconspicuous."

"You can if you have help on the inside."

"You always have the right answer." She craned around to look at the cinder-block building. "Are we going inside that?"

"No. We stay in the car, because the second we step outside its protection, we're easy targets. We're not alone, by the way. We're being watched."

Alarmed, she looked around and asked in a loud whisper, "Are you sure?"

Griffith grinned. "Relax. It's friendly. There's a security camera on the main building, which can keep most of the airfield under surveillance." Not all of it, but he didn't tell her that.

Several moments later his cell phone chirped, and he pulled it out of his pocket and flipped it open. "Where the hell are you?"

Diva's voice answered: "We're about fifteen minutes out."

"You're late," he said, trying for Fiona's sake not to sound too annoyed.

"And you're early."

"Traffic was lighter than expected."

"Everything okay?" Diva asked.

"Yeah. Just get here as soon as you can." He kept his voice neutral but trusted Diva to understand the urgency of the situation.

"Affirmative," she said.

After disconnecting, he tossed the phone on the seat between them.

There was something too easy about all this. He wanted to believe that, with a lot of skill and no small amount of luck, he'd gotten Fiona safely away without anyone following. But given how their target had been one step ahead of him from the start, and how somebody always got past his defenses, the lack of obstacles now, when it mattered most, bothered him.

After all that had happened, he couldn't see anyone just shrugging his shoulders and walking away. Not McMahon, and especially not Rainert von Lahr.

He didn't want to frighten Fiona more than he already had, but trouble was coming; he could taste it.

"This is creepy," she whispered, barely loud enough for him to hear. "And I'm not sure if it's because this old place looks like something out of a Stephen King movie, or because people with guns might be lurking just out of sight, or because there's a camera somewhere watching us. Or all of it." She sighed. "I think it's 'all of it.' "

He kept it simple. "They'll be here in about ten minutes."

"That soon?" A look of relief crossed her face. "Then it's almost over."

"Nothing's over until we're in that helicopter and in the air," he said. "The last time I thought I was in the clear in a situation like this, I lost three of my people. I'm not letting my guard down for a second."

"But nobody followed us. We'd either see or hear a car if it drove up now, even with the rain. There's only one way in here, right? Nobody can make it down this way without headlights on. The road's too overgrown for that." Fiona scooted closer to him, and he could feel her shivering. "Are we really still in danger?"

Such an innocent.

She had no reason even to think of things like night vision goggles, helicopters, or sniper rifles, and it reminded him that this woman would never be a part of his world and he couldn't ever be a part of hers.

"I think we're as safe as we can be, under the circumstances."

"I was hoping for a more comforting answer. A nice, unambiguous 'yes, we're safe' would be lovely."

She'd obviously not considered the other possibility. Griffith debated if he should tell her; it might be easier on her if he kept silent. Then again, after all he'd put her through, he owed it to her to be honest. At least this once.

He sighed. "Fiona."

She looked at him. "Mmm?"

"There's a possibility someone was here before we arrived and is only waiting to make his move. It's a slim chance, but I thought you should know about it."

He felt her body go rigid. "Then why did we come here?"

"Because there's also a chance I'm wrong. We didn't have much of a choice, and the helicopter should've gotten here first. The rain slowed them down and helped us along by cutting down on the traffic just enough to get us here earlier than planned."

"If somebody is here—" She broke off to glance around uneasily. "I don't understand why they'd wait. From what I've seen of you, I'm assuming the people in this helicopter will have enough firepower to take over a small country. I can't believe von Lahr wouldn't anticipate that you'd call in your own personal army."

He laughed; he couldn't help it. "I'm glad you're not the type to panic easily."

"Oh, there's panic, believe me. And that's not an answer to my question."

"I don't have one this time." Griffith shifted, glancing behind him. "The simplest explanation may be that no one is here but us. And if someone is already here, they could be waiting for something or someone else."

"Such as?"

"The possibility I like least is that I'm bait for the rest of my team. Taking out one of us might make a splash, but wiping out every operative called into the L.A. office would make big waves. Not to mention a hell of a dent in our personnel pool."

"That's not good."

Fiona leaned even closer, and Griffith, sensing what she needed, gave her hand a quick, reassuring squeeze and kissed her on the temple. Her skin was warm and smooth beneath his lips and he had a sudden, almost overwhelming urge to pull her into his arms. "Don't worry. They can take care of themselves; it's you we need to keep safe."

"And we're not keeping *you* safe?" she asked. "This isn't a movie. The bad guys are probably very good at hitting what they're aiming for, and you're not immune to bullets simply because you're cute."

She thought he was cute? Dumb as it was, hearing her say it lightened his mood.

Griffith thumped his chest. "Which is why I'm wearing this. And the scars on my back are proof that I already know they hit what they aim for."

"Sorry, I forgot. Why do you continue to do this, Griffith? If you really want more out of your life, get out. You can do something else."

The abrupt shift took him by surprise, as did the vehemence in her voice. To keep the mood from swinging where he didn't want it to go, he said flatly, "Maybe. But how about we postpone any retirement talk until this is over?"

"Because after this is over, I won't ever see you again."

Pretty, soft, warm; funny and smart . . . with the tenacity of a pit bull. "It's for the best, Fiona. You must know that."

"Can you at least promise me you'll think about stopping this before it gets you killed?"

He shouldn't promise her anything at all. Spontaneous heat-of-the-moment promises could come back to bite him on the ass, and haunt him. "I can't do that."

"Of course you can." She was still speaking in a loud whisper. "It's just easier for you not to."

Frowning, Griffith broke off from his surveillance to stare her down. "I am what I am, and it's too late for me to change. And what I do with my life is none of your goddamn business anyway. Don't mistake my concern for your safety for anything more. I don't love you. I don't feel anything at all for you in that way."

Silence fell between them, and he regretted the harshness, but she'd hit a nerve, and they were still in a shitload of trouble, so he didn't have time for this.

Fiona turned her head. She eased away from him. Just an inch or two, but he immediately felt the distance.

Shortly after that, he spotted the blinking of lights that signaled the approach of the helicopter. Diva must've pushed the engine to its limits. "Do you want a gun?"

That brought her attention back to him—and he thought he detected a wet sheen in her eyes.

"I don't know . . . I've never handled a gun in my life. Then again, it'd be better than standing around and doing nothing if something happened."

"So was that a yes?" he asked, patiently.

Her head bobbed up and down. "Yes, I'll take it."

He carefully passed his grandfather's Smith & Wesson over to her. "It's not much, but it'll do the job if necessary. And it's small enough for you to handle."

He tried not to smile as she took it gingerly. People unused to guns always handled them as if they would bite. He'd lived with guns so long, he could hardly remember what it was like not to feel the weight of one on his body.

"We don't have time for a full course in gun safety, so I'll keep it short and sweet: keep your fingers away from the trigger unless you intend to shoot. Pick it up only by the grip, and never, ever point it at yourself—or anybody else you don't intend to shoot. My boss'll gut me if, after all this, you accidentally kill yourself."

That finally coaxed a smile out of her. "That obit would be nearly as embarrassing as dying while naked and handcuffed to a daybed. I promise not to be excessively stupid."

"Of course you won't. You don't have a stupid bone in your body." Griffith glanced up; the blinking lights were clearer now. "The helicopter is almost here. We stay inside until it's landed and my team exits. They'll provide cover, and then I'll take you to the helicopter. If everything goes well, we hop inside, they follow, and we take off again."

"That option has my vote."

Her voice was brisk, but he could feel her trembling. Most people would've been in hysterics or too scared to talk, much less move. "Before we leave, I want you to know that you're one of the strongest women I have ever met."

She made a rude noise. "Not me. I'm ordinary and hardly brave at all—"

"Stop selling yourself short. I know strong when I see it."

Fiona's eyes widened, then she smiled. "Look who's telling me not to sell myself short: the man who couldn't even promise me he'd think about a new line of work that doesn't involve armored cars, bulletproof vests, international thugs, and secret organizations."

Twenty-three

9:20 P.M.

VON LAHR HEARD THE HELICOPTER APPROACHING and glanced at his watch.

It was about time; he didn't have all night to lounge outside dirty, rusty old hangars. He'd never get the stains out of his leather overcoat, and the cold, constant drizzle did nothing for his sinuses. He'd considered breaking into one of the hangars, but he couldn't be sure the buildings weren't booby-trapped or rigged with alarms. Nor had he had the time to find out. So the tall grass and the cover of night and the old buildings had had to be enough.

Anticipation sizzled through him like a current. It had been a long time since he had deliberately put himself in danger like this, and he'd forgotten the adrenaline high it brought. The pounding blood, the chimeralike sense of invincibility.

His mystery man had never called again but had been telling the truth. From his hiding spot behind the farthest hangar, he could just glimpse the car with Laughton and the redhead inside.

He'd briefly been tempted to shoot once Laughton had switched off the engine, but he'd known better. The moment of opportunity, the one to wait for, was when the helicopter landed and Laughton transferred the woman. Everyone except the pilot would be out in the open at that point.

Minimum effort, maximum result.

Von Lahr had no idea whether McMahon was here as well. It was likely, although he hadn't seen or heard anyone approach, and he'd been waiting for a while. Long enough to note the surveillance cameras and their blind spots, to determine that there was no location close enough to hide a car or truck.

If McMahon was here, he'd come earlier on foot from a distance, slipping through the long grass and darting from bush to scrub brush, to wait, like himself, for all the players to assemble. Von Lahr doubted McMahon had the resources, as he did, to arrive by air.

This time, at least, he was better prepared for an airfield adventure. These weren't the best conditions, and his positioning for shooting wasn't what he'd have preferred, but his choices were limited.

Von Lahr hoisted his semiautomatic Dragunov sniper rifle, with its night scope, the weight of it comfortable and familiar in his hands. The German army had trained him as a sniper long, long ago, and the skill had never left him. Or failed him when he'd needed it most.

For the hell of it, he sighted the dark interior of the car, grinned, and whispered, "Bang. Bang. You're all dead."

Twenty-four

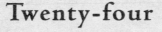

Fiona watched, mesmerized, as the helicopter approached. It was black; at first she could see nothing but the blinking lights. She could hear it, though, and as it drew near, the air circulated by its blades whipped the long grass into a frenzy.

It all seemed like a dream, but the tense warmth of the man beside her was real, as were the tight vest and the alien smoothness of the gun in her hand. She hoped she wouldn't throw up in sheer terror if someone started shooting at them.

Half the babbling she'd done all the way here, and then afterward, had been to keep herself from dwelling on how terrified she was—although she'd meant that bit about his promise to find himself a safer line of work.

She was more afraid for him than for herself. She sensed the desperate need in him to keep her safe, to the point of putting himself in harm's way for her sake, as he'd done to draw fire when they'd left the apartment building.

Telling him not to do so was pointless, and part of the reason she'd taken the gun. If it came to it, she'd try to protect him as well. He'd done things he shouldn't have, but he was trying to do right by her now and to right the wrongs of others. Maybe he wasn't a Hollywood kind of hero, but he was a man trying to do what he could. And that, she had realized on the long ride over, counted for something.

As the helicopter touched down it activated its searchlight, and suddenly the whole area lit up as if it were high noon on a sunny day. After her eyes adjusted to the sudden glare, she saw the logo on the side of the aircraft.

Fiona stared. "Did you steal a media helicopter?"

Griffith laughed softly. "It's not a news chopper; it just looks that way. Remember, things are not always what they seem."

She gazed at him, and a strange sense of fear, regret, anger, and longing washed over her. His dark hair, blue eyes, even clearer now that he'd given up the pretense of wearing glasses, and that amiable smile . . . her frat-boy mercenary. He certainly hadn't been what he'd seemed; it was a lesson she kept failing to learn.

"Ready?" Griffith asked softly.

"As I'll ever be."

The hatch on the helicopter opened, and two people jumped out. They were dressed all in black, and she could tell by their weapons that these people meant business. The searchlight swung around the area. If anyone was out there and moved into the open, he'd be spotted at once.

To her surprise, she recognized one of the figures moving toward her and Griffith—Noonie. Apparently he was back in the good graces of the powers that be.

Griffith turned to her. "Stay close to me. I'll exit first. You follow on my side, and stay between me and the car. I'll guide you to the helicopter. Keep your head down and move fast."

Fiona nodded. "I understand."

He smiled at her. "It's almost over. You're doing fine."

It was moments like these, when his warmth broke through the cool reserve, that she sensed the man he could've been had he made a few different choices.

And it made her wish she'd had a chance to get to know the real man, not the one he'd been hiding behind.

Noonie and the second man motioned for them, and Griffith ushered her out of the car, keeping her close to him. When the other two joined them, providing cover, she felt truly safe for the first time in hours.

Griffith moved her forward at nearly a run, and they were halfway to the aircraft when a sudden movement by the first hangar caught everyone's attention.

The searchlight and assault rifles swung toward the figure, and Griffith pulled her behind him. He had his gun out as well.

"What the hell?" he muttered. "Where'd he come from?"

"Please don't shoot!" The man held up his arms. "I'm not armed!"

"Identify yourself!" Griffith ordered in a tone of voice Fiona had never heard before, so harsh and cold that it gave her chills.

"Ask the lady with you. The little cat-eyed goddess."

The chill crystallized into brittle fear, and Fiona whispered, "Richard!"

Pressed against Griffith, she felt his muscles go taut as he shouted, "Are you Richard McMahon?"

"No, but I knew him very well. Sorry for the deception, Ms. Kennedy, but it was the only way I could think of to get your attention."

"Rico!" Griffith shouted at the man nearest the helicopter, whose rifle was pointed toward the figure at the edge of the light.

"Yeah?"

"Search him." Griffith glanced back at Fiona. "Do you recognize him?"

She could see, now, that this man was not Richard. Relief rushed over her, then anger. She could only shake her head.

As Rico cautiously approached the man, Griffith shouted, "You! Don't move, and keep your hands where we can see them. Who are you? What do you want?"

Obediently, the man held his hands high in the air and didn't move. "Who I am, I'll say in a minute. I want to cut a deal with Avalon."

Avalon? Fiona looked at Griffith and saw how his mouth had tightened and every line of his body had gone taut.

"What kind of deal? Give me a good reason why I shouldn't have my people shoot you right now."

"Because if you can promise me protection, I can tell you where to find Rainert von Lahr."

"What's going on?" Fiona demanded.

"Not sure," Griffith answered tersely.

A tense silence followed as Rico had the man lie down and searched him. The helicopter light kept circling, and Griffith never relaxed his watchful stance.

"He's clean," Rico yelled back at them.

"Bring him over here." Fiona saw Griffith mouth the word "fuck." He didn't look as happy as a man should, who had the focus of a five-year hunt within his grasp.

"I want you in the helicopter," he said. Before she

could say anything, he pulled her rapidly after him, pushing her head down.

The sound and the feel of the air from the rotating blades was frightening, but the strength and warmth of Griffith's supporting arm helped keep her calm.

The pilot, a woman, leaned back from the cockpit and yelled, "Is this Kennedy?"

Griffith nodded and helped Fiona climb up through the hatch. He slid the briefcase in after her.

"If there's trouble, you get out of here and make sure she's safe," he ordered. "And the manuscript, too."

"Got it."

He was leaving her? Fiona grabbed at his arm. "You're not coming? You can't stay here! What if that man's lying? What if—"

"All the possibilities have occurred to me," he said shortly. "Now sit down."

She'd promised to do as he told her; he had experience in these situations, and it would be foolish to argue. The dark-haired pilot pointed toward the far corner of the helicopter, and Fiona scrambled to the seat and sat down, her legs unsteady.

Rico and Noonie had brought their unexpected visitor closer, their rifle barrels pointing at him. Griffith stepped between the man and the hatch, and Fiona rose to get a closer look, ignoring the pilot's impatient motions for her to sit back down.

She was quite certain she'd never seen him before, yet he acted as if he knew her and even smiled at her. And of course he'd known her by a private, intimate name.

"Where is . . . Do you know where Richard is?" she called out, because she had to know, one way or another, if he was alive. "Please!"

"I'm sorry, Ms. Kennedy, but your husband is dead." The man was smiling, still holding his hands above his head. The cheery smile, incongruously coupled with his words, hit her hard. "They got him a year ago, and they're after me now. If you people help me get away to a new life, I'll tell you not only where von Lahr bases his operations now but also the name of the man who paid McMahon to forge the Marlowe. It's the same man who ordered him killed so he wouldn't talk—and who'll kill me if you don't help me out."

"Your name," Griffith said flatly.

The man considered, eyeing Griffith, and whatever he saw there must've convinced him to answer. "Oliver Hanson."

Frowning, Fiona leaned out of the helicopter to get a better look. If she could see his face more clearly, maybe she could remember having met him.

"How did you find out about this place?"

Hanson beamed. He was younger than Richard by

a good five years, although they had the same basic build and coloring, and even a vague resemblance.

"We all know about Avalon, and it was just a matter of taking a logical approach. Who would be able to move around the world so quickly and easily at a moment's notice? Who had related businesses in major cities in the US and satellite offices around the world?"

Although he had to shout over the din of the rotors, Hanson acted as if they were chatting in a coffee shop.

"I figured that had to be in the private sector, so no one would question the legitimacy of flights, passports, and visas for groups of people, and so there'd be no obvious relationship with any government organization."

He looked very proud of himself. "It didn't take me long to work out that would be a travel agency specializing in international travel, though it did take me a while to find the connections. Sheridan is good at obscuring the trail, I'll give him that."

Fiona saw Rico and the pilot glance at each other, although Griffith didn't so much as blink.

"Here's the deal. I'm tired of running. I'm tired of hiding. I want to go back to living a normal life, and normal doesn't include a prison cell. You do that for me, and you get what you want, and I keep my mouth shut. You don't, and I tell everybody the truth about Avalon and Ben Sheridan."

"Why not just go to von Lahr with your info and negotiate with him?"

"Because the second I gave him what he wanted, he'd kill me. I figure my chances are slightly better with you guys. You don't kill without provocation, right?"

For a moment, there was something about Griffith's face that said Hanson had severely miscalculated.

Then the hard expression smoothed away to a flat neutrality. "I can't make any deals with you. The best I can do is take you to Sheridan."

"And keep me alive? You'll make sure they won't get to me?"

"I'll do my best."

"This ain't good," the dark-haired woman muttered.

Griffith glanced at Noonie and Rico. "Put him into the chopper. We'll take him back and talk where it's a hell of a lot safer."

"Grif, that puts us over the weight limit," the woman said sharply.

"I'll take the car," he replied. "If anybody followed our uninvited guest, I'll take care of it."

"Not alone," the woman protested. "At least take Rico with you."

"Diva, you're the pilot. You can't keep watch and fly this thing at the same time. I'll need someone experienced to guard Hanson and someone else to protect Ms. Kennedy, and that would be Rico and Noonie, respectively."

"But—"

"I'm giving the orders."

Fiona didn't like it, and she tried to signal him with her eyes, but he wouldn't look at her. A few moments later, the still-grinning Hanson was shoved unceremoniously into the already cramped interior of the helicopter. Noonie hopped in after him. While she wanted to ask Hanson about Richard, and put to rest so many of her questions, she also wanted to kick that sleazy, annoying smile off his face.

What the hell was he smiling about, anyway?

And then Rico shouted a warning and dropped to the tarmac just as Griffith jumped in front of the open hatch, firing as he did so.

"Sonofabitch!" the pilot shouted, glaring at Hanson, who still had the smile frozen on his face. "You were followed, you dumb-ass!"

Fiona didn't understand what was happening. She hadn't heard any shots; she'd only seen Rico drop to the ground and scramble toward the parked car, combat-crawling across the pavement, and Griffith suddenly fall back against the side of the helicopter as he continued to shoot.

Twisting around, Griffith grabbed for the hatch lever to pull it shut—and Fiona saw a wet sheen on the leather sleeve of his jacket. "Diva, get them out of here!"

He was yelling over Hanson's screams, the whine of the engine increasing in pitch, and Fiona snagged Griffith's arm to try to draw him inside to safety.

Noonie was shouting at their prisoner to move away from the open hatch, and the next thing Fiona knew, Noonie dropped like a stone and Hanson had his rifle.

The smile returned, and Hanson swung the weapon toward her.

Fiona shouted a warning, fumbling in her pocket for her gun. Diva, preparing to lift off, turned to see what was happening. Before Fiona could do anything, and before Diva could clear her holster, Griffith lunged inside the helicopter.

Hanson fired.

Griffith landed on Fiona with a grunt and kicked out, catching Hanson on the leg. It was enough to make him stumble but not fall. Instead, Hanson jumped out of the chopper—and took the briefcase with him.

"Diva," Griffith yelled as he rolled out of the hatch and landed on the tarmac. "Get out of here now!"

"No!" Fiona shook her head wildly. "I don't—"

She saw a man emerge from the shadows behind the last hangar, the one set apart from the others.

The helicopter provided enough light that she could clearly make out white-blond hair and the flutter of a long, dark overcoat.

Rainert von Lahr; it had to be.

And he had a rifle.

Nobody else had noticed him. Noonie was down, too injured to move. Diva was half out of the pilot seat, wanting to help her comrades, then cursing as she sat again and prepared to lift off. Griffith was struggling on the tarmac with Hanson as Rico tried to locate the shooter, but he was facing in the wrong direction, searching the long grass. He'd never hear her shouts.

Fiona raised her gun and pointed, the barrel trembling slightly, just as the skids began to lift off the tarmac and the helicopter started to swing away from von Lahr, leaving Griffith, Rico, and Hanson wide open.

She couldn't make out details beyond that unmistakable sight of a rifle aimed directly at Griffith.

Taking a deep breath, she fired.

And missed; von Lahr was still standing.

"Goddammit!" Frustrated, she aimed again.

But she must've caught the man's attention, because now he swung the rifle scope in her direction. Fighting back a rush of panic and cold fear, she fired again; then a dark figure loomed between her and the gunman.

Griffith!

A split second later, he reeled around and dropped to one knee, firing toward the far hangar. She gave an anguished scream, knowing he'd deliberately come between her and that bullet. The helicopter rose sharply, banking to avoid the gunfire, and sent her sliding back against Noonie's inert body.

"Knock off the screaming," Diva barked from the pilot's seat. "Shut that hatch and help Noonie. Goddammit, what the hell's happening out there?"

"You can't leave them behind! Griffith was shot, and there was a man—"

"I know that, but I have my orders to get you to safety, and Noonie needs help right now. I've called for backup. If Rico can grab Grif and hold on for a little longer, they'll make it."

"I have a gun. If you circle around by the gunman, I can try to—"

"Get us shot out of the sky? Grif is giving us a chance to get away. Now shut up and do what I told you!"

Fiona shut up, then slammed the hatch closed. By then, whatever was happening below had been swallowed in the darkness.

Twenty-five

❖

SHE WAS SAFE.

It was the first thought that rang clear in his mind, a split second before he realized that, if he didn't get under cover, he was going to get shot again.

And what the fuck was going on?

It was clearly some kind of trap, and their "target" was shooting at them and at the man by the far hangar, whom Griffith had immediately recognized.

Von Lahr.

"Grif, we gotta move!"

Rico, with the M16, was returning fire as von Lahr ducked safely behind the hangar. A sniper rifle was no match for an assault rifle, so that would keep von Lahr at bay while they scrambled for cover.

Griffith had no idea where Hanson had disappeared to, but he had to be near the only other cover: the car.

He exchanged looks with Rico and nodded tersely. "The other hangar. There's no choice. You cover the front, I've got your back. Go!"

With the helicopter only a fading light in the black sky, the old airfield was smothered in darkness once again, and Griffith couldn't see worth shit. But then neither could Hanson and von Lahr.

A bullet thudded into the pavement far too close for comfort, and Griffith revised his last assumption. Apparently, von Lahr could see them pretty damn well.

Rico let loose a wide spray of bullets, then dove behind the cover of the hangar diagonal from the one shielding von Lahr. The car was plainly in sight for everyone, and Griffith caught a scurry of movement behind it.

Suddenly a shot erupted from behind the car, but it wasn't aimed at them. It was directed at the far hangar.

"What the hell is with that guy?" Rico demanded. "He asks us for help, then shoots at us. *And* he's shooting at von Lahr. That *is* von Lahr, right?"

"Yeah, it's von Lahr." The pain was more intense now; he must've been hit more seriously than he'd thought.

"Now what?" Rico muttered.

"We hold tight until help arrives. Diva would've

radioed the cops, and Sherman will get here first."

A shot winged by, and they both crouched lower, cursing. Griffith hurriedly reloaded the Jericho, trying to ignore the burning pain in his shoulder. A sting along his lower leg, which he only now noticed, signaled that a bullet had grazed him there as well. The shoulder was a definite hit, though. He could barely move his right arm—and since he was right-handed, that wasn't good.

"Grif, how bad are you hit?"

"I won't bleed to death anytime soon, but I'm losing blood fast. You?"

"Just a glancing hit to the chest. Knocked me on my ass, and I think a rib or two's bruised, but that's it. God bless Kevlar."

A barrage of bullets from the car interrupted him. Sandy dirt and rocks and bits of pavement shot upward, pelting their hands as they covered their heads and faces.

Griffith had had enough.

Angrily, he jabbed his finger toward the dark head that had popped up behind the car as Hanson took aim again. "Take him out!"

He and Rico fired together over the wail of a lone police siren in the distance. There was no sound or any movement from the hangar where von Lahr was hiding, and Griffith wanted to go after the bastard so bad he could almost taste the dark, bitter need.

"That better be Sherman," Rico said. "You think we got Hanson?"

"I saw him drop down. Whether he's hit or not, I don't know."

"You holding up?"

His vision was going blurry. "I can hold on for a little longer. Dammit . . . where's von Lahr?"

A familiar sound forced his attention upward: a helicopter with lights flashing, descending at an alarming speed.

"Jesus, did Diva come back?" Rico asked, glancing up. "What the hell? She's coming in way too fast!"

Griffith got a clearer look at the chopper. "Shit . . . that's not one of ours!"

Floodlights flared, and Griffith ducked his head, blinded by the brightness. The rotors kicked up the wind, and when he glanced up again, peering through the blinding white light, he saw von Lahr jump into the helicopter. Just as someone fired toward Rico, forcing him to drop to the ground again.

The chopper rose; then the nose swung around toward the car where Hanson was hiding. A flash of gunfire followed; then the pilot dipped low enough for another man to climb down onto the skids and reach for something.

The manuscript.

"Sonofa——" Griffith raised his gun. Even though

he could hardly see and his right arm was useless, the solid black bulk of the chopper was hard to miss. He fired with his left hand, and Rico joined in with short bursts of automatic fire, trying to hit the rotors between dodging returning fire.

The helicopter sharply pulled up, and rapidly moved out of range.

Then it was gone, with Rainert von Lahr and the manuscript, leaving darkness behind and a quiet broken by the approaching howl of the police siren and flashing lights.

Light-headed from loss of blood, Griffith fought to keep alert and leaned back against the hangar.

"Dammit, it's not fair when the bad guys have cooler toys than we do." He let out a groan of frustration. "And he got the manuscript."

Rico snorted. "But we got Kennedy out in one piece. Can't say the same for Hanson. I don't see any movement by the car."

"Looked to me like von Lahr made an extra stop to be sure he wasn't going to talk."

"I can't *believe* he got away. This is the third time we've come this close to him, and he escapes every fuckin' time."

The police cruiser had arrived, slowing as it neared the car. Rico leaned out into the view of the headlights and signaled their location, then pointed toward the car and motioned for caution. A moment later, the cruiser's door opened, and the man inside got out slowly, shotgun ready.

He crouched out of sight for a moment, then stood and called, "He's down and ain't coming up anytime soon. If ever."

Griffith tried to take a step, but dizziness overwhelmed him and he almost fell. Then Rico steadied him, slinging Griffith's arm around his own shoulder as they moved forward.

By the time they got to the car, their LAPD contact was kneeling beside Hanson's crumpled body. Patrolman Balthasar Sherman, a former marine, had deep black skin, a shaved head, a goatee, and the build of a professional wrestler.

"Dead?" Griffith asked, leaning heavily back against the bullet-pocked car while Rico dropped down beside Sherman.

"Nope. Still breathing. Don't know for how long, though." Sherman looked up. "You don't look so good yourself."

"What a coincidence. I don't feel so good, either."

His grin a brilliant flash of white, Sherman gently turned Hanson over, and the sound of his labored gasps for breath was clearer. "Shot two or three times. Sounds like maybe a lung got hit. Ambulance is on the way." Griffith could hear the distant wail of sirens.

"Grif, you better sit down before you fall down," Sherman said. "What's the story, before the others get here?"

"The usual suspected drug shit gone bad. I think maybe I will sit."

Rico helped him down, pressing Griffith's hand harder against the wound in his shoulder. "That's a lot of blood. I'm thinking you need to take a trip on the ambulance yourself."

"Yeah." Griffith rested his head back against the car as Sherman worked on Hanson. "But she got away okay. She'll be fine." He shook his head, trying to clear his clouding vision and repeated, "She'll be fine."

"You bet she will, so stop worrying about it. Diva'll take care of things while you get yourself stitched up. We'll come up with a story for her to explain what happened, and she'll be back to her little bookstore in no time."

"You guys took care of the cat?" It was harder to think, all fuzzy inside his head as darkness pushed inward.

"Yes, we took care of the cat. Not that it appreciated our efforts."

Griffith smiled. "Cats are like that."

"C'mon, Grif, hang in there." Rico's voice, distant and fading, was threaded with worry. "It's just a few more holes and scratches, nothing worse than you've had before. You'll be okay."

"I know." Griffith briefly opened his eyes, and suddenly the pain tore through him, sharp and hot. "The question is, for what?"

And then everything spun down to blackness.

Twenty-six

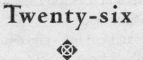

11:40 P.M.

FIONA, WRAPPED IN A BLANKET AND HOLDING A CUP OF warm tea in her trembling hands, surveyed the small, white room at the Torrance Airport. It was a bland, typical office with neutral gray carpet, partitions, and the usual desks, computers, and file cabinets.

Diva, the helicopter pilot, hadn't left her alone since they'd touched down next to a small building with a sign that read TORRANCE HELICOPTER TOURS.

An ambulance had been waiting and immediately whisked Noonie away. She'd held him the entire trip, pressing the hem of her sweater to the heavily bleeding gash across the side of his skull where the bullet had torn through flesh and grooved along bone. She'd managed to stop the bleeding, but her sweater would never be white again.

A taciturn medic had also looked over Fiona and declared her unhurt except for a few bruises and cuts, which he'd treated with a stinging antibiotic and Band-Aids. After that, he gave her a clean sweatshirt to wear. It was several sizes too large, but it was warm and not covered in blood.

They'd also taken Griffith's gun away from her.

Since then, she'd been in this room with Diva—Fiona doubted it was the woman's real name, any more than Rico and Noonie had been real names—who explained they were "waiting on news."

"You feeling okay?" Diva asked. She was a small brunette who had Latino or darker Mediterranean blood somewhere up along the family tree, judging by her olive-tinted skin. With an angular face, greenish brown eyes, short, feathery hair, and a scar across her left eyebrow to match the one on her lip, she was attractive in a scary kind of way.

Fiona nodded. "I'm not shaking as much anymore. Or light-headed."

"You're doing great. I was worried you were gonna hyperventilate on me, but you kept a level head. Good for you." Now that Diva was saying more than a word or two, Fiona detected a definite New Jersey accent. "Sorry for all the shit you had to go through. No one had any idea this might happen."

Nobody but Griffith.

"Do you think it'll be much longer before we hear back from Griffith?"

Diva regarded her with a faint frown. "We probably won't be. At this point, our associates in the LAPD will take over."

"I don't understand."

"Okay, then I'll make it really clear. From here on out, you won't hear from or see Grif again."

Fiona looked down. "You'll at least tell me if he's okay?"

"If he wasn't, I'd have heard back by now."

The woman's tone was flat, neutral, and Fiona couldn't tell if she were telling the truth or not. Maybe they all had to pass a fibbing exam.

The thought made her smile, and Diva said, "Hey, that's good . . . a smile is good."

"You know what he told me?"

"Grif?"

Fiona nodded. "He told me he didn't care about me."

"Oh." Diva looked uncomfortable. "Yeah, well, that was rude, but he was kinda preoccupied at the time. I wouldn't take it personally."

"And he also told me never to believe him."

The woman stared at her, then snorted. "And you shouldn't. That man's nothin' but a walkin' package of beautiful lies. You're better off forgetting all about him."

"I know."

Then why did she so badly want to see him one more time, if only to assure herself that he was all right?

Of course he was all right. Men like Griffith Laughton walked with the devil's own luck, and bounced back from injuries and close calls that would kill a lesser mortal being.

But the little pep talk didn't work, and suddenly an overwhelming wave of weariness rolled over her. All she wanted to do was close her eyes, crawl into a safe little corner, and let out all her pent-up fear and anger and confusion in one long, soul-cleansing crying jag.

Unfortunately, she was stuck here with a woman who looked like she'd never cried in her life and who would mock anyone who did. "What happens to me now?"

"Like I said, the police will take care of it."

"How? I disappeared from my home and business for an entire day, there was a man shot in my store, another shoot-out in an airfield outside the city, and people were hurt. How will they explain that away?"

Diva didn't answer, and Fiona looked down again, taking a deep breath. "When that man shot at me . . . right before it happened, Griffith stepped in front of me. I know he was hit."

"He was wearing protective gear. He was still on his feet. It's probably not as bad as you think."

"The man at the hangar with the rifle . . . that was Rainert von Lahr, wasn't it?"

Diva shifted, rearranging her legs slightly. She had lounging down to an almost elegant art, despite wearing a flight suit. "I can't talk about that, so don't ask."

"I noticed you didn't answer my question about how the police were going to explain away what happened to me and at my shop."

"I can't talk about that, either, except to say that you'll be compensated for any property damage or medical bills you may incur, and that they'll come up with a reasonable-sounding story. I suggest you go along with it."

"And if I don't?"

"Your choice." Diva shrugged. "But why wouldn't you?"

"I think my civil liberties have been deeply abused."

The woman laughed. "I guess that means Grif is losing his touch."

Fiona felt her face go hot. "I could sue you people. Go to the press. Accuse the police of a cover-up. This is L.A . . . it's not like a good conspiracy theory won't make the headlines."

"And what good would that do you?"

None, none at all.

All the attention, the questions from reporters, the hours talking with police investigators . . . Going through that ordeal after her husband's "car accident" had been more than enough. Richard's name would be dragged through the mud, and to what end? Did his family need the grief all over again? Did she want some crazy-sounding story to cast doubt on her reputation as a businesswoman?

Fiona held back a little sigh. "I suppose there's no record of you being on the payroll here."

"Probably not. This is a legitimate business, after all."

"And medical records can disappear, or be altered. So can police reports."

"Los Angeles is a big, busy city, with a lot of crime and a lot of emergency room trauma. Things get mixed up. The police are overworked. Some of them might be reluctant to ask too many questions if there's no good reason to. If the answers fit and there are no loose ends, that's all that matters to a lot of people."

"And nobody would believe me anyway."

"Likely not," Diva agreed cheerfully.

And Griffith would disappear, off to rescue some other ancient artifact or catch another slick smuggler or thief; to play the part of the hero he so wanted to be, and seek some sense of forgiveness for the failures he couldn't forget.

Would she be another one of those failures driving him?

"I hope you find this von Lahr fellow. He sounds like a nasty piece of work."

"You have no idea."

Even knowing she wouldn't get an answer, Fiona asked, "Were you with Griffith when Annamari and the others were killed?"

Diva's eyes widened, and she straightened, her expression hard-edged. "He told you?"

"Yes."

"Huh." Diva arched a brow and returned to her slouch. "Isn't that something."

"It is?"

Anxiety and jittery energy compelled Fiona to stand and walk around the room.

Diva was clearly surprised that Griffith had talked about his past, and Fiona was afraid to think that meant she was anything special to him.

Even considering the idea was foolish. The man had lied to her, used her, manipulated her, had sex with her for reasons that made her feel dirty and angry, and he'd disrupted her shop, kidnapped her for a day, gotten her shot at, and put her in danger—

And had taken a bullet for her, told her things he must've never told anyone else, and kept his promise to see her safely returned.

He'd told her if he had had a chance to settle

down and live a quiet life, he'd have wanted to do it with a woman like her, and then told her never to believe anything he said. And even if it meant she was a sentimental idiot, she'd sensed the weary loneliness of someone who'd taken a good look at his life, didn't like what he saw, and didn't believe in himself enough to change.

And knowing that hurt. She had met a man who, despite the lies and the danger, had touched her . . . and then he was gone, with everything between them left unfinished.

Fiona hated unfinished business.

It was almost like losing Richard again, left in limbo with unanswered questions and unsettled feelings. Would it really hurt these people to give her a simple yes or no about his safety?

A cell phone trilled, and Diva answered. A brief conversation followed, then she disconnected, turned to Fiona, and said, "The police are on the way to pick you up."

It looked as if the woman was waiting for her response, but Fiona didn't know what to say. "Oh."

Diva's brows shot upward. "It seems you were called away unexpectedly for a business matter at the Getty, with Louisa Lau of the rare books section, and—"

"I know Louisa in passing." The bitter tinge in her voice sounded strange and alien. "I suppose she's one of your associates as well? My, you secret superhero types are very efficient."

"—and while you were gone, someone broke into your store," Diva continued as if Fiona had never interrupted her. "The police were notified by a suspicious passerby, there was a struggle in the store, and the man was injured before being taken into custody. You've been with the police and your lawyer and just now got back, and you really don't know anything about what happened, but you're glad it's all over."

How . . . sanitary and convenient. There was no reason anybody would question a story like that, when the blandly ordinary could explain everything so neatly.

"You do good work. Very thorough."

Diva's flat expression never wavered. "We've had many years of experience."

"And the art world is a small one. Griffith told me that, too." She hesitated, then tried one more time. "What about Griffith and Rico? And that man who claimed to have known my husband? What will happen to him?"

"It's no longer a concern for you." Diva moved forward and took Fiona's arm. "We have to go now. A car is waiting for you outside."

Everything was turning out just like Griffith said it would. All the wishful thinking, all the what-ifs and might-have-beens meant nothing, because she had a life and she needed to get back to it. She had a vacation coming up, and she needed to plan for it.

And now she had a man in her heart that she needed to forget.

"All right." She put the tea and the blanket aside, squared her shoulders, and smoothed her hair. "I'm ready to go back."

Twenty-seven

❖

DECEMBER WAS DRAWING TO A CLOSE, A MONTH AFTER von Lahr had slipped through his fingers again, before Griffith recovered enough from his injuries to drive to the main offices of Sheridan Expeditions outside Seattle.

Ben's office on the top floor had a great view of the Puget Sound, and Griffith understood why he didn't want to be anywhere else. After years of working the field himself, Ben had found his place to belong.

A "place to belong" was something that had been on Griffith's mind. And although he'd had plenty of time to think over the last month, he still wasn't sure what he would tell Ben today.

As he walked into the bustling atmosphere of a busy travel agency, he nodded at the security guard by the main desk. The guard looked ordinary and nonthreatening, the usual rent-a-cop kind of guy, but Griffith knew better.

The general ambience of the agency suggested the man who owned it had no interest in art beyond making his business look good, and the responsibility for that had been delegated to an expensive landscaping company and an interior designer who'd opted for a rustic look.

To the casual visitor and average employee, there was nothing out of the ordinary about Sheridan Expeditions or Ben Sheridan's office. Only someone like him, who knew what to look for, would notice the tight security. Even fewer had any clue about the little extras built into the place.

"Hide in plain sight" was the motto of Ben Sheridan's other business, and Griffith had had a talent for it as well. It had helped him rise to the top of the Avalon hierarchy.

He took the elevator to the third floor and was admitted into the main reception area once he'd punched in the correct access code and had his fingerprint identified.

Ben's secretary, Ellie, was also his longtime bodyguard. She just happened to look like a young, blond, athletic suburbanite. "Hello, Griffith. We've been expecting you."

"Sorry I'm late. Traffic is a bitch, as usual. Is he in?"

"You bet." She pressed the intercom. "Grif's here, Ben. Can I send him in?"

"Hell, yes" came the gravelly reply.

Griffith arched a brow. "Sounds like he's in a bad mood. Should I expect a flaying or just an ass kicking?"

Ellie smiled. "It's not you. He lost a bet to his ex-brother-in-law and had to buy him lunch. That always leaves him in a bad mood. Go on in."

Griffith smiled back, and Ellie buzzed him inside. As the door shut quietly behind him, Griffith faced his boss: a tall, rugged-looking, dark-haired man in a suit, sitting in an office of oak floors and furniture, and high, arched windows. The ceiling fan had clear Lucite blades so as not to interfere with the view of the rough-hewn ceiling beams.

Ben lounged back in his leather desk chair, boots propped on the only clear spot of his disorganized desk, with its heaps of files, books, papers, boxes, and empty soda cans and coffee cups.

Griffith had known the man for fifteen years and respected him like he respected no one else, but how Ben managed to operate amid such a mess continually baffled him.

Smiling, he walked forward. "Hey."

"Hey yourself. If it isn't our favorite chaos magnet, up and ambulatory once again." Ben swung his boots down to the floor with a loud thump. "Sit.

You still look like shit. Want something to drink?"

"No." Griffith sat, carefully, in one of the chairs across from the desk. "Thanks for the compassion, though. I'm deeply touched."

Ben grinned, but the smile didn't quite reach his eyes. "I'd hate to lose my favorite source of entertainment. When you're in action, I never know what the hell's going to happen."

"This last time, a lot more than I'd bargained for." Griffith glanced out the window toward the sparkling blue of the Pacific. "I still can't believe I almost had him. He was right there, Ben, and he slipped through my fingers again."

"Don't be too hard on yourself. Von Lahr's been slipping past the best law enforcement agencies all over the world for years. There's comfort in numbers, I suppose, and a postmortem on a fuckup is always educational, in a painful kind of way."

"Happens a lot with him."

"It's unavoidable that we don't win 'em all, operating in the dark half the time and the other half with sketchy information. I love it when the jobs go off without a hitch, but that's seldom happened in the twenty years I've been working for Avalon. Something always goes wrong."

"I messed up on this last one, Ben. Pretty bad."

With a sigh, Ben sat back, chair springs creaking. "You didn't mess up that bad, so knock off the pity party attitude. All things considered, you did damn well. No one died, right?"

Griffith snorted. "I can always count on you to put things in perspective."

"Kennedy is safe and sound, and her life is back to normal. Hanson's talking, so we know the names of the people who were behind the Munich forgeries. The police are already starting to round them up. We may have lost von Lahr and the manuscript, but we have enough new leads and names to shut down the ring. That's what matters."

"Yeah, I know." His arm ached, and he wondered if maybe he'd been too quick to ditch that sling. "Did Hanson know where von Lahr's base was, like he'd claimed?"

"He gave us an address to a warehouse in Rio. It was empty by the time the local police got there. I'd expected as much. But if it's of any help, Ms. Kennedy will see justice for those who killed her husband. She may never know it, but you will."

Griffith nodded, looking away from Ben's sharp eyes at the second mention of Fiona. "So did Hanson finally get around to explaining what the hell he was doing that night?"

"He hasn't admitted anything outright, but I suspect it's pretty much as you already guessed. He was sick and tired of the running and the hiding, and he thought if he lured everybody into one spot with the promise of revealing secrets, he could kill all those who knew about him and be free to get on with his life."

"Ambitious of him."

Ben sent him a sour look. "Everything else Hanson told us about von Lahr, we already knew, so nothing useful on that end. Von Lahr must've suspected Hanson was lying to him all along, and my guess is that he showed up just to play his usual games and make a point of demonstrating how useless we are in his eyes."

"It worked. I was feeling goddamn useless, lying there passed out on the ground."

"It could've been a lot worse. He could've had a clear shot at you guys and you'd all be dead." Ben ran a hand through his short hair, then let out his breath. "One of these days he'll get too cocky and make a mistake, and then we'll nail him. It's just a matter of being patient."

And that was his cue, if there ever was one.

Griffith sat straighter. "About that . . . there's another reason I came to see you in person."

Ben pursed his lips. "I suspected as much. Go ahead."

"I think I want out of Avalon."

Ben nodded. "I was afraid you'd say that."

"I used to enjoy the work. Hell, I lived for it. If you'd asked me ten years ago, or even five years ago, if I'd ever want out, I'd have laughed in your face.

But everything changed after Hamburg." Griffith leaned forward, his hands clasped. "I think if I'd caught him this time, I wouldn't have brought him back alive. And no matter what he's done, it's not my right to execute him on the spot."

"I can understand why you'd feel that way. To want revenge is only human, Grif."

Griffith looked down, focusing on his hands as he flexed them. His right hand was stiff and numb, and he still couldn't make a fist. "I've done what I could to see justice done, to try to right a few wrongs out of so many that can't ever be righted. I've been shot, knifed, beaten up . . . I've lost touch with my family, and I don't even have a place to call home—just post office boxes and apartments around the world that change from one year to the next. Once, that was enough for me. But now I want something more, and I don't think I can have it if I stay with Avalon."

"Fifteen years is a long time to do this kind of work. It takes a toll. I can't deny that." Ben leaned back again. "But we've invested a lot of time and money in your training. Your experience is valuable. I'd hate to lose that."

"And I'd hate leaving you when you're already shorthanded. Then there are the others. I don't want them thinking I've turned my back on them, because I still care about the job. I still believe in what we're doing, I just—"

"Can't do it anymore," Ben finished quietly. "In the end, that's the only thing that matters. You're no good to me or your team if you can't give your two hundred percent and then some. But I need to ask you this: is what you're feeling now real and not just a by-product of frustration? Can you be sure you'll still be feeling this way five years from now? Ten?"

That was the crux of Griffith's problem, why it had taken him so long to come talk about this. "I can't be sure about anything. Nobody can, but I know what I feel and what I want, and I believe that it will be what I want five years from now, ten years . . . and for the rest of my life."

Less than a week before she was to fly to the Bahamas, Fiona stepped off a plane in Seattle and took a cab to Sheridan Expeditions.

She had overheard enough to put a few pieces together and find the wilderness expedition travel agency. That had been the easy part; gathering her courage to confront the man who owned it had been harder.

For weeks she'd debated the wisdom of making such a trip, suspecting that she'd never get anywhere near Sheridan—and even if she did, that he'd deny knowing Griffith or anything else related to this mysterious Avalon.

But the new year would soon begin, and she didn't

want to start it out with unfinished business. All she really wanted to know was if Griffith had survived his injuries. Nothing more. After what he'd done to keep her safe, it was the least she could do to make this trip.

Still, as the taxi pulled into the drive that led to Sheridan Expeditions Corporate Offices, the jitters had a firm hold. She stood at the main entrance for several minutes, taking in her surroundings as she calmed her nerves.

The building itself was beautiful. Located on prime real estate along the coast, the three-storied rustic log structure was large enough to give the impression of a thriving company yet still blend in with the office buildings around it, nothing about it hinting at its secrets.

Once through the main doors, she found that the interior carried through the log cabin theme in a very expensive, high-tech way. It fit the theme of wilderness travel, with everything wide, bright, and airy. Lots of wood in warm, golden pine tones and simple furniture that looked expensive despite its rough-hewn style. All the little decorating extras complemented that outdoorsy feel, especially the prints hanging on the walls. The focus was on world travel, with large framed posters of exotic or rugged wilderness locales, from lush jungles and arid deserts to underwater worlds and snow-topped mountain ranges.

A woman sat at the main desk opening mail, and she smiled as Fiona approached her. "Hello. May I help you?"

Here goes nothing . . .

"Yes, thank you. I want to arrange for a tour and would like to research options and ask questions. I'd like to speak to Mr. Sheridan, if I may."

"Do you have an appointment?"

"No. I was in the area and thought I'd try dropping by."

"I'm sorry, but Mr. Sheridan is a very busy man. If you'd like to make an appointment, I can—"

"No, that won't be possible. It's very important, though, that I speak with him. Can you at least call him and tell him that Fiona Kennedy-McMahon is here to see him? I think he'll see me if you tell him who I am."

The woman looked uncertain.

"Please," Fiona said again, quietly. "It's very important. If he says no, though, I'll leave."

"I'll try. But I'm not even sure if he's in the office."

"That's all right. I know I'm taking that chance."

"Wait over there, please, while I make the call. And again, you are . . . ?"

"Fiona Kennedy-McMahon. It's important you use the exact name."

The receptionist gave her a sharp, suspicious look and then jotted down the message.

Fiona headed to the waiting area and sat on one of the overstuffed chairs, with its log frame and striped upholstery in dark, earthy tones.

What a cheery, bustling place. So open and bright, to hide such dark secrets.

So far, so good, Griffith thought. Ben seemed to understand that he needed either to get out completely or to have more time to get his head straight.

He hadn't had to bring Fiona into the conversation at all, or try to explain her part in his decision.

"Grif, there *are* options we can discuss. Maybe you just need a long break, but I could transfer you out of the more dangerous regions. You might consider training, providing or acting as a consultant."

None of these suggestions roused any enthusiasm. "It's something to think about."

Ben leaned forward. "Give it more time. And then if you—" The buzz of his intercom interrupted him, and he scowled. "Ellie, I don't want to be disturbed right now."

"There's a Fiona Kennedy-McMahon in the lobby who asked to talk to you. I thought you'd want to know."

Griffith sat up straight. "Jesus Christ!" Panic seized him, then faded as he smiled. "I told you she was a smart one. Good with details."

"Maybe a little too smart," Ben retorted. "This could be a problem."

Sobering at the reminder, Griffith said, "Ben, she can't know I'm here. That would—"

"Just calm down a minute." To the intercom, he said, "Did she ask to speak with me specifically?"

"Yes."

"Is she making a scene? Can we have security toss her out?"

"I didn't get the impression from the receptionist that she's causing any trouble. She's merely insistent that she talk with you."

Ben glanced at Griffith. "Tell Ms. Kennedy that I'll be down to see her shortly."

"Will do." The connection ended.

Silence filled the office, and Ben finally said, "What do you want me to do if she asks about you? Do you want to see her?"

Slumping back in his chair, Griffith ran a hand tiredly over his face. "No."

Not now, he wasn't ready. He wasn't sure if he'd ever be ready.

Ben eyed him for a moment longer, then stood. "All right. I'll get rid of her for you and you can hide away up here."

The receptionist was on the phone again, occasionally glancing at Fiona—and then her eyebrows shot upward. After she hung up, she stood and called over to Fiona, "Ma'am, Mr. Sheridan is on his way down now."

He was coming down *to her?*

It took her a few seconds to find her voice. "Thank you very much. I appreciate your help."

"You're welcome," the receptionist said politely, then returned to opening the huge stacks of mail.

While Fiona waited, she glanced through various travel magazines left lying on the end tables, but she couldn't concentrate enough to read any of the articles.

Finally, she heard the receptionist say brightly, "Hello, Mr. Sheridan! Yes, she's right over there. The one in the gray suit."

Fiona slowly stood as Ben Sheridan walked toward her.

He wasn't quite what she'd expected. A tall, rangy, dark-haired man with shrewd, dark eyes, he had the kind of comfortable good looks that wouldn't threaten other men yet fascinated women, who'd spend hours trying to figure out what exactly about him was so attractive. He'd look as good in jeans and T-shirts as he did in his dark suit.

He appeared to be a successful businessman in his late thirties or early forties who, when not making his stockholders happy, would be content spending his days off with a cold beer and the latest in fishing pole technology. No one would ever suspect him of running an organizational hub of a secret international group of mercenaries.

"Ms. Kennedy," he said, holding out his hand.

She took it, shaking it in a firm grip before releasing it. "Thank you for seeing me."

He nodded. "Would you like something to drink? Coffee or soda? We have a cafeteria. I can send for whatever you'd like."

"I'm not thirsty, but thank you."

"How about we go over there so we can talk more privately?"

"Perhaps your office—"

"It's occupied." He led her firmly to the far side of the reception area. "I don't think this will take long."

They sat, and after several seconds passed in silence, she realized he wouldn't make the first move.

"I'm sure you have an idea of why I'm here, so I'll get right to the point. I would like to know about Griffith Laughton. I want to know how he is."

Sheridan's dark eyes were unreadable, although his expression was politely attentive. "It's against policy for me to give out private information about current company employees."

"Of course, I understand that."

She also understood that anything he told her wouldn't be straightforward: she'd have to interpret what he said and what he didn't say.

"Current employee" implied that Griffith had survived, at least.

"I know he was hurt, and I was concerned about him. And the others. It's been bothering me, so I wanted to find out."

"I can sympathize, but I still can't share that kind of information about my employees."

At that, she smiled a little. "It's quite the business you run here, Mr. Sheridan. As I'm sure you've gathered, I overheard a few things you probably wish I hadn't."

He smiled back but said nothing.

"I want you to know that I do appreciate everything you've done for me, and I won't cause you any trouble. I understand what you're working to accomplish."

"Thank you."

Facing Sheridan's gaze wasn't any easier than facing Griffith's. This man was far more dangerous than he looked, which really didn't come as a surprise.

She stood. "I'll be going, then, as I think I have the answers I came for."

Sheridan stood as well. "I'm glad to hear that."

"Please don't tell Griffith I came here asking for him. He . . . I think it would trouble him, and I don't want that."

She thought a look of surprise crossed his face, but it was too quick for her to be sure. After a moment, he said, "I'll have Lynne call you a cab."

"Thank you," Fiona said, and extended her hand.

He took her hand in his again and shook it firmly. "Good luck to you, Ms. Kennedy. I hope everything works out for you."

Then he left, spoke to the receptionist, and without a backward glance, disappeared through a big, log-hewn door.

"Well," Fiona whispered, "that was that."

While waiting for Ben to return, Griffith paced the office. His hands were shaking. Was he so afraid of seeing her that he was reduced to hiding like a coward? Especially since what he *really* wanted was to see her?

Ben wasn't gone long, and when he returned he wasn't smiling. He sat down at his desk without a word.

That sudden change of mood made Griffith uneasy.

"Did you see her?"

"Yes. A very pretty woman. You were right; the file pictures didn't do her justice. The color of her hair is amazing."

The comment brought a hundred memories rushing back, and Griffith had to look away.

The pale skin, the dusting of freckles all over her body, and how that hair had looked spread over a pillow, over the sheets. Over him. He remembered what it had felt like to be inside her.

And he remembered so much more: Fiona telling

him she didn't want him to sit at the window alone, her forthright honesty and her bravery. He recalled the shifting emotions reflected in her green eyes, from passion to wonder, from anger to fear and determination. He remembered how she'd clocked him in the shop rather than bawling or breaking into hysterics; squatted in the helicopter hatch and fired his grandpa's Magnum—wildly, missing by a mile, but still trying.

Looking back up, he smiled. "She shot at von Lahr. Did I tell you that?"

Ben rubbed his thumb across his bottom lip, a habit whenever he was deep in thought. "Rico told me. Diva was impressed with her as well, and Noonie thinks she's some kind of saint. From what I can tell, she sounds like a remarkable woman."

"That she is." He shifted, frowning, then sighed. To hell with his pride. "Did she ask about me?"

"I can't tell you that."

Griffith went still. "What do you mean, you can't tell me? Either she did or she didn't."

"She talked to me in confidence and asked that I keep that confidence." Despite Ben's neutral expression, a glint of amusement sparkled in his eyes.

And that was all it took for Griffith to understand. Something warm and light washed over him, and he couldn't help smiling. "She asked about me. She came all the way here just to ask about me."

That she'd come here made all the difference in his decision. More than he could ever make Ben understand—but he tried anyway.

"She came here for *me*, Ben. Nobody's ever done that before. Not like this. You and the others have always been there for me, but this isn't the same. She's not one of my teammates, who come and go as the years pass. It's—"

"It goes deeper than that," Ben cut in quietly. "I understand what you're saying. And I hope she returns the sentiment when you go see her."

Startled, Griffith asked, "How did you know I was—"

"I'm not blind. Your feelings are written all over your face. And considering this is *you* we're talking about, that's not something I take lightly."

"She's a . . . genuinely nice person. I know she might've come here only to see if I was okay, and maybe it doesn't mean anything beyond that. I wouldn't blame her if she didn't want to have anything to do with me."

"I think you might be surprised about that."

It wasn't like Ben to say these kinds of things. The man didn't have a sentimental bone in his body.

"I hope you're right." Griffith stood, hands shoved into the pockets of his jeans, and moved to the window overlooking the ocean. "But even if she doesn't want anything to do with me, I need to move on. I have a family I've barely talked to over the past ten years. There are fences I may never mend."

He watched the sunlight sparkle on the water and seagulls dip and glide in the blue sky. "And I need to find a place and a life for myself. A little treasure all my own, for once."

"I understand. Look, I'm not going to stop you or try to talk you out of it. But if you leave Avalon behind completely, you can't come back. You can't make any attempt to contact your former teammates or me, in any capacity other than the owner of a travel company."

This was the hardest part. He could see why Ben would shut him out, but it still hurt. Avalon had been the closest thing he'd had to a family for a very long time. "I know. It'd be too risky to have me on the outside but still involved. Especially now that you know someone's traced you and even cracked into our security."

Ben shrugged, but Griffith didn't buy into the unconcerned act. "Hanson's in no position to talk to anybody about it, is he? And I have a feeling von Lahr has had his suspicions about me for a while. It was only a matter of time before someone made the connection. Avalon's been around for almost a hundred years, it's happened before, and it'll happen again. You can't keep secrets forever."

"Except the name of the Big Boss." Griffith walked back and leaned his hip against Ben's desk. "Do *you* even know who you really work for? Who gives you the money and the resources and saves our asses when we get in too deep?"

Ben grinned. "Nope."

"And if you did, you'd never tell me."

"That's right. Otherwise, I'd have to kill you."

It was a joke with enough truth in it that it carried a hint of danger.

"I'd like at least to know if it's a man or a woman. Can you tell me that much?"

"I think you can comfortably live out the rest of your life without ever having to know."

"I knew you'd say that."

Griffith hesitated, then unholstered his Jericho guns and placed them on Ben's desk. He could've walked out with them and it wouldn't have mattered, but it was his way of making a clean break.

Then he dropped a fat envelope next to the guns. "Passports and IDs for all the other versions of Griffith Laughton. After today, there's only the one."

"Right." Ben stood and reached out his hand. As Griffith shook it, he asked, "You won't reconsider and at least stay behind to train new recruits?"

"If I leave, I leave. It's not something I can do halfway." Griffith motioned to his shoulder. "I wouldn't be much good to you. My range of motion is gone, I'll never be able to shoot like I used to. It'd make me a liability."

"That doesn't make losing you any easier. But as I said, I've seen this coming for a while. I wish you nothing but the best, Griffith. And I hope she'll give you the chance you deserve."

Ben smiled, then slapped Griffith on his back—but not too hard. "Give it your best shot, and it'll work out. You just have to believe."

And where had he heard that before?

"If you hurry, maybe you can catch her at the airport."

Griffith swallowed the lump in his throat; the last thing he wanted was some maudlin drama. He wanted to walk out of this office with his pride intact and his eyes dry. "Thanks, but I don't think the airport would be a good place for what I have in mind."

The intercom buzzed, followed by Ellie's apologetic voice. "Sorry for interrupting again, but the airport courier is here with a bunch of packages. Shall I wait or—"

"It's all right. We're done in here." Ben smoothly swept the guns and envelope into a drawer, out of sight. "You can send him in."

So this was it. The end.

It hadn't been easy, but it hadn't been as hard as he'd thought, either. With a last smile, Griffith said, "Take it easy. On your next bet with your brother-in-law, I hope you whip his ass."

Ben laughed as the door swung open, and Griffith turned away. Time to make his exit with some kind of dignity.

The courier, on the way in, stopped short when she saw him. Pretty, pert, college-aged, she couldn't be used to seeing what equated to the walking dead. She stared, mouth open, and blurted, "Whoa. You okay, mister?"

"Yeah, I'm okay."

"You sure?"

Hearing her genuine concern, he smiled again. It seemed to be the question of the day. "Never been better."

Griffith turned and left Sheridan Expeditions, knowing he'd never come back.

Twenty-eight

❖

FIONA SIGHED AND LOOKED AT THE CLOCK. IN TWENTY minutes she would lock up for two weeks, because tomorrow she was getting on a plane and heading to the sunny Bahamas.

It was raining again, and she was so damn tired of the rain. It always made her think of Griffith.

Over a month had passed since she'd last seen him, and the memory of him coming between her and the rifle was still disturbingly fresh. It would come upon her at the strangest times, leaving her staring off into the distance so that her friends and customers sometimes gave her odd looks.

They attributed her behavior to emotional trauma from the break-in of her store, an unexpected benefit of the story the devious folks at Avalon had cooked up for her. Everybody had accepted the story. Her search for a mention of it in the newspapers had led to a tiny side article about a bookstore break-in. So mundane; just another footnote of crime in the City of the Angels.

She should tell Cassie and Diana what had really happened but couldn't bring herself to do so yet. When she was ready, she would fess up.

The closest she'd come to telling them was when she'd called Cassie to quiz her about the freelancer on her staff, the one who she'd mentioned also worked for a wilderness travel tour company.

"You mean Russ Noble?" Cassie had said, puzzled. "Yeah, he still works for me off and on. Why do you ask?"

"Do you remember the name of the company he works for?"

"Sheridan Expeditions. It's in Seattle, I think. Again, why?"

Fiona had dodged answering, which had alarmed Cassie, and Fiona had ended up promising to come for a visit soon.

Cassie's answer had led Fiona to call Sheridan Expeditions, although she hadn't really expected Griffith to be there. Still, she'd had to try.

The receptionist informed her there was no one in the office named Griffith Laughton. When Fiona asked to speak to Russ Noble instead, the receptionist told her to hold and then transferred her call.

A little panicked, Fiona hung up before Noble answered. Then she called the police department and asked for the patrolman who'd returned her to her shop. Not surprisingly, she was told that no Balthasar Sherman worked for the LAPD.

She'd even made a trip to Torrance Helicopter Tours, ostensibly to ask about tours, curious to see if she'd recognize anyone or spot anything that looked . . . well, out of place. Or anything that held any connection to Griffith. Again, it was a dead end.

From Wednesday's trip to Sheridan Expeditions, she at least knew Griffith had survived.

At this point, she simply had to accept that she'd never learn the truth about him, or even what had happened that strange night to cause so much trouble.

Maybe she was better off not knowing. But times like this, with the gentle patter on the windows, she still half-expected to see Griffith walk out of the book stacks in his leather bomber jacket, his blue eyes bright and warm, cheeks grooving as he smiled.

Something large and furry brushed against her ankles, and she looked down at Faustus—who'd been thoroughly cared for, in her completely cleaned apartment, while she'd been off adventuring.

"I'm pathetic, aren't I?" she crooned at the big

cat, and Faustus rumbled and purred and butted his head against her leg again. "Who needs men, anyway? So what if all my friends are blissfully happy with their mates and humping away like bunnies? I don't need that, I have you." She frowned. "And books. And a job. And accounting software I still haven't upgraded. I'm in avoidance mode, Faustus. Very sad."

Faustus meowed, this time his deeper, growling meow that sounded like "Feed me now, or I'll scratch out your eyes."

She bent down to retrieve the bag of kitty kibbles and heard a knock on the shop's front door.

She sighed in irritation. Why was there always one customer who showed up just before she locked up? And why were they knocking? The sign plainly said OPEN.

She straightened, then headed to the door and swung it open.

And froze.

"Hi."

Griffith . . . it was *Griffith*.

"I should've called first, but I wasn't sure if you'd want to see me. I figured it'd be best if I came by in person."

She could hardly breathe, and the silence stretched on as she stood frozen, hand still clutching the doorknob.

"So," he said after a moment, a familiar half smile curving the corner of his mouth. "Are you going to invite me in out of the rain, or what?"

He was soaked through, droplets running down his face, flattening his dark hair, dampening his jeans, and slickening his leather jacket so that it gleamed under the lights.

She snapped out of her shock and stepped back, opening the door wider.

"Of course you can come in. I'm sorry, I didn't think I'd . . . I wasn't sure if . . ." She let out her breath in a short, shaky sigh. "You have managed to take me completely by surprise."

Griffith stepped in and shut the door behind him. He was so tall, so broad-shouldered, so achingly good-looking. Memories rushed back with such force that she had to look away, desperate to regain her composure.

"I know. Sorry about that, Fiona."

A hundred questions crowded in on her, and she blurted out the one that chimed loudest: "I had no idea if you were even alive or dead, or how badly you were hurt. They wouldn't tell me anything!"

"I know," he repeated, his voice gentle. "But I'm here now. You can see I'm alive and well."

"You were hurt, I know you were. I *saw* it."

And his grandpa's jacket had a patch on the right sleeve.

"Yeah, but I'm okay. Not moving too fast yet, but I'm okay."

She looked over every inch of him but couldn't see anything obviously wrong. "For real?"

He smiled. "For real."

"I have so many things I want to say . . . and I don't even know where to begin." God, she hoped that didn't sound like a wail.

"Take as long as you need. I'm not going anywhere."

She searched his face, trying to decipher what he meant, then flipped the OPEN sign to CLOSED, locked the door, and pulled the blinds. "I think I'll close a little early tonight."

Motioning for him to follow, Fiona headed back toward her desk. "I could use a drink right about now. Too bad I have only coffee and bottled water."

"Hey, Faustus." Griffith bent to rub the cat's head. "You been taking good care of your mistress?"

"It's the other way around, but we won't discuss that. It's that male pride thing."

"Ah. Something I can understand."

How calm they both sounded.

Or maybe *he* was calm; he had a lot more practice than she did at dealing with sudden crises.

He sat in the chair where he'd sat the first time he'd come to the shop. Faustus, rumbling happily for whatever reason, arched his back and rubbed against Griffith's legs.

"So," she said. "I was in Seattle on Wednesday. Talking to your boss."

She was surprised to see him smile. "I know. I was there."

"You were *there?* Then why didn't you come down and talk to me? I have been sick with worry over you! The least you could've—"

"I was afraid to," he interrupted. "I wasn't . . . ready."

He, of all people, had been afraid to see her?

Confused, she looked down. "The other people who were with you, Noonie and Rico, are they all right?"

"Yes."

"I'm glad to hear that. And that other man, Oliver Hanson. What happened to him?"

"He made it, but I don't know where he is now or what will happen to him."

"That's okay. I don't want to know any more of the truth about Richard. Call me a coward, but I'm going to do my best to remember the good he did and bury the bad."

"You're not any kind of coward, Fiona. Believe me."

She smiled, meeting his gaze. "Says the man who told me never to believe a word he said."

"That guy doesn't exist anymore. This one, though—you can believe him."

"Ah." She wished he would just come out and say why he was here. "Does this mean you've thought about trying to find that something more in your life?"

"It was time. Past time. It's something I should've done years ago, but you were the one who helped me make up my mind."

"I did?" She arched a brow. "How?"

Griffith looked uncomfortable and for once, uncertain. "Because you believed in me. It sounds melodramatic, I guess, but nobody ever told me that before. Not the way you did. Since I had plenty of time to think while I was healing up, I decided if I was going to make a change, it was now or never. What kind of change that'll be, I haven't a clue."

Fiona was too stunned by his admission to speak.

After a moment, Griffith added, "I was hoping you could use an extra hand around this place. If not, I'll be on my way. No strings attached to the offer, incidentally. You owe me nothing."

"I like the idea of a little extra help around the shop," Fiona said slowly, hoping she was correctly hearing what he'd left unsaid. "There's a lot that's not getting done because I don't have the time or the know-how. Among your skills, would making heads or tails out of accounting software be included?"

His entire body relaxed as he leaned back against the chair. "I don't know, but I can give it a try."

"How are you with repairs? A place this old always has something breaking or needing repair."

"That I can handle."

"And I was thinking I'd like to expand the non-book stock. I'd need help for that, too. Looking around, tracking down antiques . . . it takes time."

"Sounds interesting." He smiled. "My last job involved tracking down old things, and I was pretty good at it."

Fiona returned his smile. "This would be a lot less exciting, though. You'd be all right with that?"

"Yeah, I think I would."

Fiona stood, knowing that he was deliberately leaving this in her hands; he wouldn't pressure her. She walked around the desk, stopped by his chair, and gently brushed her fingers along the side of his face. "I just wanted to touch you, to see for myself that you're really safe." She paused. "I missed you, Griffith."

"Same here." He covered her hand with his and squeezed lightly as he came to his feet.

"It wasn't *all* bad, you know, our time together. Parts of it were very nice." She could've sworn a dull red flush darkened his face. "Though I could've done without the blood and the guns."

When he didn't say anything, she added, "Was it hard for you to leave? I don't know much about the people you worked for, but I wouldn't think it would be easy to walk away."

"They understood. It's done."

"Seems to me you're taking a rather big risk on a woman you hardly know."

"Back at you." He moved closer.

It felt so good to be with him again. Under all the deceptions and half-truths, what had started between them was real. New, tentative, even fragile, but real.

"Baby steps," she said, leaning against him so that she could soak in his warmth and lean strength. "We've gotta start somewhere."

Griffith held her close, his arms tight around her. "And I'd like to start here."

Then he did what she'd wanted him to do from almost the moment he'd walked through the door: he kissed her.

It was a slow, gentle kiss that gradually warmed her from head to toe. Gentleness gave way to a heated urgency, and Griffith broke the kiss to murmur, "How about we go out for dinner? Or if you'd prefer, I'll take you to that sofa bed upstairs."

Fiona smiled. "Not so fast. You're going to have to work your way back into my good graces; I'm not going to make it *that* easy." She cleared her throat. "At least not today."

He grinned, not looking in the least disappointed. "So it's dinner then. Where to?"

"Surprise me. Do you think you're up to the challenge?"

"Let's find out."

"Oooh, I like that. By the way, do you have a suitcase?"

Griffith blinked in surprise. "Uh, yeah. Why?"

"Because I'm going to the Bahamas tomorrow. Would you like to come along?"

His eyes widened, then he laughed. "Hell, yes. Someone's gotta protect you from all those easy scuba instructors."

Epilogue

❖

Valentine's Day, one year later . . .

"HAVE YOU EVER BEEN TO WYOMING?" FIONA ASKED as Griffith pulled into the long, gravel drive that led to Cassie's place.

"No." He glanced at her. "I'm a city boy. Wide open spaces don't hold much appeal."

"The country has its charm."

"Not for me. I don't want to live anyplace where going out for a gallon of milk means a road trip through snowdrifts as high as my shoulders."

"You're exaggerating. It's not really that bad." She eyed him, then reached over and squeezed his hand. "Are you nervous?"

"About what?"

"Making a good impression on my friends."

"Maybe," he admitted. "A little."

Fiona smiled and gazed out ahead. There was snow all around, and it looked bitterly cold. The only greenery she could see was hardy, wind-scrubbed pines, a far cry from the palm trees of L.A.

This trip marked the first time Griffith would meet Cassie and Diana, and by extension, Alex, Jack, and the rest of Cassie's clan. Fiona had known them all for ages, and even *she* was still intimidated at times by the ebullient crush of the Parkers. And while she was quite fond of Diana's husband—Jack Austin was a born charmer—she didn't know Alex Martinelli, Cassie's fiancé, very well. Like Cassie's brother, Wyatt, Alex was rougher around the edges.

"It's a party, so everyone will be in a good mood," Fiona said, reassuring him.

The reason for today's celebration was Cassie's official engagement announcement. Cassie and Alex had finally figured out they were the only people on the planet who could put up with each other, which gave Cassie an excuse for a party and Diana and Fiona an excuse to come visit.

Up ahead Fiona could see the Parker ranch, in all its homely, haphazard charm, the result of multiple generations adding on and rebuilding without much thought for aesthetics. Still, she'd always loved the place for its simple, welcoming warmth.

There were dozens of cars and trucks already

parked outside the house and next to the fossil shop and the big, blocky warehouse that was Cassie's lab.

"Maybe while I'm here I can see Trixie," Griffith said as he switched off the engine.

"Just ask. I'm sure Cassie will be happy to show off her latest baby," Fiona said wryly, thinking of the troublesome infant *Tyrannosaurus rex* Cassie had discovered the previous year. "Trixie is very much a part of the family, despite having been dead for some seventy million years and belonging to a species that would've munched on us like appetizers. Alex has been known to show baby pictures."

Griffith laughed. "Thanks for the warning."

"Do you need a refresher course on who's who?"

"Nope. I think I have it all straight." He rubbed at his jaw, grinning. "I've been familiar with a bunch of them for a while."

"No mentioning that," Fiona said tartly as she got out of the car. "I don't want my friends to know I'm sleeping with a man who was spying on them."

"I *personally* wasn't spying on them." Griffith put his arm around her as they headed up the steps.

Then Cassie's son, Travis, whipped open the front door and yelled, "Mom, Auntie Fiona's here!"

"My God, look at you!" Fiona hugged him, then pulled back and stared at him in amazement. "When did you grow up to be such a handsome young man?"

Travis turned a little pink. "I'm a junior this year."

As he ushered them into the house, filled with the cheery din of conversation and laughter and the wonderfully rich smells of food cooking, Travis looked curiously at Griffith.

Fiona said, "Grif, this is Cassie's son, Travis. Travis, this is Griffith."

"Your boyfriend, huh?" Travis grinned. "I'm jealous. You're stealing my favorite auntie."

"I'm not your aunt! Stop saying that. It makes me sound old."

Still grinning, Travis led them into the family room, where everyone was gathered among a shocking volume of pink and white crepe-paper streamers and heart-shaped balloons.

"Dear God," Fiona said. "I feel like I've walked back in time twenty years to a high school slumber party."

Cassie stood with a shriek and dashed forward, her arms open. "Fiona, you're here! Now the party can begin for real!"

A wildly emotional few moments followed, involving a few tears, many hugs, and lots of people asking a steady barrage of questions. Through it all Fiona kept an eye on Griffith, taking it in with a smile on his face.

She could tell the laughing, friendly chaos was something he'd long wanted to be a part of, and it pleased her that she could give it to him.

Little by little they were settling into a lovely normalcy, just any other couple in love and working out the kinks of living together. The life he'd once led, and those terrifying two days she'd shared it with him, seemed like a distant dream now.

"So this is the new man in your life," said Cassie. "I'm glad to finally meet you, Griffith. Come sit down and say hello to everybody else. We're all dying to hear more about you."

Fiona exchanged glances with Griffith, and he smiled slowly.

"Hey. None of that secretive mushy glances stuff. Only Alex and I are allowed to be mushy. Not that we will be, I swear it, and I apologize for all the hideous pink. Wyatt thought it would be funny. I suspect it's some sort of revenge for all our squabbles, but he swears it's not."

Wyatt, Cassie's younger brother, was on the couch next to Travis, looking smug and amused.

After that, Griffith was introduced to Cassie's mother, her lab crew, and a few of Alex's friends whom Fiona had never met, either. Then Cassie wisely handed Griffith off to his own kind: "This is my fiancé, Alex, and this is Jack Austin, who's married to the blond bombshell over there."

She pointed at Diana, who, busy eating potato chips, waggled her fingers in a greeting.

"And this useless waste of air is Russ Noble."

Cassie motioned at a good-looking, dark-haired young man who plainly had Native Americans in his family tree. "I'm mad at Russ right now because he's leaving me to work for someone else."

"Someone who'll pay me a lot more than you can," Russ retorted, grinning. "An independently wealthy paleontologist."

As Griffith and Russ talked, Fiona became aware of an undercurrent of shared knowledge between them.

"So it sounds like you got a good job offer," Griffith said, his smile widening. "Congratulations."

"Yeah, I did." Russ smiled back. "Thanks."

"And a better salary, too. That's always a bonus."

"It is." Russ nodded, a glint of amusement in his dark eyes.

"I wish you the best of luck with the new job. I hope it's all you want it to be. I mean that."

The tenor of Russ's laugh convinced Fiona that her hunch about what they were really talking about had been correct.

"It wasn't an offer I went looking for, but you know how it is. When a good opportunity comes around, you take it."

Griffith caught Fiona's gaze and held it. "Yeah, I know how it is. Good opportunities are rare."

"I'm glad I had a chance to meet you, Griffith. I've heard a lot about you."

Griffith raised a brow. "All of it favorable, I hope."

"Near legendary might be a better way to put it."

"Really?" Diana suddenly inserted herself between the two men, and Cassie, Alex, and Jack were now watching Griffith and Russ with no small amount of interest. "I think I'll enjoy getting to know you a little better, Griffith. Fiona has been rather secretive about you."

Cassie laughed. "That's because she's embarrassed at having sex with a man she'd only known for a few hours."

As heat rushed to Fiona's cheeks, Griffith said, "I'm the very persuasive type. And I like cats."

Exasperated, Fiona jabbed him with her elbow and then glared at Cassie. "I can't believe you just said that!"

Unrepentant, Cassie grinned. "Wow, I'm glad someone besides me gets that sharp elbow. Griffith, I am delighted you're with Fiona. You'll save me from many years of bruises on my arms."

Despite her embarrassment, Fiona couldn't help smiling. "Only because your mouth outruns your common sense, more times than not."

Alex winked at Cassie. "That's part of her charm."

"Spoken like a man in love," Jack said, and laughed.

"Why are you laughing when you say that word?" Diana asked archly. "And be very careful how you answer."

"You are all crazy," Travis pronounced in utter seriousness. "And chicks are scary. I'm never getting married."

"Ah, you say that now. Just you wait." Alex picked up his beer can and held it high. "Let's get this celebration rolling and make a toast!"

Fiona drew closer to Griffith as Cassie raised her beer and exclaimed, "To love!"

Alex clinked his beer can to hers. "And all that other mushy shit. Where would we be without it?"

Griffith pulled Fiona against him and whispered, "In a place where we don't want to be. Have I told you lately that I love you?"

She smiled. "Yes, but you can tell me again. I don't mind."

Diana had raised her wineglass. "And here's to marriage! It's wonderful."

Jack touched his beer to his wife's wine. "And she's not just talking about the sex."

"You taking notes, Wyatt? I think you could learn something," Russ called, but he lifted his beer along with the toast and said, "Hear, hear."

Wyatt echoed this, along with Travis, and then everybody turned to face Fiona and Griffith.

As he handed her a glass of wine, Fiona met his gaze and said, "Here's to always having a place to go home to, where the lights are always on."

Griffith touched his glass to hers. "And to second chances."

"Hear, hear!" Cassie agreed. "God knows we've all needed that at some point in our lives. And now that the serious stuff is done . . . let's eat!"

With several dozen people gathered around tables all over the room, conversation never ebbed, and Fiona was glad to see Griffith jump right in. Every now and then he and Russ Noble exchanged veiled references and innuendos, but no one except her seemed to notice.

As the night wound down, Fiona heard all about Trixie, about Alex and Cassie's plans to work together, and how Cassie's studies were progressing. She heard about Jack working to rebuild his research lab in New Orleans after the devastation of Hurricane Katrina, and that Diana was still tracking down antiques looted from several galleries in New Orleans. There was also good news: Diana's friend on the New Orleans police force, a good-looking blond detective named Bobby Halloran, was recently engaged.

"Thank God," Diana said wryly. "He needs a woman in his life to make sure he dresses right. I hope Emma burns all of his ties."

The laughter and celebrating continued unabated, and sometime after midnight Fiona realized Griffith was not in the main room. She went looking for him, and when she noticed his jacket was no longer hanging with all the others, she pulled on her coat and slipped outside.

He was standing on the front porch, leaning against the railing, hands in his coat pockets, looking up at the brilliant splash of stars in the sky.

She quietly stood beside him, and the pale puff of her breath mingled with his as he pulled her into his arms. Had he needed an escape from the cheerful din, or had he wanted to get her alone for a few moments?

"The stars are so much brighter away from the city. And there are so many of them." He was still looking upward. "I forget how many, until I see them like this."

"It's kind of humbling," she said softly, resting her head against his chest, hearing the solid, comforting beat of his heart.

"It makes me think."

Glancing up, Fiona saw a small smile lift the corner of his mouth. "Good thoughts, I hope."

"You have very nice friends."

"The best. And now they're your friends, too. For better or for worse, they'll adopt you as long as you're with me."

Griffith wrapped his arms more tightly around her, and from the warm, strong shelter of his embrace, she gave a little purr of contentment.

"That's just one more reason to make sure you keep me around for a long, long time."

She tipped her head toward his, and the intimate

heat that flared in his gaze made her hot. He bent, kissing her. At first it was a soft, gentle kiss, then it turned hungry and demanding, until nothing else existed in her world but his mouth on hers, his arms around her, and the hard warmth of his chest pressed against her.

After a moment she pulled back and said breathlessly, "Keep kissing me like that, and I guarantee I'll keep you around for a long, long time."

He grinned. "And just how long is a long time?"

Was he asking what she thought . . . ?

Anticipation tingled, and she said lightly, "I'm not sure. Did you have a time frame in mind?"

"How does forever sound?"

A rush of joy and excitement and wonder swept through her, and hot tears stung at the back of her eyes. "It sounds perfect, Grif."

He let out his held breath, then kissed her again. "Where I belong is here with you. Right now, five years from now, ten years . . . the rest of my life. I want to marry you, Fiona. What do you say?"

"Yes, yes!" With a laugh and a little bounce of excitement, Fiona slipped her hands under the back of his jacket, hugging him closer. "I thought you'd never ask."

Laughter rumbled deep in his chest.

"Me, too. And tonight I started wondering what the hell I was waiting for. What they all have . . . I wanted it, too. Then it hit me, that there was nothing stopping me from having it. Not anymore." He paused. "And I was thinking, too, we could go back to that hotel in the Bahamas. Do you remember?"

Did she ever.

"Mmmm, yes, and the Bahamas sounds *really* good right about now."

"Cold? We can go back in and—"

"Not so fast." Fiona held him firmly in place, and as he rubbed his hand lazily along her back, she closed her eyes and smiled. "It's all warm and bright out here, too. Let's stay just like this . . . for a little while longer."

"As long as you'd like." Griffith kissed the top of her head. "I'm not going anywhere without you."

POCKET BOOKS
PROUDLY PRESENTS

the next book by author

Michele Albert

Coming soon from
Pocket Books

Turn the page for a preview!

"Will."

He turned, his shirt already unbuttoned—and his smile faded when he saw her face. "What's wrong?"

"That's something you need to tell me. What was all that earlier, with Vanessa? She acted as if . . ." Mia hesitated, frowning. "As if she was afraid of you."

He tossed his shirt aside, his expression faintly questioning. "I don't know what you're talking about."

Mia pushed up from the couch and walked over to the window, brushing aside the curtain panel. Outside, a few cars rolled by, and an old woman moved laboriously along the sidewalk with a panting Pomeranian on a pink leash. "I know you, Will, and there's something not right here."

She was too nervous to face him, but so acutely aware of his presence that she could hear each breath and the slightest brush of denim as he moved toward her, then stopped.

"Know me? You haven't seen me since I was

twenty-one, back when you were still the center of my life. That was a long time ago."

Taken aback by the cooler tone of his voice, Mia turned. He was standing only a few feet away, bare-chested, hands shoved in the pockets of his jeans, which hung low around his hips, revealing a flash of blue and khaki boxers.

After a moment, he added more gently, "If anything's not right here, it's probably just me not matching up to the memories. That's all."

Could the answer be so simple? She couldn't deny that her memories were probably rose-colored, and that things would naturally change in twelve years.

But no—it was more than that.

She shook her head. "That was fear in her eyes. I know fear when I see it. Why on earth would she be afraid of you?"

Will shrugged, his muscles moving with fluid strength—and despite her better intentions, desire snared her with a low, warm hook. It was all she could do not to go to him, letting the comfort of those strong arms help her to forget her worries. "You're imagining things."

Mia met his flat gaze. "I saw what I saw. Now answer me."

Silence—and the longer it stretched on, the deeper her hopes sank. If he had nothing to hide, he would've given her an explanation by now.

"You're not really here to do an article on Haddington Reproductions, are you?"

His eyes suddenly seemed sharper, and his brows drew together in a small frown. When she couldn't stand the tense silence any longer, she turned away—just as he let out his breath and said quietly, "No, I'm not."

She twisted back around, staring, uncertain she'd heard him correctly.

"I'm not a journalist." Despite his calm tone, she could see the sinews and veins standing out in the muscles of his arms and shoulders as he clenched and unclenched his fists in his pockets. "*Antiquities Review Magazine* isn't real. The website and phone calls, the portfolio . . . none of it was real."

Her mouth was dry, her throat tight. "So why are you here?"

"I'm investigating a suspected forgery—and a theft that's planned to take place very soon."

"You're a *cop*?"

"No. Not a Fed, either. I work for a private organization."

It was too much. Mia sank down on the couch. Confusion pressing down on her like a dulling weight, she whispered, "Is somebody going to steal the Eudoxia Reliquary? Or the entire collection?"

Forgery.

An ugly, ugly word; a gross perversion of her work,

her dedication to her craft. The implication hit her hard, making her tremble from head to toe.

"We believe so."

"And you came here to catch a thief."

"Yes." Will hesitated, running a hand through his hair, then leaned against the kitchen partition, arms folded across his chest. "I needed to find out who was involved."

Mia raised her head to meet his eyes, shocked. "You thought *I* was?"

"Initially everyone was a suspect. It was the usual process of elimination," he said evenly.

"You *slept* with me, thinking I was a thief?" She could hear her voice rising, sharpening.

"I was only doing what I had to do."

"How could you believe that of me?" She squeezed her eyes shut, forcing back hot, angry tears. "How could you do that to me?"

"It wasn't like that, Mia. I knew almost right away that you and Hugh weren't involved, and what happened between us . . . it wasn't something I planned." His gaze briefly slid away. "It just happened. And you wanted it as much as I did."

"*Almost* right away," she repeated. "But not from the start. You still had sex with me, thinking I was going to steal from my own client! My God, what would you have done if I'd—"

"If you'd been guilty, I'd have taken you down." To

his credit, he didn't avoid meeting her eyes and he didn't look happy. "I'd have done it, though it would've hurt like hell."

As if that made it all better.

A sudden sinking feeling swept over her. "You think it's Vanessa? No, no. It's not possible. I've worked with her for over five years. She's a friend."

"Mia, the facts I have are indisputable. I don't make mistakes like this, I assure you."

"Facts? What *facts?*"

"I can't share that kind of information with—"

"Vanessa would never do anything like that. I don't believe you."

"Not on her own, no, but she's not working alone." He made a gesture of frustration. "You have a lot of reasons to be mad at me, but not for this. You asked for the truth. I told you."

And right now, she wished she'd never asked him anything.

"If you're not a cop or with the FBI, then what kind of authority do you have?"

"I'm in private enforcement." He let out a sigh. "Technically, I'm a mercenary."

Mia stared. "A mercenary? Here, in *Boston?* Aren't mercenaries supposed to be prowling about third world countries or South American jungles or wherever there's dictators and nasty little wars?"

"The people I'm with specialize in retrieving

stolen art and antiquities, tracing forgeries, and tracking down bands of organized looters and smugglers, among other things. This takes us from Boston to London to Rome to Baghdad to Bangladesh. All over the world. Greed is the great equalizer."

She didn't miss the sarcasm—or what his admission really meant. "Then you're not operating within established laws."

Will resumed his nonchalant slouch, hands back in his pockets, but tension still etched every line of his body. He wasn't as casual about this as he wanted her to think.

"No, but neither do thieves and smugglers," he said, his tone terse. "These people are highly organized, well armed, and dangerous. They kill, and move freely across borders, which makes catching them an international nightmare—and they know that and use it to their advantage. Putting them out of business sometimes requires working outside the law."

"Vanessa—"

"Vanessa is a pawn," he interrupted, pushing away from the wall and walking toward Mia. "She's a weak, gullible woman who got involved with the wrong man, and right now all she cares about is proving to him how much she loves him. Even if that's through grand larceny."

Mia blinked. She'd met Vanessa's boyfriend several

times. Good-looking, a recent immigrant—he'd seemed nice enough, if too young. Mia's only worry had been that he was sponging off of Vanessa's income.

"Kos is a thief?"

"Kostandin Vulaj has ties to the Albanian mafia, and to the black market art trade in Europe and the States."

Mafia!

Mia went cold. "Has she . . . taken anything yet?"

"Not that I'm aware of, no."

"Then you can stop her before she does." Mia shot up from the couch, grabbing his upper arms. "She doesn't understand, Will. I'm sure of it. Talk to her, make her see reason. *Please.*"

"It's too late for that. I'm sorry." After a moment, he added quietly, "I need Vanessa to get to Vulaj; he can lead me to the person who set this up. If it's who we think it is, he is a very dangerous individual. These people belong in police custody, and what I'm doing will put them there. Legally."

Mia dropped her hands and stepped back, staring in disbelief. "You're using her," she whispered. "Just like him, you're using her."

Will's dark eyes narrowed. "You seem to be forgetting she's made this choice of her own free will. No one's holding a gun to her head and forcing her to steal from people who've put their trust in her. I'm not the one in the wrong here."

"You just told me she's been manipulated." She was still close enough that she could feel his heat—and the tension radiating off him so strongly it tingled along her skin. "You don't know what kind of hold he has over her."

"And it doesn't matter. If she'd walked away from this, then I'd have nothing on her and I'd have to let her go. But she hasn't done that, and she won't. Within the next twenty-four hours she'll make her move, and when she does, I'll be waiting."

"How can you so cold-bloodedly . . ." Mia trailed off, her voice shaking. "All right, I agree she's been stupid, she's pathetic, desperate to find someone to love her. But is that any excuse for you to stand aside and let her destroy her whole life just so you can catch her boyfriend? What gives you the right?"

"Jesus Christ, Mia," Will snapped back. "So she's had a shitty life! Lots of people have shitty lives, but most of them find other ways to cope than by stealing or killing. Bad luck with men doesn't give anyone the right to steal or kill."

"I am fully aware of that, Will. Don't patronize me."

He was shaking his head before she even finished speaking. "You don't know what these people are like, or what they're capable of. I do. Vanessa's not your friend. Not anymore."

Memories crowded her: lunches and gossipy tea

breaks, shopping and watching movies, long talks on the phone, at the bar . . .

"I can't believe that. She's been my friend for years. It can't all be a lie."

Concern briefly softened his frown. "If Vulaj told her to, Vanessa would put you in harm's way without thinking twice. The girlfriend thing is just an act now."

Anger, irrational and hot, made her lash out, "And you haven't been putting on an act from the minute we met?"

"Who are you really feeling sorry for here? Vanessa? Or yourself, because you've been played for a fool?"

Before she could answer, he moved toward her so quickly, and with such a focused, frightening intensity that Mia backed away rapidly, almost tripping over the coffee table.

Anger flared in his eyes. "I took a huge risk in telling you the truth. I did it because you deserved to know, because I felt guilty for deceiving you, and because once, a long time ago, I loved you."

Will forced her backward, slowly and steadily, and Mia put her hands on his chest to try to signal him to stop, that he was scaring her.

It didn't work. She bumped against the living room wall, the rough plaster scraping through the thin silk of her tank top.

"Giving you this information breaks every rule I've sworn to obey and puts me in a bad situation. One careless word from you, and it's all over. They'll disappear and surface somewhere else, and there'll be more and more victims until they're stopped. That's the reality," he said, his voice as hard and unyielding as the wall at her back.

She didn't understand how his eyes could be so cold and his body so warm. "There has to be another way."

"Don't even think about talking to her. I mean it, Mia. Don't make me regret being honest with you, or trusting you."

Trapped between his powerful body and the wall, she couldn't move, and she gasped when he seized her wrists and pinned them above her head. Fear flashed through her, mixed with anger and a confusing ache of a hot, bone-deep desire.

And then, inexplicably, grief.

This wasn't her Ohio boy. She'd wanted to believe he hadn't changed so much, that it was possible to go back to that magical time and pick up where they'd left off, before things had gone so wrong.

But she didn't know this man. There was nothing in him of that sweet, rough-edged boy who'd taught her all about the excitement of falling in love and the wonders of sex.

"What happened to you, that you ended up like this?" she whispered.

"Nothing at all. I just got older. Wiser." With each word, his breath brushed against her hair. "I need you to promise me you won't interfere."

Although furious with herself for still wanting him, for still feeling this pang of need even after what he'd told her, she refused to turn her face away from his. "Let me go. I don't want you touching me ever again."

He went very still for a moment. Then his lips brushed against hers and she almost forgot to breathe, her face hot with shame because her body was so quick to prove her a liar.

He pulled back to look at her, his expression unreadable. "You're angry and upset right now. I can't blame you for that, but I'm not the bad guy here. You need to understand that."

"I understand what they're doing is wrong and what you intend is right, but I don't have to like it or approve of how you're going about it. The Eudoxia Reliquary . . . it's old and it's valuable and it's beautiful, but it's just a thing." Mia's voice thickened. "She's a human being, and people have disappointed her all her life. If you were such a good guy," she whispered, "you could've found another way."

After a moment, he said flatly, "You promise?"

"I promise. Now get out."

Who says romance is dead?

Bestselling romances from Pocket Books

Otherwise Engaged
Eileen Goudge
Would you trade places
with your best friend if
you could?

Only With a Highlander
Janet Chapman
Can fiery Winter
MacKeage resist the
passionate pursuit of a
timeless warrior?

Kill Me Twice
Roxanne St. Claire
She has a body to kill
for...and a bodyguard
to die for.

Holly
Jude Deveraux
On a starry winter night,
will her heart choose
privilege—or passion?

**Big Guns Out
of Uniform**
*Sherrilyn Kenyon, Liz
Carlyle, and Nicole Camden*
Out of uniform and
under the covers...three
tales of sizzling romance
from three of today's
hottest writers.

**Hot Whispers of
an Irishman**
Dorien Kelly
Can a hunt for magical
treasure uncover a love to
last a lifetime?

Carolina Isle
Jude Deveraux
When two cousins switch
identities, anything can
happen. Even love...

*A love like you've never known
is closer than you think...*

Bestselling Romances from Pocket Books

The Nosy Neighbor
Fern Michaels
Sometimes love is right
next door...

Run No More
Catherine Mulvany
How do you outrun your
past when your future is just
as deadly?

Never Look Back
Linda Lael Miller
When someone wants you
to pay for the past, you can
never look back...

The Dangerous Protector
Janet Chapman
The desires he ignites in
her make him the most
dangerous man in
the world...

Blaze
JoAnn Ross
They're out to stop a deadly
arsonist...and find that
passion burns even hotter
than revenge.

The Next Mrs. Blackthorne
Joan Johnston
Texas rancher Clay
Blackthorne is about to
wed his new wife. The only
question is...who will she be?

Born to be BAD
Sherrilyn Kenyon
Being bad has never felt
so right.

Have Glass Slippers,
Will Travel
Lisa Cach
Single twenty-something
seeks Prince Charming.
(Those without royal castles
need not apply.)

POCKET BOOKS
A Division of Simon & Schuster
A VIACOM COMPANY

POCKET
STAR BOOKS
A Division of Simon & Schuster
A VIACOM COMPANY

www.simonsayslove.com

12909